MR BLANK

JUSTIN ROBINSON

First edition published 2012.

Or possibly that's just what they want you to think.

For information, address
Candlemark & Gleam LLC,
104 Morgan Street, Bennington, VT 05201
info@candlemarkandgleam.com

Library of Congress Cataloging-in-Publication Data
In Progress

ISBN:978-1-936460-36-6
eISBN: 978-1-936460-35-9

Cover art and design by Kate Sullivan

Book design and composition by Kate Sullivan
Typeface: Droid Serif

Editors: Kate Sullivan and AnnaLinden Weller

Copy Editor: Laura Duncan

www.candlemarkandgleam.com

To the prettiest one.
(That’s you, Lauri. That’s always you.)

EVERY CONSPIRACY NEEDS A GUY LIKE ME.

I do the scut work, the crap no one else wants to do. I don't fly the black helicopters, I don't mutilate any cattle, and I sure as hell don't kill anybody. But if you need your lone nut's gun conveniently lost, I can do that. If you need a witness to get a weird visit from someone who might or might not be from the government, I have a suit one size too small and some gray pancake makeup in my trunk. I can't find the Ark of the Covenant, but if you need it FedExed somewhere, I'm your guy. If you need someone found, followed, called, hung up on, put in the dark, initiated, or just driven to the airport, I can do that, too. It's these kinds of unglamorous errands that keep the shadow governments moving, and without guys like me, nothing would get done at all.

Yeah, every conspiracy needs a guy like me. Problem is, they all have one.

Me.

I'm a Rosicrucian, a Freemason, a Templar, and a Hospitaler. I have links to double-black agencies in the CIA, the ONI, the NSA, and the Secret Service. I'm connected to the Mexican Mafia, the Triad, the Cosa and Kosher Nostras. I'm an agent of the Vatican, the Servants of Shub-Internet, a Discordian, and an Assassin. I'm a Knight of the Sacred Chao, a Brother of the Magic Bullet, and an Illuminated Seer of Bavaria. I can find Symbionia, Thule, Shangri-La, and the entrance to the Hollow Earth on a map. I know who really killed both Kennedys, MLK, Marilyn Monroe, and Castro. Yeah, Castro's dead—that double was doing a mean Tevye on the dinner theatre circuit when we found him. I've met Little Green Men, Atlanteans, and two of Oswald's clones. I've seen Bigfoot's W-2. The only thing I've never met is a vampire, because there's no such thing, no matter what anyone says.

I'm a member of these organizations, but I'm not high on the totem pole. I'm pretty much one step up from innocent bystander in all of them. Ever been to a fancy party? One of the really nice ones where waiters in crisp black and white wander around with trays of crab puffs and champagne flutes and there's not a single red plastic cup to be seen. Think of one of the waiter's faces. You can't, can you? No one can. The human mind has finite space to use, and it's going to ignore whatever it thinks it can, and that includes people who do menial work. Safer for the waiters, too—and no one at that party was planning to sacrifice them to some Elder God they just resurrected out of old computer parts. Anonymity is better than a bulletproof vest down in the information underground.

I live in Los Angeles. Since the beginning, LA has been open territory; that's how how Mickey Cohen ran it for years with only Dragna giving him a hard time. The Cosa Nostra is just the most visible of underground secret societies, and they've always been trendsetters, so before long, every conspiracy worth the name had an office out here. They used the city as a place where business could be conducted with the side benefits of mild weather, good food, and lots of ridiculously attractive people with serious self-esteem problems.

I work for every conspiracy, secret society, and mystery cult you can think of; a few you've never heard of; and at least one I wish didn't exist. I do the work no one else can be bothered to do. Adding up all the jobs, the hours aren't bad and the pay is damn good. There's just a lot of info to keep straight.

Such as the question I'm always asking myself: *What does this guy think my name is?*

"Sam, good to see you," he said. Sam. That was it. Sam Smiley of Palos Verdes.

The man asking the question was a Satanist, and I'm not being judgmental. He was honestly a loyal member of the First Reformed Church of the Antichrist. Like any person of faith, he was inordinately proud of his membership in good standing, despite the fact that all he had to do was act superior toward anyone not in his sect. Well, that and the occasional blood sacrifice.

Now, when I say "Satanist," most people picture someone like Ming the Merciless drinking red wine out of a virgin's skull. This guy looked like an entertainment lawyer, which if you ask me is about a hundred times worse.

He and I weren't on great terms. He thought I was a dilettante, which I was, and I thought he was the kind of guy who'd take advantage of a drunk woman with Farrah hair, which I had no evidence for or against. In any case, I didn't think he really meant that it was good to see me, but whatever. It's not like there was a Satanist softball team we played on together. Besides, if he wanted the goat's blood, he could play nice.

"Delivery's here," I said.

He squinted at the truck behind me. "I can see that."

Task number one for the day was: pick up goat's blood, deliver goat's blood, don't ask questions. Which was good, because I didn't have any that I wanted answered.

Mission accomplished, I drove the truck back into the city and dropped it off. My car was waiting for me: a hybrid with a couple of bumper stickers on the back. One look in my car and I was a slob. A closer look, and I was a collector. Those were real Styrofoam Big Mac boxes, and yes, I knew the one McDonald's that still used them. There was the open briefcase stuffed with papers. There was the hula girl on the dash, the rosary hanging from the rearview, brass washers in the change tray. My radio still had the factory settings, which in LA meant five Spanish oompah stations and KROQ, which meant I owned an iPod.

On the stereo: "More Than a Feeling."

My second job for the day was pure information. A contact of mine had something he just *had* to tell me. Ever been to a bar in Eagle Rock before noon? Probably one of the more depressing places on the planet. The lights were low, so when that door opened into the yellow morning, it was like a supernova in your retinas. The few guys in there were so listless they made Keanu Reeves look like Samuel L. Jackson. In other words, no one searching for my contact would look for him there.

"Hey, Hasim, how's it hanging?"

"Tripped over it on the way in." Hasim was the kind of guy that gets randomly selected for a strip search every time he flies. It's ridiculous. He was born in Lebanon, but there's no bigger Clipper fan on the planet. Of course, the guy *was* an Assassin, so maybe strip-searching him was a good idea.

"What do you have for me?"

Hasim took a sip out of the tiki party in front of him. "Big contract came down the pipes. That name you flagged for me.

Quackenbush."

"Contract on Quackenbush?"

He nodded. "Already taken, too. By a bad, bad man."

"Who?"

"Tariq Suliman."

My voice, in a monotone, echoed through the bar. "That's fabulous news." Tariq Suliman was a spook story to most of the information underground, and half of them thought he was made up to keep everyone scared of the Assassins. I met the guy once. It was like meeting a combination of the Zodiac and the Dude.

"I checked the name, Quackenbush. It says he's some retired security consultant?"

I nodded. Hasim didn't need to know the whole story behind Irving Quackenbush. Really, no one actually knew the whole story, or if they did, they weren't copping to it. The rumors said he was the guy behind Dulles, the man responsible for turning the wartime OSS into the peacetime CIA. Quackenbush supposedly retired in the '70s and went into the private sector. He started up a private security firm, which is what you call mercenaries in mixed company, and used his contacts to get every plum government contract he could. If there's something worth guarding in the US, Quackenbush's guys are the ones guarding it. Calling Irving Quackenbush a "retired security consultant" was sort of like calling Genghis Khan a tourist with a mild interest in politics. But for me, the most important thing was that on the first Tuesday of every month, there was an envelope full of cash waiting for me at the South Pasadena Post Office, courtesy of Irving Quackenbush. The guy wanted eyes on the street, and two of those eyes were mine.

"So what do you care if some security guy is getting the Al-Amout Handshake?" Hasim asked.

"Who set it up?" I knew he wasn't going to answer.

He smiled and shook his head. "Think I'm going to tell that to an infidel?"

I stood up and dropped two twenties on the table. "Smoke something before you head back home. You smell like a distillery."

Hasim made a gesture that convinced me he was drunker than he was letting on. I thought about reminding him that the Prophet forbids wine, but chances are the Assassins were too high to care.

I called Quackenbush's office and got the girl with the sexy voice. I was sure what I pictured when I talked to her wasn't even close to reality. She probably looked like Conan the Barbarian.

"Yes?" she said. It was very nearly a purr. I thought about promising her some insurance money and an anklet.

"Assassins have a target on Quackenbush. Tariq Suliman took the contract."

"Thank you, Mr. Levitt."

"No problem. Listen, I..."

Click. Buzz.

Yeah.

Third job was easier, but it was also more annoying. First, I had to talk to someone I found intensely unpleasant. Oana Constantinescu had taken the bronze in the women's individual all-around in Sydney and was still bitter about it. She was tiny, had olive skin, and despite a neck like a bodybuilder's thigh, was pretty enough. She wore her hair in a ridiculous ponytail with bangs that made me think of the '80s. At first glance, she looked fifteen. Second glance aged her five years, third a couple more. She always had a look on her face like she disapproved of everything she could see, and was imagining a few more things to be pissed off with. Oana was one of the more mobile members of V.E.N.U.S., which is to say she didn't own a Rascal.

She wanted to meet me at a vegan restaurant in Alhambra. I ate before I got there.

I sat down across from her. "Hey, Oana." We were the only two people in there who weren't Buddhist monks.

She looked me over. "Hello, Jonah. I was beginning to think you wouldn't show." Her Romanian accent made her sound like Dracula.

I was ten minutes late. I let her eat her stir-fry and contemplate that for a minute.

She slid an envelope across the table. "Our employers want you to deliver this."

I picked it up without even the briefest flicker of curiosity; whatever was in there was between V.E.N.U.S. and the Clone Wolves. I pocketed the envelope and left without saying anything that she could misinterpret.

I drove to the appropriate address at Caltech. My contact was waiting outside. When he saw me, he shuffled over, but never made eye contact. His name was Brian. He was like a socially awkward wall. I handed him the envelope. He took it and walked away. Didn't say a word. I shrugged.

Fourth job was even easier, although no less annoying. It required a drive out to Azusa, which is a special kind of hell. I heard one time that Azusa, which is an entirely created suburb east of LA, was named because it had everything from A to Z in the USA. Yeah, I know.

The Brotherhood of Sisterhood's headquarters was a mechanic's garage that used to be a gas station. The front was decorated with this avant-garde artwork that looked like something you'd find in Pinhead's bathroom. There was a car with its engine being rebuilt next to where the pumps used to be. I'm not a car guy, but I knew '70s muscle when I saw it.

The greasemonkeys were a pair of blondes that looked like they should be giving dumb answers to dumber questions. The truly weird thing was they both had Flock of Seagulls haircuts.

"Zeke!" the first one said. She seemed happy.

The other one looked like she wanted to see what my insides looked like. They didn't bother to check for tails, never did, and brought me to the trunk of the car they were working on.

The happy one had GOOD tattooed on the knuckles of her left hand and FISH across the right. She wore a charm bracelet on her wrist that featured what looked like a Nazi iron cross. I didn't bring that up. Never talk about religion, politics, or hate group affiliation.

"Ladies," I said. I winced immediately. I sounded like a sex criminal. "Uh... what am I here for?"

"Be careful. We're pretty sure the vampires are on the move."

I rolled my eyes. What was it about vampires that turned everyone into fourteen-year-old girls?

They gave me the goods and my instructions, and I hit the road. Getting to the reservoir part of Silver Lake was also annoying as hell, but again, not difficult. First, it meant a little under an hour in the car, and then it was going to involve barbed wire and trespassing. Silver Lake is a section of town that was first settled by Mexicans, then gays, then finally hipsters—three tribes I didn't really get, but all of which had excellent taste in food. The park there is formed of three parts. Down below there's a rec center. A hill leads up to the second part, a fenced-off dog park. These two sections are next to a fence and a steep hill that leads up to the reservoir. Past that, there's some scrub and trees, which is where the Flock of Seagulls wannabes wanted their box deposited.

I wasn't looking forward to this part. I parked over in the residential sections, where there was some open land. Pine trees gave me a blanket of needles that led out to a grassy section. Not exactly incognito, but who wanted to break into the reservoir? I hoped that the case wasn't full of LSD or something. They had to have grown out of that by now. At least, I hoped so.

I took the floor mat out of the backseat and threw it over the barbed wire at the top of the fence. I pushed the box up over the fence and let it slam down onto the other side. I followed it, and then stashed it just out of sight behind some bushes.

I hopped the fence again and retrieved my mat. The shadows were getting a bit longer and I really wanted to be done for the day. Problem was, I'd saved the worst job for last. I had to head to West LA, which is always a great idea around four in the afternoon. There's an old LA joke about the 405 freeway. They say it's called that because you only go "four o' five miles an hour." I'd say that's being generous. There are people in LA who spend their entire lives avoiding the 405. It's considered a mark of intelligence.

Fortunately, I only needed to go two or so exits, which only took two or so hours. Driving on the west side is hell, because the average driver makes around half a million a year and drives like Jack Bauer with diarrhea. They can afford accidents, but what they can't afford is being late. It's not a good idea to point out that accidents take time, either.

I pulled up a couple of blocks from the police station. I threw on a tie and sportcoat I had stashed in the trunk and clipped my badge to the belt. Breaking into a police station would be hard with a fake badge. Fortunately, I sidestepped that by having a real one. Not that I had made it through the academy—that probably would have killed me. No, I got it a couple years back when Big Oil controlled the cops. Their crowning achievement was replacing a third of the police fleet with SUVs.

I walked right through the front door. A combination of things got me past the desk sergeant. The badge was the most obvious, although equally as important was the haircut: vintage Ronald Reagan, although some of the younger kids thought it was Stephen Colbert. None of it would have worked without the look on my face, my speed, and my posture. If cops carried clipboards, I would have been carrying one. The trick is to seem annoyed and in a hurry. People don't hassle you. Of course, this doesn't hold one hundred percent true. You also have to look vaguely like you belong. For instance, if you're trying to get to a Thuggee chief, board shorts and a Party Naked shirt will get you strangled and dumped in the Ganges. But if you've got the turban and your ceremonial kukri, you're all set.

Fortunately, none of the cops looked for a gun. I wasn't carrying one. Never do. I flashed my badge at anyone who gave me more than one glance. I had a pretty convincing ID in there if they cared to look, but no one did. I made my way to the case files. From there, it was a matter of waiting until the shift change and walking right past.

I didn't know whose semen it was. I didn't ask. It was just a series of test results that all led to the same guy. I uploaded it into their system. Whatever the hell guy who'd felt the need to spray his genetic code over that ceiling fan was off the hook, and I had just set up someone else to take the fall in his place. I hoped it was someone that at least slightly deserved it, but if I'd been the type to actually do anything about injustice, I would have found another line of work.

Dinnertime took me to a pizza parlor in Westwood. I was near enough to UCLA so that the place was full of college girls and I got to look at nubile flesh and feel old. It was a good combination. I had to wait for traffic to die down before I went home, anyway.

Home was in Los Feliz, a neighborhood right next to Hollywood that I was getting too old to live in. If you've seen *Swingers*, you've seen Los Feliz. I was on the creaky side of thirty, but not too far gone yet. Eventually, I'd need to buy a house just so I would have a lawn that I could keep local kids off. Along the way home, I stopped at the Echo Park Post Office to pick up a wad of cash from the Knights of Malta. I always hoped they'd get letterhead with a falcon on it, but they lacked both a sense of humor and an appreciation for the classics.

I lived in a Spanish-style complex with nice big apartments set around a central courtyard. I was on the second floor in back. From my front windows, I could see the entry into the courtyard, and my back windows dropped into the alley behind the place, beyond which was a series of easily hoppable wooden fences and one-stories with enough greenery to hide in. My living room had a window that opened up onto a tiny wrought-iron balcony. I kept two things out there: a chair and an Army-surplus footlocker with a rope ladder in it. Those were my concessions to paranoia, but I'd been doing this for seven years, and I had yet to get any inconvenient visitors.

The living room was pretty obviously a bachelor pad. Not that I'm a slob—it's just that I've never really decorated. There was a comfortable sofa and a recliner that didn't match. I had my framed *Reservoir Dogs* and *Big Lebowski* posters that I'd gotten in college (the *Princess Bride* one hid in the bedroom). A giant TV was hooked up to the stereo. I hadn't replaced the venetian blinds on all the windows because I liked the way the shadows made me feel like a noir anti-hero. I had an aquarium with three axolotls in one corner, and my girlfriend, the computer, in another. To the right, a small kitchen where I kept my frozen meals and the New Beverly schedule. To the left, a hallway that led to a bathroom and bedroom that would have depressed me if I ever thought about it for more than a few minutes at a time.

My bedroom closet was stacked waist-high with small bills.

I had neighbors, but we never got past the waving stage. I would have liked to have kept it at slight nods and grunts under the breath, but there was nothing I could do about that. The damage had been done. The guy that smelled like Old Spice, the single mom, the hipster couple: they could do without knowing the guy in 4B.

I booted up the computer and pulled a case from under the couch and opened it. Cellphones. These were not disposable. Each was registered to one of my aliases. I was gonna need a bigger case. I replaced the phones mapped to the organizations that I'd worked for that day. Then I dialed voicemail on each phone in the case as I checked my fifty-odd email accounts. When I was finished, I had my jobs for tomorrow. A couple simple ones: a Huxley and a Bavarian Telephone. A light day. Perfect for a Friday.

Maybe I could catch a movie.

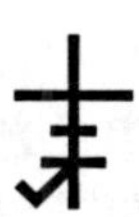

There's more than just secret societies in the information underground. Monsters are a real thing, too—although the preferred term is "cryptid," mostly so grown men don't have to stand around saying "monster." They have a weird relationship with the various conspiracies. Some of them are pets or watchdogs, others run the groups, and others have the kind of relationship you hear about on daytime talk shows right before everyone starts throwing hands. You've got little green men, sasquatches, lake monsters, and the occasional creepy gnome. Supposedly, there was a Gill Man out in Reseda, but he turned out to be an auto mechanic with a severe skin condition. Still, almost anything that someone has snapped a grainy picture of is real.

Some cryptids are dangerous as hell. Others are more like giant, horrifying teddy bears.

Strictly speaking, none of them should exist. At least, that's how the human brain reacts when seeing them. There's this instinctive terror screaming at you to do something useful like poop or run away. Sometimes you want to control this reaction, since it's generally considered to be poor form to indulge in the middle of a fancy dinner party, even if Spring-Heeled Jack is the guest of honor and he won't stop breathing fire.

Most of my jobs, thankfully, do not involve cryptids. That doesn't mean they're not horrifying, though, or that my brain doesn't sometimes throw a little fit about dealing with them. Even the simple ones can throw you for a loop sometimes, if you think too much about what you're doing.

Friday morning, I decided to get the disgusting job out of the way first. The less thought about it, the better.

Commercial candy is allowed to have up to five rat droppings per ounce by law. What they don't say is what kind of rat droppings or whose job it is to put them in there.

Which is how I wound up at the rat farm in Northridge around eight in the morning. From the outside, it looked like any of the other houses, that horrible architecture that sprung up in the early '80s where everything looks like it's in an *E.T.* knockoff. The stone wall outside was still cracked in half from the quake in '94.

I knocked on the door, and when it opened, the aroma of rat piss hit me like a right hook. It's an unfortunate aspect of this job that I have a scale of animal piss ranked from most to least offensive. Rat is in the top three, behind cat and orca. I really regret having an opinion on orca urine.

The man that answered the door looked like what you'd expect. Hair that should be white, smudged to smoker's yellow, a forehead like a deflated beach ball, and eyes that rolled in their sockets like they were trying to escape. He gave me a look up and down. "You Lohr?"

I nodded. I would have answered to any name he gave, no matter how ridiculous. As far as I knew, he was waiting on Bruce Boxleitner.

I hoped he wasn't going to invite me in, so of course he

did. The stench of rat piss got stronger as I followed him down the hallway. The house was serious hoarder territory: stacks of newspapers and unopened mail everywhere. There were paths through the stuff, almost like all the detritus were snowbanks. Hell, it was as close as Northridge would ever get.

He led me into what should have been a den. What it was instead was whatever you'd call a room stacked floor to ceiling with rat cages. I wondered what I would be doing if I had a normal job. Filing something maybe. Copying something. Having a meeting with my boss as he talked to me about the "incident" I'd caused in the breakroom.

The man pointed to a cardboard box in the center of the room. "A solid diet of mandrake. Made it a little runny at times, but they said mandrake, so there it is."

I looked at the box of shit. "That's just wonderful."

He smiled, showing off his receding gums. "Isn't it?"

I picked it up and hoped I was imagining the moist bottom. The box went into the trunk and I delivered it to the Ross Chocolate factory. I'd sworn off candy bars awhile back, but this made me renew the vow. It was like candy and I were an estranged couple that was thinking about a night of drunken sex together, but I'd just found out that candy had taken up fucking clinical test subjects for smack money.

On the stereo: "Rock and Roll Band."

Now I was Colin Reznick. This was an ID I remembered easily. Not my first, but definitely one from the early days, back when I still tried to think of cool names. After the first couple, I started to get a little lazy. It's a wonder I never resorted to borrowing every fake name Bart ever used on Moe.

I rolled up to the Temple in Burbank a little past noon. Burbank existed entirely for the purpose of destroying any lingering belief that the world was a beautiful place. Every building was a colorless box set in a little cracked parking lot.

The few trees seemed to resent being there. The sun was high in the sky. It was going to be hot and smoggy today, so I was briefly happy that I'd finished with the rat turds before the day turned on me. Walking through the Temple's door was like having a refrigerated hood thrown over my head. It took a minute for my eyes to adjust, but I was in the antechamber.

There was a guard. There always was. He wasn't much to look at: balding, a little overweight, with a head that looked like a tomato with a mustache.

I flashed the secret sign at him, even though he recognized me. He stood aside and I walked past. Past the antechamber was the temple, but not the good part of it where they kept the Indiana Jones stuff.

Stan Brizendine, or just sir to me, was waiting.

"Thank you for coming, Brother Reznick."

Stan Brizendine looked like a retired cop: gray hair, gray mustache, corded arms set off from a loosening gut. He dressed like one, too, in polo shirts and khakis. He wasn't wearing the ceremonial apron, which I thought was odd.

The room itself was a meeting hall. There was a pulpit at one end like a proper church, and an open area that could be either meeting hall or rows of pews depending. The pews were down that day, with folding chairs to make up seating in the back. The walls were hung with thick cloth, and here and there were the ceremonial symbols: the angle, the compass, the knife. Most of the organization's money was gone, or at the very least reserved for people more important than me.

And in the middle, Stan Brizendine with his old cop face trying to smile at me like he knew I was a person.

I said, "I come at the request of the master." Ritual statement, but I knew Brizendine loved it.

"You are still only second degree, is that right?"

I nodded.

"After so much loyal service, I would think you would be deemed ready to learn our deeper mysteries."

"I was deemed. I just... ah... I wanted to make sure I was ready."

He thought about this. "It's good that you treat the wisdom with such reverence. Still, one would think that you would be ready after six years."

"Is that what I'm here for today?"

He reached down and picked up a manila envelope and a locker key that had been sitting out of sight on the pew next to him. "I need you to make a delivery."

"Anything that is needed," I said. Not ritual, but it sounded like it could be.

"Union Station. The lockers at the entrance to the Gold Line."

"Locker 23?"

"Seventeen," he said. "When you're finished, we should have a talk about your future with us."

"I'd like that," I said. It wasn't an icicle that went through my heart, but it was the shadow of one. It was the way he said "your future." Made me think that future involved something unpleasant, like torture or a promotion.

From there I drove back downtown, right next to Olvera Street, where La Ciudad de la Reina de los Angeles had originally been founded. It's a little street made up to look like the original pueblo. You can get pretty good tacos there, but honestly, this is LA. You can get pretty good tacos almost everywhere.

Across the street, Union Station was a building out of time. It looked like a Spanish mission crossed with a Bogart film. On the outside: beige stucco and maroon tiles. On the inside: deep, rich browns. No matter what kind of shoe you wear, your footsteps echo in the most satisfying way.

I went in, past the few people who were there for Amtrak. I took a right past the ticket kiosks and ended up in the section they built in the early '90s. Going down an escalator landed me at what passed for a subway in LA.

It's impossible to know the history of the metrolink. Most cities have some kind of train, because most cities make sense. There's a nice large middle section and then there are suburbs, and these are on a finite grid. LA doesn't work like that. Once the water problem was solved—which was solved the way we solve everything down here, through outright theft—LA just expanded like a rash. All of the suburbanites had to get to jobs, and since the jobs were scattered all over the place, people had to commute. That meant gridlock and air pollution. In any situation like that, a train is the sane response, which meant that it could never have come from bureaucracy. Somehow, the metrolink was the brainchild of one of LA's conspiracies, but no one knew which, since no one was taking credit. The one good thing they'd accomplished, and no one wanted to slap their name on it.

My money was on some kind of mole-people group I hadn't even heard of.

The lockers were against one wall. I found number seventeen, opened it, and stuck the envelope inside.

That's when I heard a sound like a giant bumblebee whizzing for my right ear. I knew enough not to look. I just dove away.

I heard a loud clank. A woman screamed. I turned, still scrambling away.

I saw a rock, gray and the size of a Swedish baby. A chain was bolted to its side, but not a new one. It was old, rusted. It ran up to...

A man. He wore a black trenchcoat. Of course. He had to hide his giant fucking rock and chain somewhere, after all.

His skin was light brown, eyes vacant under a full head of black hair that hadn't been washed in a couple days and a face that hadn't been shaved in just as long. The good news was that he was smaller than me in every dimension. He spun the chain around, ready for another swing at me.

I got to my feet, backing off, hands up. "It's cool, man. Whoever you think I am, I'm not." The crowd was thin down here, and what was there was giving us plenty of room.

He just kept staring right through me. The rock whirred over his head like a helicopter rotor.

"Come on, I—"

And the rock lashed out. I jumped back, but I felt the rock's wake. He was getting closer and I was running out of places to back up into. It wasn't like I had another option.

I don't carry any weapons. No guns, no knives, no clubs, no chainsaws, no nothing. The downside is, as soon as someone starts waving a weapon at me, they tend to win whatever argument we were having. The upside is, they're way less likely to actually do anything more unpleasant than point the thing at me.

Apparently, this didn't apply in every situation.

He swung the rock with his right hand, held the slack on the chain with his left. He wasn't talking. He wasn't planning to reason with me. I'd seen that vacant look once or twice before. He'd be stronger than he looked, and stronger than I was.

I could wait for the cops and try to explain the three fake IDs in my pocket, or I could do something really dangerous.

I looked at the chain and made a guess. I hoped it would be a good one.

Soot from the chain was rubbing into his palm. I kept a five-foot cushion between us, watching his right hand warily. That rock would crush my skull in one hit. I tried to ignore that, but it was difficult.

Cops would be showing up soon. If I was going to do something, it would have to be now.

His right hand tensed.

The rock flung outward.

I faked a stumble and got six inches closer to a bludgeoning death.

I really hoped I'd estimated the play on the chain right.

The rock whooshed toward my head. My knees gave out in a desperate limbo. The rock was getting closer. I shut my eyes and hoped I wasn't an idiot.

I felt the wind from the rock first on the side of my face, then across my right cheek, then across the tip of my nose.

Missed.

I fell to the ground, playing dead. I tried to sell it. I tried to channel Olivier, Crowe, Hanks, even Reeves. I fluttered my eyes like an unconscious man, so I could peek at the lone nut through my lashes. He was above me, spinning the rock, ready for a killing blow. I waited. It was one of the hardest things I've ever had to do. It was worse than being six years old, looking at a huge stack of presents three days before Christmas and not touching them. It was worse than walking past an open bank vault. It was worse than passing a midget at the supermarket and not turning around for a second look.

He tensed, and brought the flail straight down, trying to cave my skull in from the forehead. I rolled. It hit the concrete next to me. The concrete shuddered, cracked.

I grabbed the chain, yanked as hard as I could, and put up a foot.

Crotch soccer might not be honorable, but sometimes it's the only option. When my foot slammed into his groin, it was all I could do not to holler, "Gooooooaaaaaal!"

He buckled. I rolled and got to my feet, and then I was running up the escalator as fast as I could. There were people in my way that could have stopped me, but they were confused. I wasn't acting like an innocent man, so there were a few half-hearted attempts to intervene, but I was running full tilt and carrying one hundred eighty pounds before lunch. I didn't look back at my attacker. Best pretend he was right behind me.

I slowed at the top. Up there, they wouldn't know who had been attacked. I ducked into the men's room and dried my face and neck, washed my hands, and tried to walk out as casually as I could.

Security was running toward the escalators. No one from the gathering crowds was looking at me.

Out the front door, into the car.

My mind started working: an assassin at the drop point. Stan Brizendine setting me up? That's what he wanted to talk about—only he didn't want to talk. He wanted me to know how smart he was that he figured me out and sent one of his empty-eyed goons to drop me. Brizendine had figured out I was playing both sides, and he was cleaning up his leak.

But the question was: which side did he figure out? And why bother with the envelope?

And what the hell was with that rock?

I'M NOT A BIG FAN OF ALMOST GETTING KILLED.

Since I started my life in the information underground, I had almost been killed three times, and the crazy guy with the rock made four. This was enough to develop an opinion on the matter, but not enough to turn a murder attempt into something that happens on Fridays. Someone trying to kill me was still an interesting, unique, and terrifying event that I should probably start paying more attention to.

The other three tries had been different. It wasn't like someone wanted me dead personally for something I had done. They were all of the "wrong place wrong time big mouth" variety.

Taking them in chronological order:

A Satanist tried to take a sacrificial dagger to my favorite spine right before a Black Mass. Because of my green eyes, the local antipriest had decided I was good luck. So, for a period of about a month and a half, I was shadowing him every other day as his personal lucky rabbit's foot. Bear in mind that these were very traditional Satanists.

They weren't fans of the recent attempt to recast Lucifer as a misunderstood rebel; they looked at the devil as the embodiment of evil. Needless to say, it's not a healthy work environment. Because they're so old-school, the way to rise in the ranks is through the ritual sacrifice of a superior, proving that you have Satan's blessing. The welcome side effect of this method of succession is that the Satanists had traditionally been led by meatheads. They can be very predictable and their ideas of evil are pretty pedestrian—or, at least, they were until Paul Tallutto took over. I'm still unclear on how he did it.

In any case, succession was what my potential murderer was up to, but first he had to take out the antipriest's security, which was me. I had turned to speak to the door, behind which the big boss was getting blown or changed (I didn't ask), when I heard a floorboard creak. I turned, and the knife came down. Still have a hell of a scar on my shoulder from that one. The guy didn't want me dead specifically. He just wanted to take out the guard at the door so he could get to the very real business of cutting his boss apart.

The next time was about a year later. When people hear "Russian mob," they immediately think "bored KGB agent." While there are some ex-KGB in the Organizatsiya, by and large, it's a Jewish mob. The Kosher Nostra has always been powerful out west, first with Mickey Cohen and Bugsy Siegel. Now the new heavy hitters are Russians coming into the States on Israeli passports. My very first job was with them. It was with a sense of Ricklesian irony that they hired a Gentile to do their money laundering, but that's neither here nor there.

By the time of my brush with death, I had moved from accounting to just working as an informant for one of the local capos, a guy named Vassily "the Whale" Zhukovsky. He had a dive bar out in San Pedro that he liked, supposedly because he could hear the creak of the cargo ships. I was sitting down at his table to deliver some information about some of the local Salvadoran gangs all living in houses owned by the same shell corporation, when a guy came in and just opened fire. He hosed the place down with a Tec9 until one of the Whale's bodyguards tackled him. The only thing on me that got hurt was my chin, which I hit on the table when I tried to duck under it. That guy wasn't after me either. That was wrong place, wrong time.

The last time was my fault. Long story short: don't call a Templar Knight "shitbird" unless you know how to use a broadsword.

In all three of those cases, killing me wasn't the goal. Even the third was more about respect. This time, though—this was different. The guy at Union Station was a full-blown Manchurian Candidate. He had the blank eyes and the robot strength. This was a guy who had been brainwashed and conditioned to become the perfect assassin. He probably escaped from the train station and woke up someplace awhile later with no idea why he had my footprint on his crotch. But the fact of the matter is, when someone sends a Candidate after you, they really want you dead. They're not joking. They paid good money, or else used an asset they'd been cultivating over many years, all to take you out.

Only a couple organizations know how to make the Candidates: there are a few tried and true ways, and those that use them often hire their Candidates out to the highest bidder. It's a serious, delicate, lucrative business, and now I was on the wrong side of the accounting somehow. Brizendine found out that I worked for someone, probably recently, and contacted the CIA or the Assassins and hired himself a Candidate. A Candidate who used a goddamn rock on a chain. No two ways about it—that was odd.

I checked the numbers on my Mason phone. Brizendine was in there, but a taunting call to him just seemed like a dick move. I scrolled through the contact list. Someone in there had to be okay with my continued existence.

Neil. That would be Neil Greene. He and I were on good terms. I remembered when he joined and, of course, when he passed me on the ladder. I called him.

"Yeah?" he said.

"It's Colin," I said.

"What's going on?"

"Can we meet?"

"It's the middle of the day," he said.

"I know that. We're in the same time zone."

"No, I mean I'm at work."

"The man lies in the temple, his guts over his shoulder." A ritual plea.

Neil's voice changed: "I could probably take a long lunch."

There's a Jewish legend about the Tzadikim. The story goes that in each generation, there are thirty-nine truly selfless people, and it is because of these people that the world keeps turning. The idea is that the rest of the world is so venal and selfish that anything less and the whole thing turns into Thunderdome. Cities function in much the same way. There are seventeen desks that control each city (and twenty-three in Wilmington, Delaware, for some reason). These desks are attached to gray jobs, the kind of work no one really thinks about. These aren't city planners. These aren't cops or councilmen. These are the bureaucrats between the other organizations, the ones responsible for passing paper along the chain. These people can pass along what they like, shred what they don't, and alter whatever they please. These seventeen desks are the carotids and jugulars of the body politic.

Neil sat behind one of these desks and controlled it for the Masons.

At the moment, however, he was sitting on the hood of his car, eating the sandwich I had bought him from the Armenian deli on Doran. I was staying the hell out of Burbank until this thing got solved, so we were in a parking lot in Glendale. Trees blocked the sun, and it would have almost been a pleasant day if not for the reason that I brought him out there.

"A... what?" he said finally.

"A Manchurian Candidate."

"Like the movie with Denzel?" he said.

"Yeah, sure." That line of thought probably led nowhere profitable. First off, I'd probably have had to explain that Frank Sinatra was also an actor. "Do you know if the... if we have access to anything like that?"

"I haven't heard anything."

"Has Stan mentioned anything about new members? Ones with CIA connections, maybe?"

Neil thought about that one. "I don't think so. What makes you think these Manchurian Candidates are real?"

Explaining to him that I'd seen parts of their creation wouldn't help. "Rumors, mostly," I said.

He took another bite of the sandwich. Around a white bolus, he asked, "Who do you think sent him?"

"Stan."

I thought for a second I was going to get to see prosciutto come out of his nose.

"Stan Brizendine? Why would he want you dead?"

Well, Neil, I could have said, *you know all those stories about* them? *About the aliens and devil-worshipers and New World Order Trilateralists? Well, that's all me. I have just as much loyalty to them as I do to you, and incidentally, they're no worse than you are, and in many cases, they have a good bit more conscience then your standard one of "us."*

Instead, I just shrugged.

He said, "Did you spill anything?"

"I don't know anything to spill!"

"Maybe you do. Maybe you know more than you know you know. You know?"

I did know. "No."

"Can you be sure? I've seen what you do. You put things in place. You make things easier for us. You find things. It's possible you found the wrong thing, right?"

Oh, I could have said. *You mean like the headquarters of the Rose Cross, where they let me in without conversation, where I even have some food with my name on it in the break-room fridge?*

Instead, I just shrugged.

"What do you want from me?" Neil asked.

"I need you to find out if Stan tried to have me killed. Scratch that. I need you to find out if any one of us tried to have me killed. You're, what..."

"Seventeenth degree."

"That's high enough for that, isn't it?"

"Should be. No offense, but if they wanted you dead, it probably wouldn't be a big secret to anyone above fifth." He chewed his sandwich. "Colin," he said. "If you thought we were trying to kill you, why call me?"

There was a long answer to that. I gave him the short version. "Calculated risk. The... uh... *we're* so secretive, that it's not like I'm going to find out about it without help. And if this thing is because of a leak, which I think it might be, I need to find the source of that leak, which I'm also not going to do without inside help."

"Yeah, but why me? I mean, I could be the leak, right?" He waggled his eyebrows like a pervy uncle.

I pointed at the caterpillars above his eyes. "Because of that. You can't lie."

He looked a little disappointed. It's a truism in this business that the desk guys all want to be field guys and the field guys are looking forward to becoming desk guys.

"Okay. I'll ask around, see what I can see. What are you going to do?"

"Try not to go crazy."

THE LONGER VERSION OF THE ANSWER TO NEIL'S question had to do with paranoia. Paranoia can be a useful and constructive state of mind. It can also turn you into a quivering lump that can't even muster up the courage to walk to the bathroom. The key is walking that tightrope. Don't get so secure that you wind up taking stupid risks and don't get locked into self-defeating loops of paralyzing logic. Either extreme, and you end up face-down in your own fluids.

So I had to do something, just not something stupid. There was the temptation to hole up at home. Maybe check into a motel. For a brief moment, I thought of fleeing town. Every one of these options was wrong. It gave the initiative to the guy who wanted me dead, and he already had too much initiative to begin with.

I had a couple moves available. Might as well take them. I changed my shirt right in that Glendale parking lot. I had a fresh one, still in the plastic from the store. Then I put on my movie star disguise: big shades and sportcoat. I didn't look like a different guy, but at first glance, all you'd see would be the hair and the shades. That would have to do.

There were good odds that the envelope I'd planted was actually for someone, rather than just being a dummy prop. I had felt the thing and there was something in it. A sheaf of papers, probably a paperclip judging by the way it scraped along the inside. Of course, I wouldn't put it past Stan to give me an envelope stuffed with blank papers. It wasn't that he had style; it was that he lacked the imagination to fill the paper up.

But like I said, there were good odds that the envelope was destined for a particular recipient. The information underground runs on efficiency. If Stan was setting me up to die, he might as well get another errand done at the same time.

Back into Union Station. The first thing I noticed was the utter lack of cops. It was hard not to be a little offended. After all, I'd nearly been killed, and not in a nice way. Not that I would have expected them to ignore it if I'd been shot at with a gun. But my attacker packed a homemade flail. Even for me, that was weird.

But there was no fuss at all.

I walked through the entrance hall a little gingerly. Even as I tried to force myself to act casual, I felt like everyone was looking right at me, and tried to ignore the sensation. I walked past the chairs that looked molded into the ground, past the gift kiosk, then turned around and bought a magazine without looking at it. Past the ticket booths, and I was at the top of the escalator. The lockers were down below. For a moment, I thought I heard the carpenter-bee sound of the chain. A glance behind me showed that the bad paranoia was creeping into the little bones in my ear.

The Candidate would be long gone. In fact, he would probably, at that very moment, be lying down in his hyperbaric chamber right next to Walt Disney's head and getting a good night's sleep for a long day of fluoridating.

That thought moved my feet. Good thing, too. One more glare of someone squeezing past me on the escalator, and the paranoia would have come back like Jason Voorhees. I looked down: the damage from the rock was visible. Locker seventeen was nearly caved in and the floor in front of it was cracked in a neat pattern. No police tape, either. The locker damage had been ignored, but there was a wet-floor janitor cone next to the floor's wound.

Covered up. Almost everyone in the underground had the juice to cover up a lone nut attack, especially if both sides got away and no celebrities were involved.

Score one for the amateur detective: I'd successfully added "Everyone" to my list of suspects.

I walked first to the broken floor. A janitor was mopping nearby. The broken section was covered in a thin gray dust, but I didn't see the Virgin Mary in the break. The rock had really done a number on the floor, probably more than a sledgehammer could have.

I asked the janitor, "What happened here?"

He shrugged. "Someone dropped something, I guess."

"Obviously, you're not a golfer."

I walked away to have a look at the locker. The denting looked a little strange to me. I traced it with my fingers. They came away covered in the same gray dust. I sniffed it. I had no idea what I expected to learn from that, other than the fact that it smelled like rock. I walked away to lean against the wall.

It wasn't my first stakeout. In my years of work, I had sat in cars and watched cameras. I had crouched in bushes outside of apartments. I had waited in bathrooms. A couple of times, I had hidden in crawlspaces. None of that makes me sound very good, but in my defense, I'm not a very good person.

I picked a wall with a good view of the locker, just below the escalator. Whoever went to the locker would have his back to me. Now, to look unobtrusive. I brought the magazine up and...

20 Ways To Know He Loves You.

Son of a bitch. It was a *Cosmo*.

Screw it. As it turned out, the twenty ways weren't variations on "He remembers your name." That was the problem with those magazines. You got women who don't understand men writing for women who *really* don't understand men. There's at least two layers of bullshit to wade through in those situations. Women don't want to know the truth: we're not that complicated, we're not that interesting, and we react to the most simple of stimuli. In short, we're not women.

The sad part was, I ended up getting interested enough in the article that I nearly missed the mark.

If it weren't for the red hair, I wouldn't have looked up at all. Like I said, simple creatures.

A little too short to call it long, but it definitely wasn't short. What it was was shiny. What it was was hypnotic. What it was was completely distracting me from what I should have been doing.

I tossed the magazine away, tried to take in the rest of her, and there was a hell of a lot to take in. Not chunky exactly, though an asshole might call her that; she had too much grace to be accurately described that way. She definitely had a waist, but it probably measured more like the hips on an average LA woman: the Monroe hourglass. She didn't seem at all ashamed of that, either, like that magazine I had just tossed would like her to be. Her blouse and skirt hugged that figure, showing every bountiful curve. It had just become a very good day to be me.

She was at locker seventeen, fishing out the envelope I planted.

"Excuse me," I said.

She turned around. She really looked familiar, but that could have just been wishful thinking. Still, I could have sworn on a polygraph I'd seen those big blue eyes somewhere, but the way my heart was pounding, it would read like a lie.

"Yes?" she said. Polite. Calm.

I tried to concentrate. There was part of me that thought she might be a ghost of a starlet from the '50s. I thought better of trying to pinch her. The downside of all of this was that I completely forgot what I planned to say.

Okay, first, figure out if she's connected, and if so, with who.

"Do I know you?" I hated myself as soon as that came out of my mouth, and it must have shown on my face.

She said, "No. Just one of those asses."

"Wait, what?"

"Listen, it's fun getting hit on, but this is the metro and I'm a little busy."

This was rapidly getting out of hand. "Oh no. I'm not hitting on you."

"Sure seems like it."

It clicked right then and there. I knew who she was, and where she was going. It didn't explain the envelope, but I wasn't going to get anywhere standing around, especially with the way she was looking at me.

"My mistake, I just could have sworn you and I were both on the Finnish biathlon team." I turned and double-timed it up and out.

It was a quick car ride from there to Mount Washington, the collective name for a bunch of hills in East LA. The house was hidden amongst these hills. It was almost a commune, with multiple levels and tiny stinking gardens. It was the local headquarters of V.E.N.U.S., and unless my instincts were completely off, it was Red's destination.

I drove past the house and made a U-turn so my car was above the house and facing downhill, then walked to the gate. The intercom was old, but it worked, and I buzzed.

A male voice said, "Hello?"

"It's Jonah Bailey. Let me in."

The gate buzzed again and creaked open. There was a short path up to the house. Because this was Southern California and I was on hippie land, the path was hot and dusty, and the vegetation looked sick and natural. They were on the porch that day. If I had to guess, I would have said that there was a shade over two tons resting on there. Good thing it was concrete.

There were four of them, lounging on pillows that looked like they were in pain. They were women, and in their humble estimation, the most beautiful things in all the world. See, V.E.N.U.S. got its name from the first artwork produced by human hands, figurines of obese women with breasts like battleships. It was the contention of V.E.N.U.S. that this meant the truly desirable physique involved big breasts, big hips, and a pregnant belly. If you weren't pregnant, the belly was to be simulated. It wasn't an entirely crazy concept; it's just that the people on top took it a little too far. They had that in common with every organization in the history of the world.

V.E.N.U.S. was also an acronym. I can never actually bring myself to say what it stands for out loud, but anyone with a pulse could probably figure out what the V was.

One of them looked me over with eyes half-closed by fat. "What a blessing that you should arrive when you aren't called, Mr. Bailey."

A man emerged from the house, dressed in some kind of weird toga. Their men came in looking different, but before long, they were beaten into the same shape: rangy, hunched shoulders and downcast eyes, and for some reason, balding heads and full beards. The man was carrying a tray of goblets. I wondered if they were full of raw lard.

"I thought I'd come back to see if anything needed doing."

The look she gave me would haunt me for the rest of my days. "Finally accepting what millions of years of evolution has been telling your eyes?"

"No, I still think you're all basically planetoids who are about a week from achieving their own gravitational pull."

In the brief silence that followed, I could hear a dog barking a couple blocks over.

"We don't need you today, or any other day."

"You'll need me as soon as you need someone ambulatory. I know, I know, I'll show myself out."

I turned and walked away, reflecting about how that could have gone better. By the time I made it to the gate, I had thought of eight things I could have done differently. Pretty soon I was going to have to alphabetize them just to keep track. I was ready to push the gate when it opened on its own.

I thought it was sort of silly that she drove a Prius. Granted, next to the landmasses on the porch, she looked positively petite, but in the real world, she was a big girl. It was Red, of course.

I smiled and waved.

She pulled through the gate and stopped. Her window slowly dropped. She looked at me over her Audrey sunglasses.

"Who are you?" She actually sounded a little impressed, throwing some extra mustard on *are*.

"Have you opened the envelope yet?"

Her brain found the track. "No, of course not. Daphne wanted it closed."

"Do you know who told her it would be there?"

She shook her head. "Who are you?"

"I just compared your bosses to moons. Comets. Large asteroids. So I'm not really welcome up there at the moment."

"I... see. And why did you do that?"

"Turns out I'm not that bright. Who knew? Look, I want to know what's in that envelope. Are you opening it with Daphne? Which one's Daphne?"

"The... uh... the blonde."

"There's a blonde?"

She nodded. Apparently there was a blonde.

"Are you? Opening it with her?"

"I think so. What's in it that you need to know?"

I glanced up the path. They were probably wondering where she was. "I'm parked up the street. Gray Toyota. When you're done here, come meet me there, and don't mention it to them, okay?"

She looked me up and down. She didn't seem to notice the hair. Damn. "Maybe."

"That's the best I'm gonna get, isn't it?"

"Yep."

"Fair enough."

So I got to wait in my car for Red, who might or might not come. This was the destination of the envelope, but there was a distinct lack of apparent desire to kill me, no matter how many insults I threw their way. I was fairly comfortable putting V.E.N.U.S. in the safe pile. That meant my suspects were everyone minus one, which still sounded depressing.

Red left the compound and looked around before spotting my car. The hill was pretty steep, and she was a little out of breath when she got to me. I got out of the car.

"Jonah Bailey," she said.

"Sure, why not?"

She frowned at me, but stuck her hand out. "Mina Duplessis."

Her hands felt like silk. “Nice to meet you. So, about the envelope?”

“What do you know about it?”

“Tell you what. You tell me what you know, I’ll tell you what I know.”

She said, “Do you know who the Anas are?”

“Ana” was a pejorative term for members of a sect called the Guardian Servitors of the Anorectic Praxis. They worshiped a goddess they called Anamadim, sort of a high-fashion nymph type. More importantly for Mina’s purposes, the Anas were V.E.N.U.S.’s opposite number. The Anamadim Cult had been around since the late ’60s, but really started to come into its own in the internet age. They believed that anorexia was a lifestyle choice rather than a clinical illness. They were constantly at war with V.E.N.U.S. over the female psyche and proper representation of woman. V.E.N.U.S. gave us Sophia. The Anas countered with Twiggy. V.E.N.U.S. gave us Anna. Anas struck back with Kate.

“Yeah, vaguely. They’re the... uh... bad guys.” Low-levels loved the term “bad guys.” They used it before they got to understand that good and bad were mostly relative terms.

“Right,” she said. “We’ve had a ceasefire since the most recent assassinations.”

“Assassinations?”

She got a look like she’d just spilled the beans, but to her credit, she bulled ahead. “Come on, Jonah. There’s more out there than you realize. Think back a couple years. A large actress would die, then a skinny model. It was like homicidal badminton.”

I honestly hadn’t put that together. My work with both groups was pretty arm’s length. I was even lower with them than with most, simply because I couldn’t stomach the higher-ups for too long. I kept wanting to order a pizza for one side and tell the other side about how much weight Jared lost.

"Right, so there was a ceasefire."

She nodded. "But in the envelope, there were documents. Expense reports, bills, that kind of thing. It points to an offensive. It could mean they're ready to go after some of our people. Monica, Christina... probably not me, but maybe."

"You? What do you do?"

She blushed a little. "I'm a... uh... model."

"A model? But you're so..."

"Fat?"

"I was going to say short."

"I'm five-eight."

"Right. I meant in comparison. You know, to a basketball player."

She gave me a glare.

I said, "So you're a model, then?"

"I'm a plus-sized model."

And that's when I figured out where I knew her from. It was a commercial that had been running for a couple weeks. A young woman, babysitting her brother's kids; she doesn't know how to cook, but hey! No problem. There's Casseroller! The casserole that's easy and fun!

I must have made the recognition eyes at her. She nodded, and in the breathy voice she used on TV, "It's so easy!"

"So you're here to..."

She finished for me, like she was quoting: "To promote a more positive image of femininity and to return the aesthetic to what the Goddess intends."

I had to admit, if more of the V.E.N.U.S. women looked like her, I could see myself becoming a fanatic. I thought about wearing a suicide vest stuffed with ice cream bars and charging into runway shows.

"So how's that working out for you?"

"I get more gigs than I did before. What about you? I shared. Your turn."

It's a good policy not to let a pretty face get you stupid, but in my defense, she had pretty other things, too. We were five seconds from her giving me an "I'm up here."

Deep breath. "I planted the envelope."

"You. You!" She stumbled backward and turned to run.

I couldn't think of what to do, so I grabbed her. "Wait, Mina!" Turned out, that was a mistake. She hit me in the gut with an elbow, turned and punted my head like a football, then ran back down the hill for the gate.

I lay there for a second, trying to catch my breath around the sheepshank her elbow had planted in my lungs. I wasn't sure if the compound was going to empty onto the street to collect me. There was a decent chance I was about to be surrounded by soft-eyed and bearded men with Uzis. As fun as that sounded...

I rolled over and stumbled to my car, hit the ignition, and sped back down the hill.

EVOLUTION PUT SOME SHORTCUTS INTO THE human brain that probably seemed like a good idea at the time, but can be manipulated if you know how. It's about finding the cracks, usually in the interplay between belief and perception and how one bolsters or destroys the other. Some people call it magic, some call it a con game, and some call it New Age psychology.

Belief means different things to different people. When I use it, I'm not talking about expectations based on experience. I'm talking about expectations based on ephemera. Take my haircut, for example. People trust it because it reminds them of Ronald Reagan, and everyone knows that Reagan was a tireless champion of human rights, the guy who brought down the Berlin Wall and the Soviet Union and saved a bunch of hostages from Iran. This belief really isn't based on anything solid. In fact, Reagan was responsible for the creation of twenty-three FEMA-controlled concentration camps within the U.S. and kept Saddam Hussein, the Ayatollah Khomeini, and Osama bin Laden on the CIA payroll. Seriously, look it up. That's the whole point: the reality of the situation and the belief about the situation have nothing to do with one another. People believe Reagan was a good guy, and so the haircut, his most identifiable physical trait, gets associated with good guys. Belief allows you to ignore facts in favor of what sounds right. It can also allow you to see something that's not really there, but that's slightly more complex. Where there's smoke, there's fire. Well, not always, but belief can manufacture the perception of the same. Plant a cause, and people will remember the effect.

Which is why I looked like a Phil Collins video.

Mina had kicked me right along my jawline. Her foot didn't land flush, thank my lack of belief in God. If it had, I probably would have been knocked cold instead of just being dazed. The bruise was red, and would probably turn good and purple before dinner. On that subject, chewing would be fun.

The Masons were trying to fan the flames between V.E.N.U.S. and the Anas. As I drove, I tried to think of a good reason for that.

On the stereo: "Amanda."

I couldn't think of one, beyond some paranoid fantasy about a gender war.

That left the Candidate. If there was a contract out on me—or, more accurately, out on Colin Reznick— it was probably sent to several different groups. Going to the Assassins themselves would be like marching into the lion's den covered with lamb chops and barbecue sauce. There was a next best thing, though.

Besides, a nice sea breeze sounded good right about now.

I pulled over near the onramp to the Old Pasadena Freeway, popped my trunk and fished around until I found a small locked box. Opened it. Jewelry. Not nice jewelry, either. Man jewelry was basically glazed testicles worn on the fingers or around the neck. In my box, there were class rings from every school worth mentioning and a few that didn't exist. There were gold chains. There was even a fake clip-on diamond tooth. I picked a gold rope and unbuttoned my top two buttons. I checked the look in the mirror.

Hello, Nicky Zorotovich.

I wished I'd picked up a nickname, but this ID wasn't even Russian. Wasn't Jewish, either. That's the trick with a good ID. Don't want to be too good to be true, especially if all you're after are scraps.

Still, a nickname would have been cool. Nicky "the Butcher" Zorotovich. Nicky "the Red Menace" Zorotovich. Nicky "Nicky" Zotorovich was the best I'd done so far.

I never liked visiting Vassily "the Whale" Zhukovsky. Unlike most of the people I worked with, Vassily was actually dangerous in an immediate sense. I worried that if I moved too slowly, he'd just eat me.

I'd be in San Pedro in the late afternoon, which would mean there was one place I could find Vassily: the one place I never liked to go. Meeting Vassily for lunch, great. Dinner, even better, assuming you liked cognac and caviar. Meeting Vassily for a nightcap, sure, even if it did lead to awkward side-by-side lap dances by strippers with bullet scars. There were two times never to meet the man. Before and after dinner. Both watching him work up an appetite and digest were repulsive.

Possible scenarios to keep my mind off Vassily: the Masons wanted me dead for divided loyalties and did the two-in-one. The Anas found out I was going to start a war and headed me off with a male assassin that couldn't be traced to them. V.E.N.U.S. found out and did the same, only their motive was to catch me in the process so they could wave a bloody shirt in front of the Anas. This wasn't helping. Wasn't an investigation supposed to *eliminate* suspects?

The Barbary Coast was a section of San Francisco in the latter part of the 19th century. Supposedly, it was the most debauched place on earth. You could get hookers of every flavor, gamble away your life savings, and watch no-holds-barred unarmed combat. It was like a hillbilly Caligula's wet dream.

Vassily came over from Russia with this very idea. He'd spent his life trying to recreate the Barbary Coast just south of the harbor. He had been partially successful, proving that the American Dream wasn't dead, just a little sticky. When I got there, he would be getting ready for the night: watching his dealers set up, scaring his whores, and fixing the fights.

From the outside, the new Barbary Coast didn't look like much. Just some warehouses that scary Russians liked to loiter in front of, smoking. They returned my nods.

I picked the least scary-looking one of them, which was like selecting the least horrifying stage mom. "I'm looking for Vassily."

"What the fuck happened to you? Get in a fight?" His accent was pretty thick. Stereotypical Southern Russian.

I touched Mina's autograph. "You should see the other guy." Seriously. The other guy was a hot girl. "Where's Vassily?"

"He's with dogs."

"What, no rats?"

"Traps been bare for days, except for couple raccoons and a possum. Last time we try them, no good."

I went past him. This section of the warehouse was the casino. The only sounds were a pit boss's rusty murmur, the purr of the cards, clinks of glass from the bar. I walked past this low-rent Vegas to a padded door. The muscle stood aside. I opened it.

Sounds: barking. Smells: blood, shit. God, I hated this part of the place.

I knew some murderers. Vassily had killed people. I wouldn't have been surprised if Stan Brizendine had done the big deed at one time. Hasim was an Assassin, so it was pretty much a job requirement. The saving grace was something John Gotti supposedly said to a scared lawyer. He leaned across the table and offered what he thought was a comforting smile and said, "Don't worry, we only kill each other."

That's mostly true. Not me, of course. I'd probably throw up if I pointed a gun at someone, and that would reflect badly on me and my employers. Who wanted to pay the Puking Hitman? I wanted a nickname, but not that bad.

Like I said, Gotti's theory was mostly true—just not in Vassily's case. Coming in here, seeing the chainlink cages stuffed with dogs—it bugged the shit out of me. These were dogs. Animals. There was no element of choice there. They were going to kill each other and they never got a vote in the matter. All they had done to die was get born a dog, then meet Vassily. The point is, I couldn't stop thinking about what amounted to a bunch of mentally challenged wolves, and it bugged me more that Vassily was hurting them than that he was hurting people. It seemed like I should think about my priorities, or even sic the ASPCA or PETA on him. PETA vs. the Russian mob. Yeah, I'd pay to see that.

I saw Vassily through several layers of fence. He was looking at one of the dogs, a snarling and snapping black-and-tan that might have been a Rottweiler. He was speaking to a short, balding man with what looked like carpal tunnel braces on both forearms.

There's an element to a good nickname. If it makes you laugh whenever you hear it, it's a good nickname. If different people at different times bestow the same nickname on the same guy, it's a good one. If you hear about someone by that nickname, then see the guy, and you can immediately deduce that that's the guy, it's a good nickname.

Vassily the Whale might as well have been born at sea. Calling him big didn't cut it. He was about six-ten, but walked in a rolling hunch that made him look rounder. I had no idea how much the man weighed, but he looked like the Kingpin. His bald head was almost impossibly shiny, and he wore that kind of suit that only gangsters wear, the sort that shined like it was wet, like he had just surfaced from the depths. His meaty hands gave the impression of flippers.

The guy was a fucking whale on two legs.

He was also the scariest man this side of Brighton Beach. Vassily was the kind of guy that couldn't help but have legends made up about him. Legends about his strength, like the time he got drunk and fell in the bear cage at the zoo and ended up beating the shit out of the bear. The thing about Vassily was that you sort of believed the stories, no matter how weird they got.

"I don't see it," Vassily said.

"Trust me," said the trainer. "He's vicious."

I cleared my throat.

Suddenly, I had Vassily's undivided attention. I realized that I hadn't thought this through.

"Nicky Z! Someone give you trouble outside?" I realized he was commenting on my jaw.

"No, that's from earlier. Can I talk to you?"

Vassily said, "Not here." He led me back into the casino and up to the bar. "I'm glad you come, actually. Saves me trouble of calling you."

"Oh?"

"You first. You made drive. Wait. You want something?"

"Sure, how about a..."

Vassily was already waving at the bartender, who was already pouring two cognacs. Russians.

Vassily said, "Talk."

"Right. Has anyone talked to you about a hit on a Colin Reznick?"

Vassily's face was blank. "Who is Colin Reznick?"

Me, you psycho. "A friend of mine. He's into me for ten large, and he's getting skittish. I think he might be into someone else for more, but I can't be sure. If he was, I thought that someone might be less patient than I am."

"Ten large?"

"Gambling." Sometimes it worried me how easily I lie.

Vassily nodded. "I never heard this name before now. If someone wants him dead, they don't talk to me."

"What about the... uh..." I pointed to my head and made a swishing motion.

"The towelheads? No way little fish gets on their bad side."

I shrugged. "Being thorough."

"There's more to being thorough than just me and Abduls."

"What do you mean?"

"New players in town. Maybe old players who are good at hiding. Hitters out there that don't belong to either."

There are those that would think freelance assassins would lead to another form of organized crime, but that's for the people who had never traced the tentacles of the octopus back to the central mass like I had.

"Who, then?"

Vassily shrugged. "No one you have to worry about. Ten large isn't too much to lose."

"You're sure? Nothing on Reznick?"

Vassily gestured at me with a tumbler that looked like a

thimble in his flipper. “Don’t get so attached, Nicky. Eventually these fuckers make you do something bad, and you do it. Minute you pussy out is minute you lose power. You have to take things one step further than anyone thought you could.”

“Thanks, coach.”

“Poor Nicky. It’s funny, though, that you come to me asking about this Reznor.” I didn’t bother to correct him. Best he forget that name, and soon.

“What’s that supposed to mean?”

“A hit come to me just this afternoon. I was going to call you tomorrow to track this person, but here you are.”

He’d never called me about something like this. It might have been bad timing, or Vassily might have started to trust me. Either way, bad news.

“Just tracking?”

“You don’t pull any triggers. Not yet, anyway.”

“What’s the name?”

“Some model. Mina Duplessis.”

I’d never been strangled by cognac, but that mouthful tried its damnedest with hands made out of battery acid.

“You know this person?”

“No, no. Sorry. Wrong pipe.”

Vassily watched me. I couldn’t tell if he bought my bullshit. “Okay. You track this person, you find her, you call me, I send someone.”

Fuck that. “Who hired us?”

“Never seen him before. Little blond guy, mustache, skinny as a fucking rail. He smelled Fed to me.”

“Fed? You’re sure this isn’t a setup?”

“Open your shirt, Nicky.”

I laughed.

He said: “Not joking.” He loomed over me like an angry eclipse.

"It's cool," I said. It hadn't worked on the Candidate, and it didn't work on Vassily. Very carefully, I opened my shirt and held up the back.

Vassily grinned. "I was mostly joking. Still, can never be too careful."

The true irony is that I *was* a Fed, sort of. I was technically in the employ of six different alphabet agencies, and the minute Vassily found out about one was the minute he made good on his unspoken threats.

"Right. I'll track her down and call you."

Vassily was already ignoring me. His cognac was much more interesting. "Good."

I walked from the casino out into the evening. I didn't start to run until I was out of sight.

☥

FINDING PEOPLE IS PATHETICALLY EASY. MINA might as well have been Lojacked. First, I checked to see if she was listed. She wasn't, of course. Then, the magical tool of a magical age: Google. I set my laptop up in a coffee shop and got to work. I wasn't looking for her address, because that wouldn't be on there, but I knew what would be.

Her agency. Mina was a working model. She needed to be hired for bookings. I found her listing, along with her vitals and some glamour shots. I avoided going through those in too much detail. After being kicked in the face by someone, objectifying them becomes that much more difficult. There was also the fact that I was in a coffee shop, and there was a table of two mothers and three kids behind me that would probably not react well to a weird guy perusing cheesecake.

Agent first. Tried to hire her for an emergency booking, got told she was busy, found out where. It was past dark, and the bruise on my jawline was really coming in nicely. Getting into a fancy affair with something like that would be difficult at best, so I had to do something I really hated doing.

Put on makeup.

Even if it's not noticeable to anyone else, *you* know when you're wearing makeup. I don't know how women do it. It drives me insane. I feel like I'm melting.

I had to shave first, which was an adventure. I went home. Pressing the shaver to my jaw provoked the first curse of the evening. I fixed my hair and changed into something a bit nicer. I hoped the event wasn't black tie. I tried a suit that said "Hollywood player": dark colors and lots of them. That usually worked in a pinch. Chances were I'd be overdressed or underdressed, but not by much.

What to tell her? She thought I was an agent of the Anas. There was no guarantee she wouldn't freak the hell out as soon as she saw me. I had to explain that there was a hit on her, and if the Russian mob knew about it, the Assassins did, too. Explaining exactly how I knew this without getting another kick to the face would be a challenge.

I straightened my tie and tried to think of an end to the evening that didn't involve me missing teeth. I said goodbye to them just in case. We'd had a good run.

Yes, I was planning to warn her. I couldn't just let her die. I'd met her, after all. She had a name, a face, and a size seven foot. Maybe more importantly, the hit on Mina meant that both of the people who went to that locker were marked. It possibly meant a common enemy. Find the Fed that tried to have Mina killed, maybe find the empty-eyed man that tried to air out my brain. Could be the Masons wanted her dead to provoke V.E.N.U.S., could be V.E.N.U.S. wanted a martyr, could be the Anas wanted to drop a rising star, could be the Feds... oh, who the fuck knew what the Feds ever wanted.

I fed the axolotls and told them daddy would be home later.

The party was in Beverly Hills, of course. Might as well go

as Jonah Bailey, since that was the name she knew. I wasn't attached to a job, but I could easily fake one. Speak in generalities and look predatory and I'd fit right in.

The party was a release for Sultry, some new plus-sized label that Mina was supposed to be the face for. It looked like some kind of '50s revival. There had been some shots on Mina's site. She looked great. Not that I'd looked.

I rolled up good and late. It was a private home, an estate really, complete with valets. I don't like valets. They have entirely too much power for how much they get paid. "Keep it close, please."

The guy looked at the McDonald's boxes, but he didn't say anything. I made a mental note to give him a couple extra bucks for that.

There was a man at the door checking invitations. Go for broke. I waited until there was another party about ten seconds behind me, then I walked up to the doorman, looking not at him, but through the door.

"Excuse me, is Reed here yet?"

"Reed?"

"Sue's husband. Oh, right, there he is. Reed!"

He got out a "sir!" before he was knee-deep in the people behind me.

I headed inside. The foyer was huge, complete with one of those carpeted staircases that was perfect for making an entrance. I wouldn't call the people there beautiful exactly. A few, certainly; any gathering like that one brings out the trophy wives. But the graybeards on whose arms they draped brought the average appearance from a solid B+ to a gentleman's C.

I didn't belong. The concealer on my jaw stank. I tried to calm down. Search the crowd. How many players? I spotted a V.E.N.U.S. enforcer skulking around the stairs almost immediately. Bald, skinny, bearded, unmistakable. He didn't see me. I had to find Mina, and if I had the score, she was the guest of honor.

I walked through the double doors straight ahead under the twin staircases. The owners of the house probably called the place a living room, but it was more like a ballroom. It had been cleared out in the center, with antique chairs and settees facing inward: here would be the big reveal. I scanned the crowd. No Mina.

It hit me in the chest like a Nolan Ryan fastball. I ducked back behind the door. He didn't see me. Did he?

Stan fucking Brizendine was in the ballroom chatting, a smile plastered all over that cop face. There was a part of my mind that flashed on an absurd thought: he might not try to kill me in such a public place. Right. Because Dealey Plaza was so intimate.

Past Stan, drapes were hung around the far side of the room, forming a natural entryway. This would be where Mina would come from. A few guests gave me funny looks. I tried to avoid touching the makeup on my jaw. What I really wanted to do was let loose a stream of expletives that would have made Carlin blush, but there was work to be done.

Not technically work. I mean, I wasn't getting paid for this. The opposite, actually.

I backed off and looked through the door from a distance. I pinpointed Stan's location and waited. He was laughing and drinking and chatting with the graybeard set. Probably selling them on that burger chain he owned. I think they had about three restaurants. I hated to admit it, but they did this great burger with feta cheese. I wondered if Stan was Greek.

I had to get my head into the game. So Stan was here. So he was, in all probability, trying to have me killed. It didn't mean that I couldn't cross a room.

Turns out I didn't have to.

I found them outside. Smokers. In California, no one smokes inside. Those that do get the kinds of looks that one would usually reserve for someone who brought a duck into your living room and began vigorously sodomizing it. Smokers, like duck-sodomites, did their dirty little business outside. A side effect of this was a growing camaraderie between smokers. They all had it bad, and so they understood one another.

My mark was youngish, and he immediately smiled shyly at me. I said, "Hey, can I bum a smoke?"

He handed me one. "So, it's crazy in..."

But I was already back inside, the cigarette in my hand. A glance told me that Stan was where I left him. Now to get lost. I went right, into a sitting room, then through several doors. Through each, fewer and fewer guests. I was looking for the point where everyone would be in a crisp white shirt and a black bowtie.

One more door, and there it was. A staging area stuffed with silver chafing dishes and bored-looking staff. I showed off the cigarette in my hand, like I wasn't sure exactly what it was for.

"Excuse me?" to the caterer.

"Yes, sir?"

"I was looking for somewhere I could..." I finished the situation by waving my vice at him.

"Yes, sir, the front is..."

"I was asked to move. I think there's a couple people with, you know, allergies."

"Oh." He pointed at a door behind him. "Through that door, make a right and go straight. That leads to the garden in back."

"Thanks a million."

Through the door was a hallway. I made a left and started opening doors. Had to be around here somewhere. Nothing. Nothing. Nothing.

Jackpot.

Mina was leaning over, checking her makeup in a mirror surrounded by light bulbs in a room bolstered with racks of clothes that flattered the hourglass. She was wearing one of those dresses that made her look like she should be on a picnic in the '50s where everything is bright shiny colors and she keeps accidentally showing too much cleavage. I wanted to paint her on the nose of a B-52.

I shut the door.

She turned around.

"Hi," I said. Seemed neutral enough.

She looked terrified. "You... you're back."

"I don't want to alarm you or anything, but I have some bad news. Maybe you should sit down."

She was staring. I realized what she was up to. "Don't worry, I'm unarmed."

Which turned out to be the exact wrong thing to say. Mina might've been shorter than I was, but she was a formidable woman, and all twelve stone of her was coming right at me with death—or at least castration—in her eyes.

"No, wait!"

Her fist was cocked, but it didn't fall. I understood how she felt. She thought I was working for the Anas—which, in fairness, I was—and she thought I was here to finish the job she'd thought I was going to do outside of V.E.N.U.S. HQ. I sympathized. I really did.

"I'm not here to hurt you."

She had a couple options, and she landed on sarcasm. "You're not, are you? Well, that's just great. I love trusting double agents."

Double agent. That was kind of cute. “I don’t really care if you have trouble trusting me. The fact is, there’s a hit out on you that the Russian mob would just love to collect.”

“The Russian mob? What do they want from me?”

“I don’t know. Date any hockey players?”

She didn’t have a response to that.

I went on ahead. “Doesn’t matter. The point is, if the Kosher Nostra knows you’re hit-listed, so does everyone else. You’re not safe here.”

“And I’m safe, what, in your sex dungeon?”

“Sex dungeon? What the fuck are you... look, Mina, I didn’t get to finish my story this afternoon before you beat me up. What I was going to tell you was that right after I planted that envelope, I got attacked. It was definitely a professional hit, and not the normal kind. What this means is that both people who went to that locker have hits out on them.”

“Why?”

“That’s what I’m trying to figure out. I just thought that once I found out that you were targeted, I should take a little time out and warn you. Consider yourself warned.” I turned around, thought better of it. “Oh yeah. The guy I’m pretty sure set me up is here tonight.”

I put my hand on the knob, then paused. I wanted to give her some time to rethink the past five minutes and maybe say something. Anything. I was about to give up and turn the knob, when:

“Show me.”

I stopped.

She said, “Show me who set you up.”

I turned back around. Her posture said I was still a little dangerous, but I had piqued her interest enough so that she wasn’t going to cold-cock me on principle. That would have to do. “Okay, come here.”

I picked some scissors up off the table, and she flinched, but I ignored it. There was a doorway that led back into the ballroom. I opened it, finding a narrow hallway formed by those drapes that looked expensive from far away but cheap as hell up close. I cut a small hole in the curtain with the scissors and peeked through. Then I motioned to her to take the eyehole.

"Gray hair, mustache. Looks like a cop."

"I see him. Who is he?"

"Stan Brizendine. 31st Degree Mason. Runs the temple here in LA."

"Why did he want you to plant the envelope?"

"Good question."

She turned back to me. A small spot of light from the ballroom hit her right cheek. "You're a Mason?"

"Little bit."

"So you don't work for the Anas?"

"Never said that."

I took the eyehole back and nearly pissed myself at what I saw. The crowd had parted, trying not to look too closely, which was the effect he created wherever he went. He marched at the head of a bevy of bottle-redheads, looking neither left nor right, but instead up, because that was the only way for him to look. He was dressed in his specially tailored black velvet, accented by shocking silver jewelry. He was a little under three feet tall, and other than the shaved head and the black goatee, could be mistaken for an ugly child. He looked like mini-Ming. He was Paul Tallutto, the High Priest of the First Reformed Church of the Antichrist.

I turned back to Mina, whisper-yelling, "You want to tell me what the fucking *Satanists* are doing here?"

"What Satanists?" She seemed so innocent.

I motioned her to the eyehole.

"Who am I looking... oh. The midget?"

"Primordial dwarf, actually. You've never seen him before?"

She shook her head. She didn't move from the eyehole. "He's so tiny!"

"Mina, we have to go. We've got two major players here tonight. I know Paul's got a thing for redheads, but maybe that's a coincidence, and besides, that's mostly because of the legends."

"About witches?"

"About how Satan supposedly has a thing for red hair and green eyes."

"I have blue eyes," she said.

"Mazel tov. We have to go."

"I can't. This is the biggest contract of my career. V.E.N.U.S. finally got me my big shot. I'm the face of Sultry!"

"No argument there. You just have to make a decision. Do you want to be famous and dead, or unknown and alive?"

I expected her to have to think about it. After all, she *was* in LA. But she didn't. "Let's go."

"We just make a left turn and go straight and we're out the back. Do you want to get a jacket or something? I mean, it's summer, I know, but it's night and..."

"Jonah?"

"Yeah?"

"We need to go, remember?"

"Right." I opened the door and headed left. The escape was going well: no security, no handlers, no caterers. I got to the back door, a double glass number that gave me a great view of the garden out back. And that's when things went pear-shaped.

I said, "We have to turn around."

"Why?"

"Because there's an Assassin out there."

There was, and he was coming up the back porch. The first thing I saw was the cherry on the end of his smoke. Even in the dim light in the garden, I recognized him. It would be hard not to. He was the only Arab I'd ever seen with dreads. He had a scruffy beard, but other than that was dressed pretty nicely, probably to blend in with the partygoers. It was Tariq Suliman. I could think of one thing offhand that could take him, but I doubted anyone brought a chupacabra to a fashion show. We had leash laws in this town.

I grabbed Mina's hand and pulled her back. "There has to be another staircase."

"I think there's one in the kitchen. Come on." She led the way now. We went through to the other side of the house, into the kitchen. Tariq would be coming in through the rear. Caterers gave us weird looks, and we got a couple "sir?"s and "ma'am?"s as we went.

Of course. Stairs from the kitchen. I had to start hanging out with a better class of people if I wanted to think of these things—there were special stairs for the servants. Wouldn't do to have them mixing with the "real" people, after all. We went through the pantry and up. Just as we cleared it, I heard the kitchen door open, and another round of "sir?"s. Sounded like Tariq had figured out the servants' thing, too.

Up the stairs, through the door. We were in the house proper, the part that had been cordoned off, the part that the party wouldn't be in. Upside: Tariq couldn't net us in the crowd. Downside: Tariq could pretty much kill us at his leisure. We needed to get out of the house. If Tallutto and Brizendine were still in the ballroom, that was a clear path to the front...

...where the valets had my car. I swore out loud on that one.

"What happened?" Mina whispered.

"Uh... more bad news."

"This guy, he's an assassin?"

"Assassin. Big A."

"What?"

"He's a member of an Islamic cult that dates from the 9th century AD. They're the original Assassins, so they get a capital A."

"There's a thousand-year-old Muslim death cult after me?"

"Well... one member currently. His name's Tariq Suliman, but don't introduce yourself."

I opened a door. An office. That would have to do. I pulled Mina inside, hit the flimsy lock on the door, and looked around. Desk. Books. Window. A couple other doors out. I locked them, too. Then I checked the window. It was on the side of the house, and it was a sheer drop onto a concrete path.

"Jonah! He couldn't have gotten weapons past security."

"He doesn't use weapons. He likes to kill his targets with whatever's in the room. Considers it a challenge. I heard that a target once decided to hide out in a room that was stuffed entirely with feathers. Once Tariq was done with the guy, he looked like Clive Barker's pillow."

"That's horrible."

"Yeah. Shit." I was looking at the door, where I saw two parallel shadows. Tariq was standing right outside, listening.

Mina followed my eyes and hers got as big as Frisbees. The feet disappeared. On impulse, I went to the door. It would open inward.

"What are you doing?" she mouthed at me.

I counted to three and opened the door. Tariq's foot sailed through the now-open doorway. I slammed it as hard as I could. I wanted to get his head, but instead caught his leg, mid-calf. He didn't shout, but I knew it hurt when he yanked himself back through. I shut the door and locked it again, beckoning to Mina.

I opened the door to the left.

At that moment, I really hated anyone who ever had a hobby. This room was some kind of half-assed man cave, and this guy seemed to collect literally anything that could cause grievous bodily harm. There were swords on the wall, a signed baseball in a glass case, a model train with plenty of stabby bludgeony bits, a television that could easily be dropped on the head—I couldn't look anywhere without seeing my imminent and messy death.

The door to the office splintered behind me.

I yanked a katana off the wall.

Mina said, "What, are you kidding me?"

I really wanted to roll my eyes at her, but I just didn't have the time. Tariq was already on the other side of this door, and if I pulled the same trick, he'd be ready. I stabbed the doorjamb as hard as I could. The wood was strong, but the katana was stronger. The wood didn't splinter, but it gave.

Tariq kicked the door. The lock broke, but the door slammed right into three feet of folded steel.

I exclaimed, "Come on!"

I pulled Mina to the door out into the hall. A moment later, Tariq joined us, slipping out of the office door. He saw me, and his face broke into a wide smile. "What the hell? Don't I know you?"

Mina and I were backing away as he moved closer. In the hall: paintings, a fancy vase, an end table. Tariq could probably smother a guy with the Oriental rug that ran the center of the hall.

"Yeah, I do." He really did have a nice smile. Genuine.

"Sure, you're..." he snapped his fingers to remind himself. "Larry? Lenny?"

He was closer to us than we were to the stairs down.

"It's always nice to see a friendly face," he was saying. "But this contract is mine. You should fuck off downstairs or something."

I didn't have to look at Mina to know that she was looking at me in horror. I'll be the first to admit, it didn't look good. "Yeah, sorry about that. You're right."

He nodded. "Just like a school of fish. I'm the alpha fish, and you should know that."

"You're thinking of wolves." It was insane, but I was getting closer. He hadn't tensed yet.

"Right, yeah. Wolf fish. So here's what we do. You go downstairs and grab us both some of those mini-quiches. I'll kill her, I dunno." He smashed the vase with his fist and picked up a shard. "Maybe cut her throat or something. I come down, we have some quiche, then get a real meal. I'm hella hungry."

Maybe it was that he threatened Mina's life. Maybe it was that he said "hella."

The important thing was that he didn't see it coming. As he was looking down at his foot from where I stomped it, bringing up the shard to slice me open, I head-butted him.

It would have worked if it wasn't Tariq Suliman I'd tried it on. He moved back, Thufir Hawat's reed in the wind, and I was left off balance with Tariq ready to perform a makeshift appendectomy on me.

Mina did the exact right and the exact wrong thing. It really depended entirely on what her goal was. She started to run at us. Suddenly, I was an afterthought to be knocked to the ground. Tariq surged past me. I kicked the table next to him, trying to bring it down right on him. He danced aside, turning to me.

"Come on! You can't want the contract this much."

"I really, really don't."

That confused Tariq long enough to make him pause. He turned back to Mina. "Okay, Ginger, whaddya got?"

"I'll show you," she said. And then she screamed. Loud. Piercing. Bloody murder, even. The exact word, I think, since I was trying to make it out through eardrums that felt like she took a cheese grater to them, was "Security." But with that many additional vowels, it was hard to tell. She backed up, trying to get to the landing.

"Oh, come on! That's a bitch move!" Tariq said.

I grabbed Tariq's arm. He turned around, the shard raised. "Whoa!" I whispered. "I'll take her out the front—go through the back and meet me on the west side, got it?"

He nodded and bolted.

I turned around to see Mina looking at me with a mixture of wonder, horror, suspicion, and something else that I was too much of a pessimist to ID.

"We have to go, now," I said.

"What did you say to him?"

"That I was going to take you to meet him on the west side."

"And we're actually..."

"Taking my car and getting the fuck out of here."

"I like this plan."

"Thought you might."

We hit the top of the staircase. Security was coming up the stairs. Mina pointed them down the hall. My eyes went to the door. I knew the guy leaving the house. Wasn't security, valet, or waiter. Last time I saw him, I had been dodging the most terrifying DIY project outside of the Discovery Channel.

"What's wrong?" She followed my eyes. "Is he another assassin? Or Assassin?"

I nodded. "Yeah. Mine."

The Candidate glanced back to the ballroom and he went out into the night, still wrapped in that trenchcoat, and probably packing the flail. Apparently security here sucked.

Still, two players, two killers, two people marked for death. Good party.

I pulled Mina down the stairs. "Where are we going?" she asked. "Somewhere safe?"

There were eyes following us. Made sense. I was kidnapping the whole reason for them being there. If Mina had a good publicist, they could concoct some kind of story to spin this situation into fame. Maybe she was kidnapped by an international jewel thief and sold to a Saudi oil sheik, where she was imprisoned on a pleasure yacht for a week before enacting a daring escape. Or could be she was coming to the rescue of a young fan with a rare form of leukemia, the cure for which was the exclusive property of some soulless plutocrat, and Mina would have to use every ounce of brains and sex appeal to get it. Or maybe she was a costumed vigilante who had seen the Minasignal glowing in the night sky and was heading out to thwart the mayor's assassination by a team of malcontents with primary-color fixations. My point was that publicists get paid for something.

Instead of explaining this, I decided to keep it simple. I said, "The opposite. We're tailing that guy that was just here."

"Why are we doing that?"

"Because he tried to kill me this morning."

"Consider my previous question repeated."

"Because he'll lead me to his handler."

"Until further notice, assume I'm answering everything you say with the same question."

I was trying to be patient. I really was. "He leads us to the handler, maybe the handler tells us why he's trying to kill us."

"Or he tries to finish where his guy left off."

"You're just stuffed with rainbows and kittens, aren't you?"

We got to the door, and the man was in his car, driving back down the gravel driveway. I turned to the valet. "Tell me you kept it close."

He smiled. "Ten bucks close."

I flashed the Hamilton at him. "You have a big future in organized crime."

He brought me my car and I paid him. I had to drive fast to catch up with the Candidate.

On the stereo: "Peace of Mind."

The Candidate was in a beat-up Honda. There was a bumper sticker on the left side that used to read "MEAT IS MURDER. Tasty Tasty Murder," but it had been selectively vandalized, getting rid of the "AT" in "MEAT." The culprit was probably the Candidate himself, in one of his little fugue states. A cry for help and a little advertising all rolled into one. Kind of like a billboard for antidepressants.

Mina said, "Are you planning on explaining yourself?"

My mind was a blank. "I... uh... I eat a lot of lunches in the car and I don't always have time to get to a trashcan?"

"Not that. Although, wow, you could stand to put some of this in a plastic bag or something. Anyway, no, you need to explain what's going on here. You show up at the lockers, then at V.E.N.U.S., now here. You said there was a Mason and a Satanist in the crowd, and then we get attacked by Bob Marley. I think maybe you need to sing me a little conspiracy Schoolhouse Rocks."

"Okay. Ask me questions. One at a time."

"You knew that Assassin?"

"I met him one time. It was at a party... thing. Really just a bunch of guys sitting around and watching cartoons."

"Are you an Assassin?"

"I'm what they call a rafiq. Think of me as an associate. They wouldn't let me in on account of my not being Muslim."

"And how did you know about the Russian mob?"

"They told me."

"I shudder to ask the next question that springs to mind."

I didn't have to check to know the look that she was throwing at me. I decided to just get it over with and answer her. "Yeah, them, too."

"Masons and Satanists?"

"If it makes you feel any better, I also work for the Vatican and a cult that worships the Greek goddess of discord."

She said, "What about vampires? You work for them, too?"

"No. Vampires don't exist."

"I heard..."

"What the hell is it with vampires? Not real. Trust me."

"But those others. You're working for all of them."

"Yeah." I couldn't qualify that, either. It's not like you can say, "Well, yeah, I'm a Satanist, but they do a lot of great work in the community." That kind of statement never goes over well, no matter the company.

I simply said, "I work for all of them."

I watched her out of the corner of my eye. It wasn't happening like I pictured it, when I finally came clean to someone.

Not that I was coming clean. It was more like coming a little less dirty, which didn't sound good in my mind. I always expected hysterics. Some breathless accusations. Maybe a slap, possibly a punch; could be a rake across the face. About half the time, I pictured my confessor jumping from the car. Mina didn't do any of that.

Why? Wasn't that what normal people did? Normal people without ulterior motives?

Instead, she just took a deep breath. "This guy was waiting for you at the locker?"

I nodded. "He was the one that put that huge-ass dent in it."

"I was wondering about that. Are you sure he was there for you?"

"What?"

"Well, he was at my party tonight. He attacked you because you were at the locker. It's possible he meant to attack me."

"I was just thinking how much you and I look alike."

She grumbled, "Don't be a dick. What if the order he got was to off the person who went to the locker, and you show up late or he shows up early? They didn't think that he'd go after you. I mean, we know for a fact there's a price on my head, but what about you?"

She was right. I hated that she was right. A fraction of the info I had, and she was cutting right through the bullshit. I was silent, and she took that the wrong way.

"What, that's stupid, right?"

"No, I mean, I had considered it." I really hated myself for that one. "I suppose it's possible. He's a Candidate, so he's not going to be doing a lot of critical thinking."

"Candidate?"

"As in Manchurian."

She got it right away. "A brainwashed assassin. Like the

Sinatra movie."

"Exactly. The tech's been out there to do this since the original Assassins—our friend Tariq Suliman's cult—but it got rediscovered by the CIA in the '50s and '60s in a program they called MK-Ultra. They completely break these men down to their core, then build them back up from scratch, kind of how they do in fraternities and religious cults, only more extreme. These guys become complete OCD wrecks, hypnotizable at the drop of a hat, and dangerous as hell."

"You sound like you should be ranting on a street corner."

"That's a good way to get yourself killed. Anyway, this guy, in the 'Me is Murder' car, is one of those. If someone activated him and released him, it *is* possible they just gave him the locker number."

"So this guy might be after one or both of us, and you think it's a good idea to follow him?"

I gave her what I hoped was a cocky smile. "Trust me. I handle this kind of thing all the time."

She rolled her eyes.

I tailed the Candidate back through Beverly Hills and down into Hollywood. The traffic was getting good and homicidal: Hollywood on a Friday night. I put a couple of cars between the Candidate's car and mine, keeping track of him by watching a whorl of dust in the back window of his car.

We passed the crowds on the way to clubs and movies. Then we turned a corner onto a residential street, an old Hollywood kind of place where every Spanish bungalow had a bird of paradise planted right outside the front window. The street was divided into two lanes, each too small for a car. Everyone just drove down the center, weaving into driveway gaps to avoid oncoming traffic. The Candidate pulled into one of those driveways. I drove on.

"Watch him. See which house he goes into."

Mina twisted around in her seat, which created the side problem of pushing her breasts right at me. I've heard that yogis can use sheer force of will to stop bleeding, ignore pain, and even float on thin air. Fuck them. Not staring at Mina's chest showed *real* willpower.

She said, "Got it."

"Now I just have to find a place to park."

There is a group out there that claims to harvest frustration. They're a bit of a bogeyman in the information underground. They supposedly have links to all the usual suspects: CIA, Nazis, and the array of Protestant splinter sects. In my time, though, I've only ever met one person who claimed to represent them, and he was not exactly known for his trustworthiness. They're behind every loose nail, every rotten board, and the DMV. The truly paranoid even suggest that they're the reason that it rains whenever you wash your car. The parking situation in Hollywood is so bad, I could almost believe in them.

The thing is, if they really existed, I'd work for them.

The next twenty minutes were variations on this conversation:

Her: "There's a spot."

Me: "It's too small."

Her: "No it's not. This is a small car."

Me: "It's not made by Hot Wheels."

I finally did park, right under a sign that told me I needed a permit. I glanced into the window of the car in front of me, copied what I saw on a scrap of paper, and stuck it on my dashboard. It would have to do.

Getting back to the Candidate's house was a longer walk than I would have liked.

"That's the house," Mina said.

Me is Murder was already gone, which was probably

for the best.

I walked up the driveway to have a look around. The house seemed quiet from out here. Mina followed, walking like she had seen Elmer Fudd do when he was huntin' wabbit. I thought about trying to give her a crash course, but I quickly dismissed that as soon as I had a vision of us stage-whispering back and forth about the finer points of being inconspicuous. At that point, I should probably just have t-shirts made up with "BREAKING AND ENTERING, Crime for Some, Hobby for Others" emblazoned on the fronts. I checked around the back of the house and found a wooden door. I tried it.

"What are you doing?" Mina stage-whispered.

I shook my head. The lockpicks were out and I already had the lock open. That's one thing—I do actually have good hands. I catch whatever is tossed my way, and I can lift a wallet without too much trouble. Cheap locks like this one were less than a challenge.

I clicked on my penlight. The door opened into a small laundry room that led into a kitchen.

"I guess after you told me you were in the Russian mob, B and E shouldn't surprise me too much."

"You make me sound like a one-man psycho crime spree."

Impressively deadpan, she said, "Right, I keep forgetting that the Russian mob is like the March of Dimes."

"Well. Um. Just keep your voice down when you're haranguing me."

The guy's fridge was depressing, and coming from me that means the contents of the icebox would make a domestic seriously consider that life itself had no meaning.

To wit: "What does this guy eat, ketchup?" Mina was hovering over my shoulder, shaking her head sadly.

It didn't get any better in the cupboards. Lots of things in cans and boxes, nothing that looked even vaguely natural. The guy's diet made mine look like a model of the food pyramid in comparison. I was a better eater than a mind-controlled super-killer: gold star for me.

I moved into the living room, passed my light over the lumpy gray couch, over the mountain of window-envelopes that was the coffee table, over the expensive TV and cheap lounger covered in duct-tape hieroglyphs. The floors were hardwood, crunchy with crumbs or slick with magazines. Mina picked up a piece of mail.

She said, "Shine the light over here."

The guy's name was Raul Diaz. It was kind of nice to put a name to the attempted murder.

I glanced around for his weird-ass flail, even opened a closet. He probably took it with him. I mean, I would have.

I moved into the bathroom, and immediately backed out again. I really hoped the guy owned about a dozen cats, because otherwise... best not to think about it.

Then, the bedroom. It was more of a den, and not in a man-cave sort of way. It was a den better suited for the hibernation of a predator. It had the perfect amount dankness in the air. The bed was really just a mattress on the floor, and it wasn't made so much as it had some blankets piled in the center in a crusty hillock.

"So we know he's single," Mina said.

"I think that's a safe assumption."

I read the look on her face: she was picturing trying to live in this place, existing entirely on tiptoes and fingertips. The entire house was a toilet seat in a gas station bathroom.

He had shelves, or at least egg crates and cinderblocks re-purposed. In a way, it looked like an apartment out of time, before cheap furniture made everyone's place look at once expensive, sterile, and rickety. Really, his place made good sense in earthquake country. I looked the shelves over and froze.

"What?" Mina asked.

I shined the light on what I'd seen. It was a pistol, 9mm. Who owns a gun, gets activated for an assassination attempt, then thinks to himself, "Ah, the gun's so boring. You know what, I think I'm gonna go with the rock on the chain."

She murmured, "Oh."

"Yeah, I was thinking the same thing."

I left the gun where it was. On the shelves, otherwise, it was what you'd expect. *Catcher in the Rye*, a whole lot of Vonnegut, a few peeling-laminate manuals with some vaguely occult stamps on the spines, and then the blue books. As the beam of my flashlight splashed over them, I blinked. I sent it back. There were little blue spines, upwards of thirty.

"Are those..." Mina trailed off.

I took the last one off the shelf. Blue book, the same kind I'd used in college. I remember being glad that I'd never have to clamp eyes on another one of those again. I supposed that if I was going to see them again, it might as well be here.

"Yep," she said. "Is he a college professor or something?"

"What?"

"These guys, they have, like secret identities, right?"

"As long as 'drifter' is secret."

"This is a decent neighborhood. He has some source of income, and I really doubt we're going to find a W-2 with 'assassin' on the occupation line."

"Probably true."

"Deep Throat said to follow the money."

I chuckled. "I thought Deep Throat said..."

"Don't. Whatever blowjob joke you were about to make, skip it."

"Suit yourself." I opened up the blue book. I kind of wished I hadn't, because the damn thing gave me the creeps.

Didn't help that I was crouched in a room that stank of sleep sweat and reading it by flashlight with a gun somewhere above the back of my neck. I checked the last page. I found:

AE
1078 + 333 = 1
Demonstrate
Arithmetic

Then, a drawing of two stick figures on a horse.

Charles. Charles. Charles.
Charles the
Master's voice.
Time to go time to go time to go time to go time to go
Locus est terribles

I skipped back. I found:

AL AMOUT
Shub shub shub shub shub

Then, three triangles.

Those
Seers.
About how much? It will cost.
Mount
De Molay.

Then, crosses. The crosses connected, forming a cross-hatching that looked like it could comfortably crucify a centipede.

All of the writing was in a childlike cursive.

Mina, reading over my shoulder, said, “What the hell?”

I cracked up.

“What?”

I said, “That tone... it’s the one you use on the commercial. ‘It’s so easy!’” She smacked my arm. “Ow!”

“What do you... have you ever seen anything like this?”

I collected my brain. “Automatic writing. Repeated hypnosis has a way of short-circuiting the way the mind should work. It shuts down the subconscious, so the hypnotized person can’t sort through what they experience the way a normal person does, in dreams. They need an outlet. A lot of times, one of these lone nuts will compulsively write or paint. What they produce actually makes sense, but only in a sort of dream-logic way.” I flipped through the journal. There were lots of symbols implicating half a dozen societies, but one kept rearing its holier-than-thou head. I checked a few other blue books just to be sure.

I stood up, flashing the light around. “Come on.”

“You found something?”

“I think so. I want to check his mail.”

She followed me back into the living room. I passed the sofa and looked down on the coffee table. Most of it was credit card applications. I remember hearing that there were two credit cards per person in the United States. It’s a shame that most people didn’t know why that was, but they were probably happier not knowing just how real certain gods were. Other than that, there were a few bills. Right near the top, an opened letter. He had been reading it, and not too long ago. It could have been what activated him. I scanned it. Probably not.

One look told me it wasn’t his handwriting—it looked nothing like the blue book scrawls. It was block-printed with a precision to the letters that bordered on artificial. It was on a grid; the writer obviously valued the margin and wanted to keep as inviolate as a nun's panties.

"What is it?" she said.

"Love letter, I think. Listen to this: 'Dearest One. Your beauty keeps me both near and far. Near because I can't bear to be without it. Far because I fear if I approach, it will burn me up. I love you madly. Anon.'"

"That's kind of sweet."

"I saw the guy. He's not really much to look at."

Mina retorted, "There's no accounting for taste. I mean, back in school, my roommate..." and she trailed off.

Because that's when the sofa stood up and opened two giant red eyes.

I stumbled backward. Mina screamed. I would have liked to join her, but I couldn't find my tongue. All I could see were those two red eyes, big as the sun and the moon in the sky at once. They were getting closer.

I felt something grab me. I didn't fight it. Couldn't.

I was being dragged away. The thing in the living room lumbered toward me, but I was moving too fast for it to catch. Then, suddenly I was in the fresh air. The scent of jasmine brought me right back.

"Jonah! Jonah!"

Mina slapped me hard across the face. Her pinkie hit the footprint on my face.

"Son of a...!"

"Run!" She pulled me down the driveway. Some morbid impulse made me look back. I could see that dim shape in there, standing back from the window, watching us go. Mina never looked. She was smarter.

Then again, I was the one in sensible shoes.

By now, we were halfway down the block. Whatever it

was wasn't following. Mina was trying to catch her breath. "What... what the hell *was* that thing?"

"I... I don't know."

"What? I thought you knew everything!"

"It was some kind of cryptid." I could think a little, now that I was no longer looking into those twin hellpits that thing called eyes. Actually, for all I knew, it called them soul cages, but thinking like that wasn't going to calm me down.

"That was a monster!"

"Monster and cryptid mean the same thing. One's more... polite, I guess." I was trying to find some solid ground, thought maybe there was some in a pedantic lecture.

"I don't care what they're called! That was a *thing*! Unnatural!"

"Supernatural."

"That's not helping!"

I had started to calm down. Yes, what had happened was weird. Yes, what had happened was scary. But it was something I knew about, at least vaguely. I mean, on one level, it was like looking at the teeth marks in your shredded leg and being like, "Oh, it was a tiger shark that got me, not a great white!" But I had seen cryptids before—just never in the living room of a guy who had tried to kill me.

Mina craned her neck back toward Diaz's house, probably having the same sensation I did, that the big bastard would be shambling for us like Jason Voorhees. "I feel like it should be there," she said.

"It's not, right? It's not. We're okay."

"We're okay?"

"Well, you know, relatively."

I shuddered. Focus. A Candidate had a large and as yet unidentified cryptid in his living room. That added a wrinkle to the situation. We made our way back to the car, Mina looking over shoulder every couple of steps, me stubbornly refusing to, but grateful she was doing it. As we got in, one of my phones started ringing. One look at which one it was made me want to laugh. That the ringtone was "O Fortuna" was a dead giveaway.

"Hello," I said.

"Squire Max," said the voice on the other end in a shaky Brit accent. It belonged to a guy named Richard Colby. "I need you to come here, now."

"Sire, I'm on sort of a..." I glanced at Mina. "A date."

"Bring her, but tell her nothing."

I said, "Sure." Didn't feel the need to tell him I was coming anyway. He hung up without saying goodbye.

"Where are we going now?" she said.

"Medieval Castle."

There was a long pause as she processed it. Then, finally: "That tourist trap?"

There's a scene in *Alien* that always bothered me. It's not the one where the chest-burster jumps out of John Hurt, either. It's the part toward the end, right after they behead Ash. Parker and Lambert go off to stock up while Ripley sets the self-destruct and looks for her cat. Eventually, she gets in the escape pod, gets undressed, and finally defeats the alien.

What bugs me about this scene is that Ripley seems like she's *trying* to get herself killed. First she goes off alone, then she looks for her cat, then she strips down to her underwear. It's ridiculous. She did everything but have a meth-fueled threesome with Johnny Depp and Kevin Bacon. She only acted this way because she had no idea what kind of movie she was in. Had she known it was a horror movie, she probably would have put on a parka, joined a convent, and spent more of that movie gazing soulfully into the middle distance.

It's just that movies before 1996 seem to exist in this parallel world in which movies don't actually exist, or if they do, it's only the cheap public domain ones. Then again, most good movies were made before 1996, so maybe there's something to that.

I glanced at Mina out of the corner of my eye. I'd seen *Maltese Falcon*. I knew what happened to world-weary schlubs who ran into drop-dead redheads. There was only one way our relationship could end: a betrayal in the third act. We'd be on a train, or someplace high up. Somewhere suitably dramatic, where I could have a showdown with whoever had set me up. It would all be going fine—then, bam. Mina springs her trap. One way or another, her knife was going between my shoulder blades.

It would probably make more sense to cut her loose sooner rather than later. Stab her in the back before she could do the same to me.

The problem was, every time I thought about betraying her, I got sick to my stomach.

Maybe Ripley knew what kind of movie she was in, but she just had to push on ahead, find her cat, and get naked because that's just who she was. I was born a cat-loving nudist, and I supposed I might as well die that way.

"What?" Mina said.

"What?" I said.

"You keep looking at me out of the corner of your eye. It's making me nervous."

"Sorry."

Our attempted assassinations were beginning to look like the edge of something big. Still, the problem at the center of it all was: who wanted both Mina and me dead? What did we both know that had to die with us?

I asked, "How much do you deal with the Anas?"

"Not much. Why?"

"Has the peace been holding?"

"As far as I know, yes. None of us have died. That...that

sort of worries me, actually. I mean, I'm just coming out as a symbol, you know? So if the peace was going to collapse, I'd probably be the one on the block."

"You knew that going in?"

"Sure."

"And yet you did it anyway?"

"Someone has to."

I let that one go. Instead, "So, listen, they might call me 'Max,' or 'Gross' down there."

"Why would they do that?"

"Because I told them my name was Max Gross."

"Oh. Hell of a name."

"I read it on the side of a cargo container."

"Spend a lot of time down at the harbor?"

"More than I'd like."

We drove a little while in silence.

Then: "Your real name isn't Jonah, is it?"

"Based on the way you said that, it sounds like you know the answer to that one."

"Yeah," she said. I kept waiting for her to ask me my real name. I had half a dozen responses prepared for that one, and they all sounded really cool in my head. I sounded like a hard-boiled spy. I would have liked to punctuate them with a tug on some bourbon, but I was driving, and we were hitting Orange County traffic.

She didn't ask. Mina seemed to have a sixth sense about those things.

Instead, she said, "What should I call you?"

"Well, while we're down at Medieval Castle, you call me Max. When we're with your superiors at V.E.N.U.S., I'd appreciate you calling me Jonah."

"You think I'm not going to tell them about this?"

"Why would you?"

"Because you're a mercenary! You're working for the enemy."

"To be fair, the Anas could say the same thing."

"I'm not interested in being fair. There's a war going on, and, frankly, you have a penis."

"Um... yeah, I do. What's that got to do with anything?"

"Because I'm fighting for the body image of women everywhere. You're a man. You don't get a vote."

"Do the bearded castrati get a vote? Because last I checked, they were members in good standing."

She glared at the road. "Yeah, I don't like them either," she muttered.

"If my being a mercenary really bugs you, you might want to take a look around. We're all mercenaries when you get right down to it. Oh, I know, you have a higher calling to help the needy. I'm not sure when women with giant racks became a downtrodden minority, but I'll take your word on that. I'm willing to lay good odds that you don't work for free. No, you get paid for your shows, for your commercials. Every time you cram your ass into jeans two sizes too small, you're cashing a check. I just took that successful business model and applied it on a wide-ranging scale. And sure, maybe I'm not a true believer in much of anything, but let's get something crystal clear. The world could use a few more people who don't believe in anything, because of one simple fact: it's not people like me that become terrorists or mass murderers."

There was a long pause, and I regretted about half of what I said until Mina cut me wide open. "No. It's people like you that *enable* terrorists and mass murderers."

I couldn't remember Barbara Stanwyck being that annoying.

As awkward silences went, it was a doozy. There wasn't a whole lot to say after that. I just kept driving and looking straight ahead. Mina did the same.

On the stereo: "Feelin' Satisfied."

Calling Medieval Castle tacky would be missing the point. Of course, calling it classy would *really* be missing the point. Medieval Castle existed in that strange penumbra that emerged when kitsch had rebounded in on itself so many times that even hipsters couldn't quite muster the ironic detachment to appreciate it. Granted, if they knew what the so-called "Feast and Tournament" hid, they might come to it as pilgrims.

But that would be missing the point, too.

It was a castle, or at the very least, the conception of one in the mid-'80s, filtered through a limited budget, and with no desire to actually repel any invaders. One catapult would bring the whole place down, but it was the truly rare Orange County family that actually possessed siege weaponry.

The parking lot was mostly empty, except for some of the spots right next to the side entrance, where the employees went in. A casual observer might not see the pattern. A car person would immediately note the preponderance of American muscle, though not just the classic models from the '60s and '70s. Me, I always laughed a little bit when I saw the names on the backs: Charger, Mustang, Bronco.

"So who are these people?"

I quickly played through the conversation from the simple, hypothetical response, "I'm not supposed to say." It ended with blackmail. So I told her the truth: "The Knights Templar."

"You're kidding."

"No, I'm a squire."

I opened the door with my key. This was backstage, but they would be waiting for me in the main hall. I knew Richard. He liked the pomp and the circumstance, and was probably knee-deep in his usual bullshit.

"Wait, these guys are Satanists," she said.

"No, you're thinking of Paul Tallutto. Remember, the primordial dwarf?"

"Okay, so what are they, really?"

"Dangerous. They've been around for a long time, they have nearly unlimited funds, and they're experts in the kind of weapons that stopped being used because they were too brutal. If you want to yell at someone, wait until we're gone and you can yell at me again."

Mina thinking that the Templars were Satanists was due to a rumor started by the Catholic Church way back in 1312. Basically, the pope accused the Templars of worshiping Mammon instead of God, which managed to be both entirely true and entirely hypocritical. Imagine if the Catholic Church started attacking daycare centers for unsafe jungle gyms and you can get a handle on how ridiculous this accusation was. The Templars were more or less exterminated, but a couple managed to escape. They had been kicking around ever since, trying to recapture their glory days—mostly by finding excuses to wale on each other with medieval weaponry.

It was quiet backstage. I could smell makeup and steel, but I ignored that and followed the hall toward the central pit, bordered on either side with coarse curtains. Up ahead: a doorway that led out into gold. Gold sand underfoot and gold light from the floods up top. Within twenty steps, there was a clanking sound. The gold was eclipsed.

Son of a bitch.

His name was Eric Caldwell, and I had once called him "shitbird." Number three on my "times someone tried to kill me" list. He was a big guy, and even bigger when he was wrapped in steel. He had replaced his show tabard, the one with the Day-Glo colors, with a simpler one emblazoned with what looked like a Nazi iron cross, only in red—the Templar insignia. He had one of those stubble beards complete with slightly longer hair around where he should have a goatee, and dark hair like he was on the cover of a romance novel. More importantly, he was armed with three feet of steel.

"Gross. And guest?"

"Sir Richard asked to see me, and he said to bring her."

Eric turned his head to talk to someone inside. "Squire Max and guest to see you, Sire."

Richard's voice boomed out somewhere overhead. "Let them in!" Other than that ridiculous accent, he had a pretty good voice. He ordered hot wings with the authority of a man commanding a full spread of photon torpedoes.

Letting Mina in meant he was curious. It was always possible he knew about her already, if he knew about Raul Diaz and the swinging rock of death. It didn't feel like a trap, but "It didn't feel like a trap" could always be put on my tombstone. For extra fun, I could let Mina choose the name to go above it.

I gestured to her and walked toward the light. Eric loomed in close on me. I could smell his breath. Mostly rosemary—leftovers from the kitchen. I think he was trying to intimidate me, which, considering I still had a scar from our previous encounter, should have been a little easier.

"Chew some gum, Eric. For me," I said.

Then I was out in the light and before Sir Richard and there wasn't anything Eric could do within protocol.

Richard was, in many ways, the personification of this place. He looked like he had stepped right out of Boorman's *Excalibur*: same neat beard, same circa-1981 haircut, same good looks. He even had a little bit of an accent. He'd lived in LA for at least twenty years, but that damn accent was his bread and butter. I was pretty sure he was faking most of it these days, since he didn't sound like any actual British person I'd ever heard. He sat in a fake throne about fifteen feet above the floor—he was the "king" of Medieval Castle, after all. He was dressed like Eric, in plate armor with a similar tabard over it. Two knights flanked him, and two more stood in the shadows on my level.

"Thank you for coming, Squire Max. Would you be good enough to introduce your guest?"

He knew something. That's the only reason the son of a bitch would let her in. Let's lie to him and see what happens: "Sir Richard, this is Rosemary. Rosemary Lewis. My... um... friend."

"So I see. Welcome to Medieval Castle, Rosemary."

Mina gave me a look. "Uh... thanks. We're a little late for the show, I guess?"

"I'm afraid so. Come see us again another night and I would be pleased to allow you in free of charge."

"Sure." Mina's deadpan nearly made me lose it.

"Max, if you could come with me..." Richard gestured, and I took the meaning.

Between her clenched teeth, Mina hissed, "You're leaving me here?"

"You're as safe as I am," I said.

Her glare supplied the sarcastic comment.

I went backstage and climbed some stairs, joining Richard in the box. He had a look in his eye like a kid who'd just learned that the internet had a porn section. "That's quite a friend you brought us."

"I didn't really bring her to you, exactly."

The accent really slipped when he blurted: "I'm invoking the right of *droit du seigneur*."

Some people knew that as *prima noctis*, a possibly fictional tradition where the local noble was allowed to deflower the women on his land on their wedding night. I didn't bother to point out the obvious: Mina and I weren't getting married, and the probability of her still being a virgin was roughly equal to the chance of my developing the power to control the world's pelicans by thought alone.

Instead: "Yeah, have fun. That's between you and her."

He rubbed his hands together. "You're flirting with knighthood, Max."

"What a pleasant surprise."

"I have an errand for you. Something of the utmost importance. Are you familiar with the Chain of the Heretic Martyr?"

Of course I was. I wasn't born in a cave. "Somewhat."

"It was stolen, not long ago, from our French brethren. It was spotted in Los Angeles last week before it vanished again. Find it."

"Okay. Can I ask you a question first?"

Richard nodded. I raised my voice just loud enough so that the knights below could hear me. "Do we have any sleeper agents? Hypnotized assassins?"

The look on Richard's face said he had no idea what I was saying. He spoke, low, "No, nothing like that. The operation here is... small."

I heard the scrape of plate armor. "I'll find the Chain for you, Sire," I said.

Then I jumped down fifteen feet to the dirt floor. It hurt like hell, but I was hoping it looked at least a little cool. I don't think the wincing helped, though.

"Before you leave," he said, and trailed off because he was scampering toward the stairs. It was ridiculous to see a guy in full armor do that, and really, I'm not even sure how he managed it. He appeared in the hall behind Eric, and even Caldwell had to react to the way Sir Richard was mincing.

"Squire Max, if you would," and he made a shooing gesture toward Eric and me. "Miss Lewis, if I may be so bold..."

Eric was shifting his weight from foot to foot as I went to stand next to him. I gave him a once-over. "Gotta take a leak?"

"Huh? No, no, it's fine."

He didn't follow it up with an insult. He didn't loom. He didn't brandish. It was disconcerting.

I watched Mina's face go from curious to horrified to angry as Sir Richard whispered to her. Her shoulder tensed. I knew that move. Now I scampered to her side and moved in close, wrapping an arm around that hourglass waist. Mina had good heft to her, and I couldn't help but think how nice she'd feel if her dress weren't between us. The problem was, I had to head off the imminent head-off.

I said, "Well, I'm sure she'll think it over."

"She'll do a bit more than that," Richard said, and that made me want to slap him a little bit.

"Right, well, not tonight, though. She's got an early start tomorrow, and I have to drop her off so I can get on that errand, right?"

Richard looked at me, more than a little shocked. "Right, yes, of course. Well done."

I kept Mina very close as I dragged her from the center of the arena. "Come on, Rosemary. Let's get you home."

She was swearing under her breath. "Who the fuck does he think he is?"

"Jacques de Molay maybe. I'm not sure."

"He told me he has the right to..."

"Yeah, I know."

"Did he think it would work?"

"Probably has in the past. You know how women like dicks. Poor choice of words. Uh, how women like..." I tried to conjure up a noun with the frantic waving of my hand.

"Assholes?"

"I was going to say jerks, but let's use your word."

She said, "Women that do secretly think they aren't worth it."

We were out in the parking lot. The night was cooling off.

"So what did he want from you, anyway?"

"The Chain of the Heretic Martyr's gone missing."

Her eyes got big. "Holy crap."

"You know what that is?"

"Of course! If there's an artifact that both V.E.N.U.S. and the Anas would love to get their hands on, it's the Chain. I mean, this is the chain that bound St. Joan of Arc. You want to talk about a feminist icon? There you go."

"I think I already found it once."

She frowned, then, realization dawning, murmured, "The chain attached to the rock?"

I thought of the soot covering Diaz's palm. "Could be. Templars lose an artifact, then a Templar assassin shows up with something matching the description? Sir Richard didn't know what was going on, but it could have been anyone in there. An inside job."

"Makes sense."

"That's the part that bugs me. These kinds of things never actually make sense. If something has a neat little bow, you can bet pesos to pantaloons it's bullshit."

"You're a real pessimist, you know that?"

"I've heard it said."

"If the Chain's been stolen, it could be the fault of V.E.N.U.S. or the Anas," she said.

I nodded. "I never knew you guys wanted it so badly... and there's the... fuck me."

"What?" she said.

"Symbolism. Why was Kennedy killed at the triple underpass? Because it's an occult symbol. The trident. It's all about the sacrificial killing of the divine king, see. The point is, if someone was actually trying to turn you into a martyr, they couldn't pick a better weapon than the chain that helped martyr an icon associated with femininity. Plus, you know, your last name is French."

She looked terrified. "You think my name has something to do with it?"

"No, that's probably just a coincidence."

She glared, trying to figure out if I was fucking with her, or, more accurately, *when* I was fucking with her.

"Where to next?"

"Not sure yet. We're going to wait here for another..." I did the calculations in my head. "Eight or so minutes."

"What was the point of all that?"

"Would you please let my plan finish up before you criticize?"

Eight or so minutes later, I saw Eric Caldwell rushing from the side entrance. He was out of his armor, dressed in street clothes. Now, I'm not the kind of guy that uses the word "gay" as a pejorative. When I say something is gay, I mean that it has something to do with two guys having sex. I used the word gay to describe Greco-Roman wrestling, *Top Gun*, and Eric's outfit. It was nothing I could really put my finger on, but the clothes were way too tight, his hair just a little too perfectly tousled.

I said, "We're following Eric to his boss."

11

It was officially the next day. My ass was getting a bit sore from all the driving, and maybe a little in a symbolic sense. I was following Eric's Charger through the streets. Over the years, I've learned a few rules that go with good shadowing. One, keep a couple car lengths between you and the target. This buffer zone changes based on local traffic conditions. Two, stop following the guy if he's leading you off the beaten path just after he's had a phone conversation. And three, it helps to know where the guy is going before you leave.

The last is called instinct by most people who have it. As someone who didn't have that sense innately but grew into it, I have to say that's not the case. It's more about knowing the situation around the person and using that to make educated guesses. It's a good way to lose someone, but when it works, the tail is impossible to detect. A good trait, especially when the tailee is a master of the cruciform broadsword.

I paralleled him for a few blocks because I knew where he was heading in the vaguest sense. When the city tightened up, so did I, catching him again on Hollywood Boulevard. We weren't too far from Diaz's place.

I passed Eric as he was heading into a bar, looking plainly uncomfortable in his skin.

Mina said, "He's gay?"

I took in the crowd. Yeah, it was a gay bar. Either that or these were a bunch of straight guys who were into working out and personal hygiene and just really, *really* enjoyed each other's company. I said, "I guess so."

"Weird."

"What, you saw the way he was dressed."

Matter-of-fact: "Doesn't mean anything."

"Sure it does."

"Clothes don't make the man. It's more about how those clothes hang than anything else. He had this look about him like he was cross-dressing. Not that he was, but that he *felt* like he was. Like he was putting on a costume. Like you look."

I wasn't sure how to take that one. It didn't feel like a shot. The Templars had given us a common enemy, so we were able to comfortably ignore the blow-up we'd had earlier. I was still trying to think of an appropriate response to it. Maybe in a week or so, I'd call her up and say, "Hey, remember when you made me feel really bad about my life choices, well," and then I'd slay her with a *bon mot* they'd be discussing throughout the underground for generations. This was assuming I'd have her phone number. It'd be less effective if I had to call her agent.

In the meantime, I kept driving, found a parking lot, and paid nearly half a month's rent.

I said, "Let's go."

"You're not going in like that."

"Why the hell not?"

"First off, there's the Big Boy hair."

I touched the top of the swirl. It was still pretty immaculate. "What's wrong with it?"

"I thought Big Boy hair pretty well covered it."

"You're a Democrat, aren't you?"

"What's that got to do with anything? Here, let me..." She touched my hair. It crinkled. "What's in here, lacquer?"

"I have to, you know, make sure it sticks."

"That's a lot of commitment to look like this."

"You realize that you're going to give me a complex."

"Is there any water in here?" she asked.

I pointed to the sagging Mickey-D's cup in the cup holder. "The ice in there is probably melted."

She opened it up and dipped her fingers first into the cup, then into my hair. I could feel her breath on my face. I could have leaned in, but I didn't. I just stayed a foot away, concentrating on her slightly open mouth, on her blue eyes, on her smooth cheeks.

"You look a little less terrible now."

I didn't want to look away. I don't think anyone could really blame me for that. It wasn't until she pointed at the rearview mirror that I turned to have a look. It was a sort of a grown-out George-Clooney-in-the-first-season-of-*ER*.

"And the clothes? Should I...?"

"What are you wearing under that?"

"Undershirt."

"What kind? Jeez. You're not into fashion much are you?"

"What part of 'double agent' are you not getting? I spend my life trying not to get noticed, and fashion is about trying to get noticed. It's a frickin' undershirt. I don't know."

She smoothed out my collar. "This will have to do."

"Okay, so I'm supposed to pass as gay, then? What about you? You're a little... well, a whole lot..." I cleared my throat. "You're obviously not a dude, is my point."

"I believe the term is 'fag hag.'"

"Oh. Right."

We got out of the car. I took two steps.

She said, "What are you doing?"

"Walking. You know, getting into character."

"No, what you're doing is wearing gayface."

"Gayface?"

"You're doing a gay minstrel show. You're one step from full-on mincing and prancing. It's insulting."

"Oh. Um."

"Just walk like a person, please, not a cartoon. You're probably not going to pass, but we don't really need you to. We just need you not to attract too much attention."

"Says the top-heavy redhead," I muttered.

"You say something?"

"Pointing out irony under my breath."

We headed around to the front. The bouncer gave us both a look like he was trying to figure out which one of us was doing this on a dare. He checked IDs—I showed him Colin Reznick's. He gave me another once-over and shook his head.

The *Principia Discordia* describes a very simple trick known as the Turkey Curse. Now, the book is joking when it tells you to literally gobble like a turkey and wave your arms around like an epileptic with bad depth perception. What it's actually telling you to do is something completely unexpected. Bouncers expect certain things: attempts to rush past them, the occasional punch, and maybe even a macing. The *Principia* tells you to short-circuit the other guy's brain. Do something he wouldn't expect, that he flat-out *couldn't* expect, and watch his brain grope for the neuron that would explain why a person would behave like a one-eyed crack whore at a Shriner circus.

I said, "Look, I need to talk to Julian about the delivery."

He didn't react. "No Julian in there."

"I find that highly unlikely. Look, somebody wanted five tons of saltpeter, and gave this address."

"Saltpeter?"

"Yeah, saltpeter. It's in a truck out back, and I don't mind telling you I'm already out of pocket on the parking."

His face was starting to go slack: the Novocain of confusion was doing its work. "This is a bar. We don't need saltpeter."

"Then what did you order it for? I need to talk to Julian five minutes ago or somebody's losing his job."

"Not my..."

I started talking louder. "Saltpeter. You know, the Army puts this stuff in the food so the recruits lose their sex drives. I guess the implication is that Basic would just be one long Madonna concert otherwise."

"But we don't need..."

"Then you shouldn't have fucking ordered it! Either get Julian or let me go in and talk to the man!"

"You're not..."

"Your problem, I know. I'm Julian's problem. Haven't you been listening?"

He blinked, looked at the line growing behind me, then back at me. He waved me in. "Gobble gobble," I said.

"What?"

"I said thanks."

I hate feeling out of place, which I suppose is a little ironic. After all, I've spent my adult life as an insider, but even within the conspiracies, I wasn't properly inside. I wasn't out in the rain, but I was in the foyer dripping wet and looking for a place to put my umbrella. In any case, at this bar, I felt more out of place than I'd ever felt before. There was no way for me to adequately blend. I kept expecting points and laughs, or at the very least some catty comments. Getting outed as a straight guy in a gay bar was the kind of bizarre phobia that would one day get me written up in a psychological journal, alongside that Waco woman who compulsively ate batteries. I wanted to leave as soon as I could, but first I needed to know who Eric was meeting. The music pulsed in my ears, the crowd was wall to wall; finding Eric through the bass beat, sweat, and my nerves was going to be a challenge.

I felt a hand on my arm. Turned. Mina. She nodded at something deeper in the club. I followed her eyes.

Eric was in a booth in the back. I couldn't ID the man he sat across from. I had to get a better angle. I crossed to a far corner, dark enough to hide me, and I could see Eric's partner. As I moved, more of the man came into view. First, gray hair. For a minute, I thought it was Stan Brizendine. No, the hair was wavy, and missing on top in a modified George Costanza. Closer, and it was clear this guy was tall, maybe six-three minimum. Thin, too. Had an old-school look to his suit. He could have stepped right off the grassy knoll. His face came into view, and it was like a human caricature of an aging eagle. The guy looked like a poster-grandpa for freelance spooks.

"Who is he?" Mina said.

"I have no idea."

I brought up my cellphone—Reznick's specifically. Eric was talking to the guy, making some kind of panicked declaration. I flipped the phone open.

Mr. Old School turned right then. His eyes glittered under the lights. He saw me—saw right through me.

"Fuck."

I snapped the picture.

Old School was coming through the crowd, Eric trailing after him.

I grabbed Mina's hand, but she had the same idea and

a lower center of gravity. The crowd parted for her. In a flash, we were outside and running. A second later, footsteps echoed behind us. I chanced a look. Eric.

The look on his face: some fear, obviously not of us. Mostly what I saw was a sick need. God, I hated that look.

There's an old joke. Two guys are hiking through the hills when they spot a bear. At that moment, the bear spots them. One guy is getting ready to run when the other guy calmly sits down and begins putting on a pair of running shoes. The first guy is like, "You really think those shoes will help you outrun that bear?" The other guy responds, cool as a cucumber, "I don't have to outrun him. I only have to outrun *you*."

Which was my dilemma. Mina was in heels—short ones, sure, but heels, and I could tell she wasn't much of a runner to begin with. She was really just wobbling along in a barely controlled forward fall. I could leave her to Eric, or I could do something very stupid.

We turned the corner, and Eric was barely three steps behind.

I stopped.

Mina turned, wondering why I'd stopped.

I ducked low.

Eric turned the corner and I jumped right at his knees.

One leg hit me on the edge of Mina's footprint, but Eric went sailing.

It should be said that I'm not much good in a fight. I've taken some classes, but I generally learn just enough to override my natural instincts and try for something a little too complicated. So while I'm trying some intricate wristlock, the other guy is using my head like a taiko drum. But a flying tackle? That seemed to work just fine.

I heard a thunk as I got to my feet and started running again. Eric was already shaking the cobwebs from his head.

He'd ended up under a newspaper vending box that now had an Eric's-head-shaped dent in the side. Mina was at my car. I tossed her the keys and the engine was running by the time I jumped in the passenger seat. Eric took a couple of aborted steps, but the car was moving.

Mina let out a whoop. I smiled a little, winced, and touched my jaw.

"You okay?"

"Could be better."

"I think he saw the license plate." She paused. "That's not a problem, is it?"

I shook my head. "It'll lead them right to a nice taco place in Boyle Heights."

She smiled at that. "You really don't know who that guy was?"

I shook my head. "Nope." I thought about it. "Had you met any Templars before tonight?"

"No. Why would he want me dead?"

"Could be work for hire, I don't know."

"How do you advertise for something like that?"

"Craigslist."

"I really should have guessed."

I tried to trace the connection between V.E.N.U.S. and the Knights Templar, and how it would run through a guy like Old School. "Does V.E.N.U.S. have a dirty tricks specialist?"

"Why?" she asked, her voice tinged with sudden suspicion.

"Someone whose job it would be to steal something like the Chain of the Heretic Martyr."

"Someone like you?"

"Like me, but competent."

She thought about it. That wasn't exactly flattering. "Yeah. You're talking about Oana Constantinescu."

Wonderful.

She misinterpreted my look. "Yeah, the Romanian gymnast."

"You wouldn't happen to know where she lives, would you?"

"Like an address? No. I've seen her around the compound before and I talked to her once or twice, but it's not like we were in the same position. I'm on the frontlines, Oana is... well, in the shadows, I guess would be the way to put it."

"She has to have a codename. Something they call her?"

"Tuesday," Mina said a little too quickly. She didn't move to cover it, just let it hang there. Was she going to call ahead? Could I let her out of my sight?

"I need to get back into the compound," I said.

"Are you insane? They're trying to kill me!"

"Well, technically, I said they *might* be trying to kill you. Might."

"Still. Walking right into their place doesn't sound like a good idea."

"Not to put too fine a point on it, but I wasn't planning on just walking in."

"They have dogs."

"That's okay, dogs like me."

"Not these dogs."

"No, those too."

She wanted to glare, but she was watching the road. "Don't get cocky."

"Worried about me?"

"No, when you get cocky, you screw up, and this is *my* life we're talking about."

On the stereo: "Don't Look Back."

We moved into Mount Washington and I started getting a little squirrelly. Breaking and entering was one thing when no one was home, but this was a commune. There was always someone home. I had two things I needed. In and out. Then there was the gambit if I got caught. It was a lot to keep in mind.

Mina parked a block away. I would approach the commune from uphill. I thought about demanding the keys back. That way she couldn't drive off and leave me in there. Then again, it wasn't like I could take her cellphone. Even if I did, she could always use one of the jillion phones in the trunk to call the hippos inside and let them know I was coming. Besides, it would be nice to know that she was a backstabber before I got too much deeper. Let her keep the keys.

"Pop the trunk. It's the lever right by... yeah."

I got out of the car. I lost the tie. The rest of my outfit was dark enough to be black. My trunk probably would have confused most people who didn't understand what was back there. Why I had seventeen copies of *Sandman #29.* Why I would need those two-liter bottles of Diet Coke. The makeshift mug book. The changes of clothes, the religious icons, the stuffed alligator. The tire iron was pretty self-explanatory, though.

I lifted out a duffel bag. Leather wallet with picks and files. Check. Bottle of nasty. Check. Flashlight. Check.

She had gotten out of the car and was watching me. "There's a trellis on the north side that's easy to get up," she said. "And, if you get in trouble, 'Lascaux.'"

"Lascaux. Got it."

"If you're looking for the Chain, your best bet is Daphne's office. Second floor. If you get to the staircase inside, it's the first door on the right at the top."

"Daphne. The blonde, right?"

She smiled queasily. "Yeah."

Probably would be the last time I'd see her. She'd sell

me out for mercy and get her skull caved in another day. It wasn't like you needed to make time for that sort of thing.

The compound was on half an acre, separated from its neighbors by tall eucalyptus trees and high fences. There was no property that looked directly down into it. They wouldn't have chosen it had there been. The closest neighboring property had a dead zone, a section of densely planted hill bordered on both sides by fences. That would be the best way into the compound.

Of course, that plan sounded all well and good, but the brush was up to my chest in places and felt like walking through a very narrow hall bordered on both sides by angry kittens. I was covered in little cuts before I'd made it five feet. On the V.E.N.U.S. side, there was fence, then a couple feet beyond, a hill that rose up before sloping down into the compound. The section between fence and hill was a perfect dog run.

The fence was seven feet tall and wooden. I braced myself on a tree and scrambled like a drunken monkey, but made it over the other side. I paused. I heard the dogs, still far off, but chewing up ground fast. I dug out the bottle of nasty and sprayed it on the fence.

The problem with this line of work is that occasionally you need disgusting things. Rat feces, insect parts, and, in this case, cat piss. There's no better way of dealing with guard dogs than cat piss. It would keep them entertained for more than long enough. The problem is, of course, collecting it, which I won't go into. You're welcome.

I crept along the side of the hill. The dogs were closing in, their breath coming out in growls. I moved quicker. The hill sloped downward into the commune proper. It was divided into sections of garden, like they were testing to see exactly what California would support. There was a section of neat lawn that, for some reason, felt ironic. There was a cactus garden with groomed sand, almost like a Zen garden. There was a small apple orchard and a vegetable plot. There was even a section that was mostly ferns with a young redwood set in the middle.

I saw the dogs: black and tan streaks in the underbrush. Rottweilers with jaws like backhoes. They were heading to my section of fence.

I moved down past the little redwood, keeping to the sections that would put trees or high plants between the house and me. There was a dirt path all the way around, bordered with even stones. Right next to the house, I found climbing plants. I scanned the area. Mina's trellis was right in front of me.

I heard a door open. I ducked backward, hiding in the ferns, sticking close to my friend the redwood. One of the V.E.N.U.S. henchmen, yet another reedy bearded man, stepped outside. He was squinting up at where the dogs had gone, an Uzi slung over his shoulder. He started moving.

I kept still. He walked over the lawn and disappeared behind the hill.

I broke for the house. The trellis was no good now. Climb that, get stuck, and the dog man would hose me down before I could say the code word.

I picked a side door. Locked, of course. That wasn't a problem. The locks in this place were a joke; I picked this one in the dark. Through the door and into the downstairs hall. I was in a living room, all wood and handmade rugs. The whole place had the old-vomit smell of cooked lentils.

I turned right, and through a door, I found a staircase. The kind that creaks. Walking on the edge of the steps, setting my feet before planting my weight—I tried every trick. Still, every creak sounded like an air raid siren. Two steps from the top, I heard a door open and some muttering several rooms away, below me.

Dog man. Fuck.

I took the last two steps with a leap.

First door on the right. Locked. Of course it was.

I heard steps on the staircase. I hoped this lock was a joke, too. Felt it out.

He was halfway up.

The door opened and I was through it. Like I said, I have good hands.

I paused, back against the closed door. I heard dog man outside. Closer.

Then further.

I decided to start breathing again. I clicked on my flashlight. I was in an office, all right. Desk facing the door and a chair big enough for two normal asses. A couch along one side, some small chairs, bookcases, and a picture window that looked down the hill into Highland Park.

I swore at Mina as soon as I saw it: the safe. This was probably what she was talking about when she said that the Chain would be in Daphne's office. Did she think I could crack a safe with my bare hands?

Instead, I went to the computer and booted it up. Password protected. Damn.

I thought about it. V.E.N.U.S. Lascaux. Could it really be that easy?

LUCY.

The OS unlocked. I shook my head.

I opened everything I could, looking for references to Constantinescu or Tuesday. The key for this sort of thing is filtering out what doesn't fit. Mention of Tuesday on a calendar doesn't help too much. Mention of Tuesday as a noun can be illuminating. I found Daphne's address book. I shouldn't have been too surprised that the damn thing was in code. The trick would be showing it to Mina. That is, if Mina was still in the car. I dug through the desk drawers, found a CD, burned it, and pocketed the disc.

Might as well search the place. I went deeper into Daphne's desk. Notes, papers. The woman appeared to be a packrat with a filing system that went past arcane and well into illuminated territory. Receipts, but nothing overly damning. Some notes, nothing that made sense.

I opened the center drawer, checked under the organizer. Jackpot.

I pulled the sheet of paper from underneath and nearly swore out loud.

It read: "Salutations. Your price cannot be paid without delivery. Trust is difficult to come by, but you must trust me. Give me what I ask and you will get what you require."

The handwriting was block printing, the margins pristine. The same handwriting on the love note in Diaz's house. Whoever was in love with Diaz, my Manchurian Candidate, was also making deals with V.E.N.U.S. I put the note back where I found it. Now to get back out.

I listened at the door. Nothing.

I opened it. Still nothing. No telling where dog man and his gun were. I locked Daphne's office behind me. Down the stairs.

The barking and snarling made me jump back. The Rottweilers were on the other side of the door, snapping and yowling. The cat piss probably wasn't even a memory in their tiny dog brains. I heard swearing again: dog man. Closer than I thought. I had two options. I didn't like either one.

I went into the living room, picked the comfiest chair, and sank into it. I crossed my legs. Uncrossed them. Crossed looked better. I crossed them again.

Dog man's silhouette eclipsed the doorway. "Who the fuck are..."

I turned on the lamp next to me and waited for it.

He gasped. "Bailey." There it was. I probably met him at one time or another, but the beardos all ended up looking the same to me.

"Hey. Could you get Daphne for me?" I said.

The interplay of belief and perception. Belief: a man caught in my house when I have an Uzi and vicious dogs will be scared. Perception: he's not scared in the least. Result: confusion, suggestibility. Low-grade hypnosis, even.

"Don't move."

"How would Daphne find me if I did?"

He retreated like I was the one with a gun. In point of fact, all I could really do was make him smell like a litterbox. I supposed that could be intimidating.

I clamped down on the nerves. Voices multiplied throughout the house. I heard the bosses start their tectonic movement. If those were the creaks they were used to on the stairs, I might have overdone the sneaking around.

Two more of the bearded guys came in with tighty-whities and Uzis. Now *that* was intimidating.

Then Daphne. I'll be damned, she really was a blonde.

"Mr. Bailey," she said. "Want to explain why you broke in?"

"I think you know the answer to that." Before she could speak, I barreled on. "And you're welcome. Security here is, well, I'd call it a joke, but jokes are generally funny and involve one or more clergymen."

"Mr. Bailey, I'm trying to think of a reason not to have you killed. After all, you broke in; it's totally legal."

Ice, mainlined right into my aortas. "Oh. I was under the assumption you'd want to see your golden girl again. Or is it crimson girl?"

That got her. She paused, then growled, "You know where Mina is?"

I nodded. "Of course, if you kill me, then *you* won't. Ever. Besides, you should be more worried about the Anas and the status of your truce, especially when security's this bad."

This changed the look on her face. I could tell she wasn't buying quite what I was selling, but, well, I knew something she didn't know I knew.

"What do you know about the truce?"

"What your man does," I said, referring to the enforcer they'd had at Mina's party. "I imagine he told you everything, unless he decided not to mention the fact that he completely lost sight of your girl as soon as she went into her dressing room. There were signs of a struggle upstairs, sword stuck through a door, that kind of thing. It's enough to make a guy suspicious." I was onstage now. Time to sell it, go for the throat, work for the go-ahead homer and a hundred other mixed metaphors. "You know, I read something strange the other day. Did you know that gymnastics has a way of delaying sexual maturity? I'm not kidding. Gymnasts get into such weird shape, they effectively delay their periods—sometimes they don't menstruate until they hit their twenties. It's a truly bizarre phenomenon."

Daphne held a hand up. She was nibbling at the edge of what I was saying. "What's your point?"

"Some of that is the result of the exercise, granted. Increase in muscle mass means an increase in testosterone levels, so that leads to androgyny: larger waists, thicker necks, smaller breasts and hips. You get the idea. But the modern aesthetic, you know, the Karolyi thing, leads to eating disorders. You know, to keep them nice and skinny. Where's Bela Karolyi from?"

"Romania."

I snapped my fingers. "Right. I knew it was someplace like that."

"Get to your point."

"You've got a rat in the house and we both know who that rat is."

I could see the gears turning in her head. I was pretty sure I knew where she'd end up. Not the ideal, but as good as I could hope. The worst part of it was that one way or another, I was going to get beaten up by a girl. Again.

"Can you get me proof?" Daphne asked.

"Not without her address."

Daphne rattled it off. Oana Constantinecu lived down near Wilshire. "Now, Mina's location?"

"When I get back, she's all yours."

I went to the front door. "See you soon, Daphne."

And then I was outside in the night air. I heard the men bringing the dogs inside. I'd come in over the fence, but I left through the front gate. I looked up the hill. My car was still there. That was surprising.

"Well?" Mina said as I got in.

"They're sending me to be killed at Oana Constantinescu's place."

"But you sound so happy."

"It's not like I was planning on showing up."

On the stereo: "Foreplay/Long Time."

“Time for a new CD,” Mina said. I was driving now, and she took it upon herself to search the papers on the floor and the glovebox.

“It’s an iPod, actually.”

“Then it’s time to reshuffle it.”

“Go ahead, but there’s only Boston on there.”

“You’ve got to be kidding.”

“I only like Boston.”

“You know, there were these other bands around then that some people think are even better.”

“Yeah, I’ve heard the whole thing. Beatles this, Stones that.”

“More than them, too. It’s like there’s this whole history of rock from Chuck Berry to now.”

“Boston is the only band that I can stand to listen to.”

“I guess they’re okay in a cheesy kind of arena-rock way, but they’re a little soulless.”

“Exactly.”

She said, "You lost me."

"That's why I like them."

"Okay, you've got your captive audience. Out of all the bands, all the musicians that have ever existed, why is Boston the only band you like?"

"The music doesn't have any mystical subtext."

It seemed like Mina was trying to develop heat vision. "What the hell are you talking about?"

"All music is basically just a shouted occult viewpoint. They've all got, you know, links. I can't take being lectured at like that."

"You're saying the Beatles are just occult cranks?"

"Discordians, actually."

"The Stones?"

"Satanists—the Lucifer kind, not the Asmodeus kind."

"The Doors."

"CIA psych-ops. Jim Morrison was a CIA plant."

A smile tugged at the corner of her mouth.

"Bowie."

"Are you kidding me? Little Green Men."

"Modern bands, too?"

"Of course."

"U2?"

"New World Order Trilateralists."

"Radiohead."

"Servants of Shub-Internet."

"I don't even know what that is. R.E.M."

"New Camelot."

"The Police."

"The police."

She giggled. "You're crazy."

"The world gets a lot bigger and a lot smaller when you're me."

"Let me guess: Siouxsie and Robert Smith are pawns of the vampires."

"I told you: vampires don't exist. Jesus, why is everyone so fixated on fucking vampires?" I turned to catch a sparkle in one eye. She was winding me up, and I fell for it. "You're a horrible person."

"Come on, you have this giant red button marked 'vampire' and I'm not supposed to poke it?"

"If you had to deal with everyone and his doppelganger wondering what vampires were up to, you'd have the same button."

"I suppose." She yawned. "I need to get some sleep."

"Yeah, I was thinking the same thing." It was after two.

"I can't go back to my place, can I?" she said.

"Not really. Not after what I found in Daphne's desk." I told her about the note.

"Oh. That's not good at all. So it's your place, then."

She was going to see where I lived. If she really was planning to betray me, that would be the perfect time. My guard would be down. Maybe now I ought to flush her out. "Yeah. I hope that's okay."

"I haven't seen it yet."

I don't know if she meant that to sound ominous, but in my head, a bolt of lightning crawled across the sky. Clear LA nights were hell on ambience.

I drove back to my place and found a place to park. Walking along the cracked sidewalk, I felt like an idiot. She was watching her feet; I had my hands in my pockets. Body language said she was shy. I looked over her bare shoulders, the ones that had the strength to put a divot right below my sternum.

She tucked some hair behind her ear. I hadn't noticed before, but her earrings matched her eyes. The fact that I noticed that now made me want to hit myself with a hammer.

We were nearing the entrance to the courtyard. Suddenly, she stopped. "This, uh... this isn't romantic. Just, you know, to be clear."

"Romance has nothing to do with it. I'm just trying to get you in my sex dungeon."

Her eyes went wide, then searched for it, found it, and she laughed. "Right, sorry. This has been a crazy night—scary, fun, I dunno. I don't want you to get the wrong idea."

"That's good, because I don't really have any moves. I'd just end up embarrassing us both."

We kept walking. No sex, just a knife between my ribs. I had a set of carving knives, too, right there on the counter. Why the fuck did I have knives? I didn't cook. Were they a gift? Did they come with the apartment?

I took her upstairs and unlocked my door. Like I said, my apartment wasn't dirty, but it wasn't clean, either. I was a bachelor who wasn't home very often.

"So no girlfriend," she said.

"How the hell can you tell that with one foot in the door?"

"No woman's been in here since you cleaned last, which I'm guessing was during the Bush administration. The first one."

"Har har."

I turned on some lights, and yeah, it did have a bit of a bachelor feel. The axolotls floated in their tank; one wiggled away when I passed.

"What are those? They look like little pink tadpoles with legs," she said.

"Axolotls," I said. It wasn't really an answer, since anyone who knew what that meant wouldn't ask the question. "They're salamanders, but they never mature past the larval state. They've always got those gills—that's the feathery-looking mane they've got."

"They live underwater their whole lives? Where do they come from?"

"Well, these came from the pet store, but their natural habitat is the lake under Mexico City. That's why their skin is pink. They don't really get any sun."

She leaned down and peered in the tank. "When they face you, it looks like they're smiling."

"Yeah, they sort of do."

"Do they have names?"

"They do, but they keep changing."

She fake-glared at me.

I continued, "Anyway, the bedroom is through there. If you get hungry, the kitchen is that way. If you want something that's not frozen pizza, I can't help you." The knives would be in plain view, if she were so inclined. I thought about laying the big one on the counter, just to get it over with.

"I don't suppose you have something I could sleep in?"

"Check the dresser. Second drawer is shirts, fourth for sweats."

"Don't suppose you've got something I can wear tomorrow."

"Oh, no way. You're doing the walk of shame in front of my neighbors."

"Good night," she said, and headed down the hall. I hit the light and collapsed on the couch. Measuring all the stupid things I'd done that day would take awhile. I'd probably need an audit. I heard the sink running and tried to remember if there was anything super-embarrassing about the bathroom. I really hoped that none of the mold in there had developed sentience.

I shut my eyes. Sleeping was going to be interesting, even as tired as I was. Sounds kept filtering through. The sink, the hum of the aquarium's filter. I heard the bathroom door open and shut, then Mina rummaging around in my dresser. Then I heard the sound of cloth. She was undressing. She was in my room, and half-naked, maybe more. After that, I could mostly hear the blood pounding in my head. I started running down a list of sexual fantasies. I stopped right around the one where I was Batman and she was Poison Ivy out of sheer self-loathing.

I opened my eyes. Sleeping was going to be impossible.

My front door splintered inward in the path of a big gray rock. That made me sit up.

Raul Diaz.

Son of a bitch knew where I lived. He stepped into the living room. I had to keep his eyes on me. The last thing I needed was him focusing on Mina.

"Hey, Raul," I said.

He had the same vacant look from the subway station, and of course the same rock that he was pulling out of the wrecked remains of my door. He choked up on the chain, ready to start swinging it around. I started thinking about propellers. Then I started thinking about the big Nazi in *Raiders of the Lost Ark*. I didn't like where this was going for either of us.

He brought the stone down overhand, in an arc. I counted on the simple fact that my rent wasn't all that high and lunged. The rock hit the doorjamb and dropped next to him. I hit Raul. It was a good punch, my whole weight behind it, and I was jumping forward like Superman. Got him right on the chin, too. He stumbled back, bounced off the wall, and focused on me again.

I looked at my fist. Was that thing loaded?

He advanced. Wouldn't make that mistake again. My old gambit of not packing weapons didn't work with these death zombies. It wasn't like a gun would make him more or less violent. The only thing that would calm him down was my head as a piece of modern art.

Maybe I could snap him out of it.

"Hey, Raul. Lascaux." Nothing. "Lucy. Sky. Diamonds. Malta. Fucking... whoa!" I jumped forward again. The rock whizzed over my head—stupid high ceilings—and slammed into the aquarium. Stinking salamander water slithered out over my floor, followed by the flopping pink tadpoles. I got to my feet. He swung again, cracking a hole in my floor. I heard the rock whooshing behind me.

I turned. It was coming at my head. I staggered back. This was getting very bad very quickly. I had my back to the kitchen. Maybe I could get in there and do something with one of the kitchen knives. Stabbing the guy wasn't going to be something I could undo, but the choices were that or dead.

This time he was Gogo Yubari, throwing the stone outward in a horizontal arc, smashing through a section of my wall. I backed off into the kitchen. Closer in here, harder to swing that thing, but nowhere for me to back up, either. Great choices. I pulled a knife from the block. I really did not want to stab him.

Diaz came around the corner.

I should have attacked right then, just stuck the knife through his chest. The problem was, I hesitated. I imagined it going in and I couldn't do it.

That's when something slammed into the back of his head and he went down in a heap. Mina stood there, holding my bowling ball in both hands and looking down at Diaz, who was now sleeping soundly. My breath caught: she had taken an old shirt of mine and stretched it over her, too tight on top, a little loose around the waist. She was wearing a pair of my sweatpants, too, and that was probably what did it. There was a strange intimacy to it, her in my clothes. That, combined with her freshly scrubbed face, made her look normal, like someone I could meet in my life.

The fact was, I *did* meet her in my life.

Reality chose that moment to tap me on the shoulder and point out that my pets were dying.

"Oh, shit!" I ran past her and scooped up the flopping axolotls. I had to be gentle. Their gills were fragile things, very sensitive. The upside was that they could regenerate just about anything, but I didn't want to put that to the test. I dumped them on the counter.

"Mina, get the door!"

She rushed to it.

I blocked the drain and filled up my sink. Not ideal. They wouldn't like it, especially with the state of LA tapwater, but then again, their natural habitat was below Mexico City, so I hoped they had a little tolerance for pollution. I dumped the little guys in the sink. They calmed down, returning to their usual positions, standing lightly on the ground at the bottom.

One down.

I dragged Raul into the kitchen. There was the matter of his weapon. I picked it up. Heavy.

Mina was murmuring by the door, talking to someone. I hoped she was a good liar. Then again, if she was, she could play me as long as she liked before the inevitable betrayal.

The chain left streaks of soot on my hand. I didn't know what to do. I put it in the fridge. Seemed as good a place as any.

Mina came back into the kitchen. "Your downstairs neighbor asked us to keep it down."

"I'm not expecting any other assassins.".

"I didn't tell him that."

"In the hall closet, on the bottom shelf, there should be a

roll of duct tape. Could you get it for me?"

She returned with it as I dragged my desk chair into the kitchen. We lifted Raul into the chair, and I taped him down, arms to the arms and ankles to the base, making sure his toes couldn't touch the ground. I topped that off with a strip across his mouth.

"This isn't the first time you've taped someone to a chair, is it?" she asked.

"Um... no."

"Should I be worried?"

"I only have the one chair."

She looked at me and at Raul.

We wheeled Raul into the living room. I cleaned up the water and broken glass as best I could, considering I didn't own a mop and was out of paper towels. I put some of the rocks from the tank into the kitchen sink. Maybe that would make the axolotls feel better about their sudden move.

"He looks normal," Mina said.

"He was, at one time, before whoever it was got their hooks into him. Probably some ex-CIA spook or something, making himself a private army of these guys. Eric or his buddy from the gay bar."

"You might want to tone down the paranoia a bit."

I shrugged. "It's not paranoia when that," I gestured to my living room and the unconscious would-be assassin, "happens."

The door was crushed, just about. It was still on the hinges, but it would only close in the loosest sense of the term. This wasn't something to call the landlord about, either. I closed it and, after a minute, dragged my couch over to barricade it. There was something odd about the wound in my door. I looked closer: where the flail had hit, I saw the same gray dust that I saw at the impact sites at Union Station. I went to the break in the doorjamb, the hole in my floor, and the chunk out of my wall. All coated with that dust.

Mina said, "That's weird."

"What?"

She pointed. On the inside of Raul's trench coat, the right side, there was a thick gray crust. It looked a little like cement, but once I got closer, I could see it was smoother, pitted, and faintly glowing. It was right where the rock would have rested when he was hiding it in the coat.

I went to the fridge. The gray dust had settled. I took the weapon out and brought it back into the living room.

Mina and I stood in front of Raul, staring at him. His weapon of choice was sitting in front of him, nice and cool from the fridge.

Mina murmured, "So that's it?"

"Hmm?" She was gazing at the weapon—more specifically, at the Chain. "Yeah, I guess it is."

She touched it. "I thought I'd feel something."

"What, like girl power?"

"Sort of. I mean, this artifact has real importance. It martyred a saint, and not just a Christian one. Joan feels more like ours than theirs." She thought about it. "Who bolts it to a rock?"

"We should wake him up and ask him," I said.

"Do you have smelling salts or something?"

I held a bath towel soaked in old salamander water under his nose. That got him stirring. He looked up at us, blinking. There was something there this time: the "No" had been turned on where just the "Vacancy" had been before.

I put a finger to my lips. He nodded. I ripped the tape off his face. "Sorry about that," I said.

He said, "What's going on?"

Mina tugged on my shirt. I leaned in close and smelled my

bath soap on her face. I don't think I ever really appreciated Irish Spring until that moment. A whisper: "How much does someone like this know?"

"You're thinking he's lying."

She shrugged. "I would in his situation."

I tried not to attach too much significance to that.

"You're tied to a chair because you tried to hit me with that." I pointed at the rock.

"What? No. No, I never did that," Raul protested.

I spun the chair, first to the hole by the back hall, then to the smashed aquarium, then to the floor, then to the hole in the kitchen door. "You did that. That. That. And that."

"Oh," he said. "If you say so." Weird resignation in his voice; I didn't like it at all.

"What the hell do you mean, 'If I say so'?"

"I don't remember doing any of that."

I held up the rock and chain. "You remember this?"

"Yeah. That was in my house. I think... I think I brought it home."

"You think you brought it home. You've tried to kill me with it. Twice."

"If you say so."

"Stop saying that." I straightened up and walked a few steps away. I wanted to pace. I thought about it. "What's the last thing you remember before you woke up in this chair?"

His eyes unfocused. "The girl. The girl. The girl."

Eric Caldwell was many things, but he was definitely not a girl.

"Hey." Nothing. "Hey!" I snapped my fingers in his face. "This girl, did she have red hair?"

Mina smacked me. "I'm right here."

"There are other redheads in the world." This was technically true, but we both knew I wasn't talking about them.

I tried to sweeten the pot: "Paul Tallutto is surrounded by redheads."

Raul shook his head. "No. She was... blonde, I think. I think."

"Did she happen to be four hundred pounds?"

"No. Thin. Very thin."

Mina and I shared a significant look. Eventually I was going to have to deal with those ascetorexics.

"We should take him home," Mina said.

Now I was the one whispering at her. "Are you out of your mind? He's tried to kill me twice!"

"What, you're going to leave him taped to a chair?"

"Well... no."

"You're going to kill him?"

"No."

"That leaves letting him go." She had a point. I really hated that. She went on: "We let him go and wait 'til this skinny bitch shows up at his place and we grab her. Or we grab your friend Eric and he leads us to her. Either way, we get deeper than we were."

I wanted to punch a hole in her plan, but I couldn't think of one. I thought about chalking that up to almost losing my salamanders, but even I couldn't sink to that level of self-deception.

"I guess we're letting him go."

She didn't gloat, but I did catch her beaming. "I need to get changed."

"I don't know, I think that look kind of works for you. Sort of modern frump."

The look she gave me could have stripped paint off a car.

I told her, "Change in the bathroom. I have to get some things out of the bedroom."

She did, and I opened up the closet and started stuffing

small bills into a backpack. With no door and my address now possibly public knowledge in the information underground, I needed to get as much cash as I could out of there. One backpack and two duffel bags later and I didn't even have half of it. I even stuck to the tens and twenties. Oh, well. I was going to make some burglar very happy.

Mina came out of the bathroom, once again poured into her fashion-show dress. She looked vulnerable in it now, with her makeup scrubbed away and her hair beginning to fall naturally. I thought about what she had said about Eric Caldwell, and it applied: she had been wearing it as a costume, but now, this was for real. I handed her two of the bags. "Carry these, would you?"

"Uh... okay."

I picked up the rock and chain and shoved it into the backpack. A murder weapon and a pile of cash: all I needed was some cooked books and I had the mother of all RICO cases. I looked down at Raul. "You planning to kill us when I let you go?"

He was about to respond. "Oh, never mind," I said. "Who answers that question honestly if the answer's yes?"

I took the kitchen knife that an hour ago I was thinking about shoving in his heart and cut him loose instead. An all-purpose tool if ever there was one.

"What now?" he said. He didn't rub his wrists or flex his ankles like a normal person would have.

"Now we take you home."

"Oh. I live at 12—"

"I know where you live." I paused. "Do you have a roommate? Seven feet tall, glowing red eyes?"

The look he gave me was priceless. "No."

"Oh, good."

I moved the couch and the door drifted open. Mina asked,

"What's in the bags?"

"Money. Lots of money." Then: "Raul. You first." Raul obeyed, shuffling in front of us. It was different from his zombie walk. That helped me trust him, at least to the point of not expecting him to murder me right this second. Considering how our relationship had started, that was a pretty big step.

There were lights on in other apartments. My neighbors weren't staring, exactly, but I could see movement behind some of the curtains. Freaky three-way interrupted? Probably strange for them, since I was chiefly known for not being known. Of course, that probably put me on the radar for being most likely to be convicted of serial murder.

We got to the car, and Mina went to the passenger side. I handed her the keys. "You're driving. I'm in the back, watching Raul."

Raul was quiet as a mouse. Subdued. "How's your head?" Mina asked softly.

He said, "Hurts a little."

"Put some ice on it when you get home," she said.

"Okay." It sounded like the acquiescence to a hypnotic command. There were definitely more damaging commands out there.

On the stereo: "Hitch a Ride."

Mina turned it off. "Not while I'm driving."

We drove into Hollywood. We were coming up on sunrise. My arms started feeling heavy. Sleep was going to be a precious commodity. Sleeping in the car with Mina wasn't going to be possible. I wished I drove a gas-guzzler with a backseat like Godzilla's sofa.

Mina found Diaz's house without any trouble. Diaz, high-pitched and dreamy: "Okay, this is me. It was nice meeting you." He sounded like we were dropping him off after a nice movie and some late-night nachos at the local diner.

Mina double-parked. "We'll make sure you get in."

Diaz got out of the car and shuffled up to the house. I saw him produce the key.

She muttered, "You think that thing is still in there?"

"God, I hope not."

"What if it is?"

Diaz was poking at the door like a stubborn prom date. The key wasn't working. A light came on in the house. The door opened.

And Diaz stood in the doorway. The guy could have been a twin, except he was clean-cut, wearing pajamas and a robe. For a second, I couldn't believe what I was seeing until Mina said, "Holy crap."

"Yeah."

Alpha-Diaz tried to force his way in, but Beta-Diaz stopped him. I saw other shapes now, behind Beta-Diaz. A wife. Kids. I had been in that house only a couple hours ago. I would have remembered them. I got out of the car. The Diazes were fighting.

Beta-Diaz said, "Honey, call the police!"

I heard sirens. Too close. Before they called, even. I got back in the car.

"We need to go. Now."

Mina eased into the gas, passing the cops as they converged on "our" Diaz.

"What just happened?" she said.

"Lone nuts have doubles."

"Then they aren't exactly 'lone,' are they?"

"Try telling that to the Warren Commission."

THERE'S A SUCKER BORN EVERY MINUTE.

P.T. Barnum said that. He was talking about the world of the 19th century, and considering some of the stuff they believed, he wasn't far off. If he lived a century and a half later and knew what I did, he would have said the same thing. He just would have meant something entirely different.

Danny Casolaro was going to write a book about a conspiracy he uncovered about some shady deal between some computer programmers, an Indian tribe, and (of course) the CIA. Then he was found in a bathtub with his wrists nearly hacked through, which was officially ruled a suicide. The title of this book was *The Octopus*. That's because conspiracies are like octopi. They sit in the darkness. They've got a central mass that holds a brain that's never felt endorphins. From there, tentacles reach into every nook and cranny, grabbing whatever they can. And how does it hold on?

Suckers.

Suckers like me.

Mina and I were parked at Santa Monica beach. Sunrise

would be in an hour or so. I felt like I was about half a minute from passing out. Mina was dozing in the front seat; I was leaning against the car, trying to let the before-dawn chill keep me awake, but the white noise of the surf was doing the exact opposite. I probably should have had some coffee or something. I couldn't quite force myself to hit a 7-Eleven on the way, mostly because a 7-Eleven at four in the morning is one of the saddest places on earth, edging out "Thai child brothel" for the third spot on the most-horrible list.

I had to make a phone call, but I wasn't looking forward to it.

Mina rubbed her eyes, coming out of her doze. Glassy, bleary, she was having a hell of a time staying awake. "So Raul Diaz is, what, a clone?"

"Probably."

"That can't be too common."

"You'd be surprised. This town is swarming with clones. It's kept under wraps for the most part."

"But the technology is rare, right? I mean, if people knew that human cloning was going on all over the place, wouldn't they freak out?"

"It's not *that* rare. The Clone Wolves can do it. So can the Little Green Men, the Goys from Brazil, and the Knights of Malta. The Nazis were pretty far along, which means Odessa and the CIA have some inkling of how to do it."

"That's troubling."

"Yeah. I need to make a call, okay? I have to meet someone."

"Dangerous?"

"Not really."

"Do you need me up for this?" she asked.

"In fact, it might be safer if you were passed out."

She got out of the car. "That's good news." She opened up

the back and swept as much of the junk as she could onto the floor. "I didn't think they even made these anymore," she said, waving one of the Styrofoam McDonald's containers at me.

"They don't."

"There's a whole long reason for this, isn't there? And if I ask, you're either going to do one of those one-liners where I'm not sure you're joking and I feel dumb, or you're going to launch into a long lecture that makes me a little sorry I asked."

"Wow. Fatigue makes you mean."

"Honest."

"And mean."

She shrugged. "I was up early today." She tried to stretch out back there and was probably wishing that I drove something a little bigger.

Actually, when I started, I thought of getting something flashy and vintage, cruising around in a real piece of Detroit steel. But then I started meeting more and more people who were okay with killing, and I thought a lower profile might work better. It's hard to second-guess something that's caused little to no trouble in over half a decade. It wasn't like I knew that, at some point, a plus-sized model and possible author of my assassination was going to need to get some shut-eye back there. I mean, if I'd known that, maybe the decision would have been a tougher one. The salesman never pitches you on how many assassins can sleep in the backseat.

I went into the trunk and sifted through the phones until I found the one I wanted. I put the battery back in, and dialed the only number in the phone.

"Yeah?" The voice was hollow and quiet.

"Is this Frank's Place?"

"3rd and Pacific. Parking garage."

She hung up.

I got back in the car and drove. It wasn't too far, which made me think they knew where I was. I pulled over, took the battery out of the phone, and got back to driving.

The parking garage was automated. It had the kind of fluorescent lighting that suggested suicide, or at the very least a David Fincher movie. It was clean, as these things went, and very nearly empty. I picked a space near the top where the cars were thickest.

Mina let out a little snore. It was funny, a woman like that snoring.

Now I was waiting, trying to keep my eyes open. Fortunately, I didn't have to wait long. A black Lexus slid into the space next to me. I got out. It was my handler, and she looked like I had gotten her out of bed. She'd made an attempt to corral her hair into a ponytail, but that wasn't working out, and at night, she couldn't wear the government-issued shades, so I could see the dark rings under her eyes. She had a little scar on the right side of her lip that gave her a cockeyed look. She had an earpiece in and a pistol in a shoulder holster.

We both got out of the car. "Dave," she said to me. It was her version of hello.

My handler worked for the Hermetic Secret Service, and I worked for her as a street-level informant. A snitch, rat, a stool pigeon—pick your favorite unflattering term. The HSS traces its history to 1865, right after Lincoln's assassination. Their original purpose was to ensure that the president was never killed again.

They don't have the best track record.

Around the '50s, they ended up getting absorbed into the Office of Naval Intelligence. In all the catastrophic Men-in-Black conspiracies, people lump the HSS under the heading of "good guys." It's not entirely true, but they *are* better than most. They have yet to assassinate anyone else's presidents, which is the gold standard for assholes in intelligence.

I said, "How are you?"

"Who's sleeping beauty?" she said.

"A friend of mine. She took about six Ambien, so she's out like a light."

Stonefaced: "What did you want?"

"According to Tom Noguchi, bullets don't go in circles."

She didn't appreciate the joke, but really, who likes RFK jokes? "You're saying there's a chance for another Ambassador Hotel?"

"Yeah. Someone is trafficking in Sirhans."

"Fucking Cubans," she said. Up until that moment, I'd always thought *she* was Cuban.

"Not Cubans, but this guy might be a Fair Play for Cuba guy. At least back in the day."

"Where did you find this?"

"Grapevine, mostly. Old stuff you told me to look out for. There's been mention of a girl, but this time she's white. Blonde. That's all I have. Except for this." I produced Jonah Bailey's phone. "I followed a tip..."

"Tip?"

"That's all I'm going to say about my contacts. I got a picture of someone." I showed her the picture of the old guy from the gay bar. "He looks like a skinny version of Statler."

She frowned.

I tried to clarify. "The Muppet. Statler and Waldorf? Come on, you remember, the heckler guys on *The Muppet Show*."

"I don't watch TV." There was literally no way to say that sentence and not sound smug.

"Yeah, okay. So who is he?"

She looked at the phone and I thought a flash of recognition went across her face. I could have been imagining it. She said, "No idea. But if this tip is good and we can find your

Statham...”

“Statler.”

“Whatever. If we find him, and your tip is good, we might have saved the president.”

That’s all well and good, but I wanted to save myself. It wasn’t like I had a vice-me that could take over in the event of my untimely death. “Fabulous.”

“Thanks again, Dave.” She cocked her head slightly, listening to her earpiece. “Were you followed?”

Probably. “I don’t think so.”

She ran for her car. I ran for mine. She was a better driver than I was. She spun her wheel and was screaming for the exit by the time I put my car into reverse.

Mina snorted, sleepy. “What’s going on?”

“I hope nothing,” I said. I wheeled the car around and hit the gas. “But, you know, keep your head down, just in case.”

My handler was far ahead of me, a little over a full branch of the garage. I spun around the corner. Mina swore. My handler headed right toward the exit.

That’s when the gunfire started. And not a single pistol shooting a couple times. This was Sonny-at-the-toll-booth. This was Frank Nitti taking out Sean Connery. This was Rambo against the NVA. My handler’s car sprouted silver holes. The engine let out a stream of white smoke. The windshield pocked and turned to sugar.

Now I swore. “We need another way out of here.”

“Who is it?” Mina was screaming.

I flipped the car around. There was a good chance my handler was nothing more than an insurance claim now. I gunned the engine and went up another level and parked.

“Come on! We’re ditching the car!”

I jumped out; Mina followed. Her eyes were big. There had been something surreal about before, about being threatened by a Muslim fanatic armed with a broken vase, chased by a possible closet-case Templar, clubbing a man armed with a weapon Cain would have considered cutting-edge. But this... this was gunfire. This was real.

I ran for the corner stairs, diagonally opposite from the entrance below, where my handler had been caught in the gunfire. If we got lucky, they were just watching her car bleed. If we were really lucky, they were only after her. In other news, I'd just won the lottery, been struck by lightning, and fucked a real live unicorn on the hood of my Batmobile.

I threw open the fire door. It was a pretty good garage; the stairwell only barely smelled like piss. "Jonah..." Mina said.

I turned back and gave her what was hopefully an encouraging nod. Of course, my eyes were like ping-pong balls with a berserk thyroid, so I might have done more harm than good.

I led the way down the stairs. Two flights to the bottom. Then, either a lead rain or a balls-out run to safety, if safety was anywhere close by.

I turned. The fire door at the bottom of the staircase was in view. It opened. I whirled around, ran into Mina, physically pushed her backward to hustle her back up the stairs. I heard hushed voices, the near-monotones of spooks talking into their throat mikes.

I didn't bother to hide my footsteps. I just wanted Mina to run. She wasn't the fastest woman on the planet, and these guys probably had some kind of government-sponsored fitness program. Wonderful. As we passed the door to the second floor, where the car was, Mina stopped. I grabbed her hand and kept running. The spooks, or whoever they were, were only one flight behind us, and it was a lead-pipe cinch they knew where we were.

Third floor. I burst through the fire door. Gunfire. I flinched.

It was at the bottom of the parking garage—sounded like right about where my handler had been shot. I hoped she was giving them a little bit of hell, or at least her friends were. She was closer to a good person than a bad one.

There were a few cars up here, a couple a quick run away. That would have to do. One SUV, one sedan. Might work as a hiding place. The alternative was sticking where I was and fighting a couple of trained spooks who probably knew some kind of martial art that involved beating me about the head with my own kidneys. Yeah, no fighting today.

I ran for the cars. We were behind the SUV when the fire door slammed open. I peeked. Two guys.

The SUV had a blinking alarm. The sedan didn't. I picked its door open. Good hands. "Get in." I followed Mina.

I waited. The spooks were walking slower when they came out of the door. They were being cautious.

At street level, the chattering of the machine guns was joined by the car-backfire sound of a shotgun.

I started to play with wires. I started thinking about those yellow-and-blue-make-green bags. I was wondering if my life was flashing before my eyes, and all that was coming was awkwardness and commercials. Hell of a life.

Five. Four. Three.

I twisted the wires together. I had a new car. "Head down," I said.

I hit the gas, roaring around the SUV. There's nothing more wonderful than a look of surprise on the face of someone who's used to being in control. The spooks were giving me that look now. They fired pistols, but were too busy getting the hell out of the way to aim and hit anything important. I roared up the ramp onto the roof. The sky was beginning to change colors over the hills to the east. The moon was still high in the sky. The sounds: gunfire, surf.

I went to the top of the garage, turned the car around, and left it running when I got out.

Confused, Mina asked, "Where are you going?"

I needed a distraction, and a big one. There would be weather damage on the roof. The concrete markers would be worn up here. Hopefully worn enough. First one, cracked but not too bad. Second one looked new. Third was broken. Below, I saw the agents running upward. I kicked the third concrete barrier. Kicked it again. My foot hurt from where I landed on it at Medieval Castle. I kept kicking.

A chunk came loose. I picked it up. Weight the gas, let the car hit the side, maybe break through, we'd buy a little bit of time. Maybe even enough.

I ran back for the car. "Mina! Get out!"

Gunshots cracked behind me. The car sprouted two new holes. Mina ducked down in the back. I dove between two parked cars. The agents were advancing slowly, guns leveled at both of us. To my right: the fire door that would lead all the way down. In front: the car. To my left: the spooks. I crouched between the cars. I had a rock now, and in fairness, that had been enough for Diaz. Then again, Diaz failed. Twice. And his rock was bigger than mine.

I heard the fire door open.

The agents shouted and fired.

The early morning turned into high noon.

I looked up.

It wasn't the first time I'd seen a UFO. I'd seen the American-built ones that liked to buzz the Nevada desert. I'd seen the old Nazi prototypes that kept order in Pinochet's Chile. I'd even seen the real thing once.

This was the real thing. Not a perfect disk, but a triangle: one side of a pyramid, to be more accurate. It looked like it was formed from quicksilver, at least the part I could see. In the center, a single blinding light, like an eye. The heat was unbearable, and I felt my hair turning to a crisp. Great, I'd live through the guns only to die from prostate cancer because of some joyriding Zetas.

I half-stood. Mina was in the car, looking around, terrified. She caught my eye, opened her mouth to scream...

...and was gone.

I blinked. Fuck. I took one step toward the car, and the white light engulfed my vision, and there was nothing at all.

THERE'S ONE STRING OF FACTS THAT GRABS every nascent conspiracy buff. Everyone who had an email address in 1999 probably got this forward. It's the synchronicities between the Lincoln and Kennedy assassinations. It goes like this.

Lincoln has seven letters. Kennedy has seven letters.

They were elected to Congress one hundred years apart: Lincoln in 1846, Kennedy in 1946. They were elected president one hundred years apart: 1860 and 1960.

Both men won their elections partly on the strength of highly publicized debates: Lincoln/Douglas, Kennedy/Nixon. Both were stuck in unpopular wars: the Civil War and Vietnam (both of which began in earnest just after their inaugurations). Both were known for championing the civil rights of blacks and were highly unpopular in the South for doing so. Both men lost a son while in office.

Lincoln had a secretary named Kennedy who warned him not to go to the theatre that night. Kennedy had a secretary named Lincoln who warned him not to go to Dallas. Both men had premonitions of their deaths.

John Wilkes Booth and Lee Harvey Oswald both have fifteen-letter names. They were born a hundred years apart (1839 and 1939, respectively). Booth and Oswald were both Southerners.

Lincoln and Kennedy were both shot in the head on a Friday while sitting next to their wives. Lincoln was shot in Ford's Theatre. Kennedy was shot in a Lincoln, which is made by Ford. Booth shot Lincoln in a theatre and fled to a warehouse. Oswald shot Kennedy from a warehouse and fled to a theatre. Both Lincoln and Kennedy were sitting by men with eight-letter names (Rathbone and Connally). Both Rathbone and Connally were injured in the assassination, while both first ladies escaped unharmed. Oswald and Booth were both killed before they could stand trial.

Lincoln and Kennedy were both succeeded by Southerners named Johnson. Both Johnsons were born one hundred years apart (1808 and 1908). Both men were known for drinking and crude behavior. Both have thirteen-letter names.

There is of course, the favorite one to end with: a month before he was killed, Lincoln was in Monroe, Maryland. A month before he was killed, Kennedy was in Marilyn Monroe.

That last one is bullshit. Kennedy died in November 1963, and Marilyn in August of '62. At least, I hope it's bullshit.

But that's the whole point. This sort of thing is donuts and coffee for conspiracy nuts. But what possible reason for the synchronicities could there be? Was there really a shadow agency that made sure that everyone had the same number of letters in their names? No, the lesson of the whole thing is this: sometimes a coincidence is just a cigar.

Other times, though...

My head felt like a five-pound bag trying to hold onto ten pounds of cotton, all of which was soaked in cayenne pepper and on fire. I tried to move. Couldn't. I looked down.

I was taped to a fucking chair.

How was that for instant karma? Coincidence or conspiracy? At my level, all that mattered was that I was the one with the splitting headache, flypapered to furniture.

I looked up. The world lurched and I immediately regretted that decision. I saw a shape, probably a man, moving away from me, toward a door. It looked like I was in a bomb shelter. The door closed. I blinked, trying to keep what little food I had in my belly where it was. The walls were concrete and had some nice graffiti over them. Hidden amongst the tags were the equivalent of hobo signs for the information underground. I saw messages that gave me an approximate location, and other marks claiming this place for the ONI, the CIA, the Knights of Malta, and the Vors V Zakonye. The room was rectangular, maybe fifteen by fifteen. There was a ratty blanket in a corner; someone had slept here. Illumination was two worklights strung up at angles, plugged into a small generator, and the feeling that I'd been there before. The door was steel, rusted, and had an eye spray-painted at chest level. It was watching me.

I looked down again, and regretted that action too, but less so. My head was clearing, and there was just a dull ache back there now. I pictured the worst: a skull cracked like a good loaf of French bread, only this loaf was stuffed with gray jelly. The chair I was in looked like cutting-edge office furniture from 1945. It was solid wood, and appeared to have new rollers on the bottom. My arms were securely duct-taped to its arms, legs to the little column. It was like they'd studied my chair-taping technique. I hoped it just *looked* like that. Otherwise this would get creepier than it was, and I was already feeling like the third-billed actor in an Eli Roth movie.

I really hoped that moisture on my neck was sweat and

not blood.

The door opened. I wasn't really prepared for what came through it.

The first man, and I knew he was first because I saw swaying shadows behind him, had a black suit that screamed "spook," topped off with sunglasses. He was nearly six feet tall, thin as a reed, with skin that could charitably be called pasty. His short blond hair was slightly tousled, and he'd grown a wispy mustache over his thin lips. He stared at me, or appeared to, the reflections of the worklights in his shades giving the illusion of eyes. It clicked in my head: I didn't know this man, but I knew who he was.

Vassily "the Whale" Zhukovsky was next, getting through the door without the aid of a shoehorn, a crowbar, or lubricant. That was impressive. The Russian lumbered forward, his flipper-hands clasped together like he was crushing mice in them. He had a look on his face that made me think the rest of my life was going to be measured in minutes. So that was two of the conspirators in Mina's assassination in one place—the Fed who ordered it and the Russian gangster who took the job.

Next was a man I didn't recognize, but who was smiling openly at me, his eyes behind Tom-Cruise-in-*Risky-Business* shades. He wore a black suit one size too small, a starched white shirt, black tie, and black fedora. Under the hat, I was pretty sure he was bald as an egg, unless he had some weird Whoville topknot. His facial features were large; he looked like a flesh-and-blood cartoon of a man. The grayish skin didn't help, either. He looked like he might want to shake my hand. That worried me more than Vassily's glare.

Following him: Oana Constantinescu, V.E.N.U.S.'s dirty tricks specialist. Two people who wanted Mina dead and one that wanted the same for me.

I recognized the last man, and he looked serious, but he wouldn't look right at me. It was Neil Greene, my Mason contact, the man who was trying to see if Stan Brizendine wanted me dead. Still possible Stan did and Neil had retained these two to make it happen. Instead of his usual cube-rat clothes, Neil was dressed like the Unabomber.

The blond man spoke first, in a raspy whisper. "So what do we call you? David Antonucci? Colin Reznick? Jonah Bailey?"

At least they'd left out a few. "Any one of those is fine."

Vassily tapped the top of my head with a finger that felt like a ball-peen hammer. "You want me to hit you again?"

"That was you? What'd you use, a brick?"

Vassily brandished a watermelon-sized fist.

"Right, a brick," I said.

Neil spoke up, looking at me for the first time. "Wherever you go, bad things happen. You've been at the center of gunfights, a couple of assassination attempts. Something happens, we go check it out and look, there's 'Colin.'" He even made the quotes around Colin with his hands. Were his feelings hurt?

"Not all of that is my fault."

The grinning man asked, "Who's trying to give you the dirt nap, see?" If I hadn't been sure about who he worked for before, I was now.

"You're assuming it's just one person. You've obviously pooled some notes here. You know the names; you know I'm a—what, quintuple agent? So someone else figures it out and targets me." I was fishing, sure, but it was better than getting fished with. We were close to the water, and Vassily *was* in the mob, after all.

They exchanged looks. I was calming down. As long as they wanted information, I could stay alive, which is right where I wanted to be.

"Humbug," said the grinning man.

"My colleague is correct," said the blond man. "You're after something. Some artifact went missing, you sniffed after it, someone found you."

I was impressed. That was partly true, even. I said, "That's crazy."

"You're sweating," Oana said.

"I'm bleeding," I said to her.

She touched the back of my head. There was a little red, but not as much as I was afraid of. She showed her hand to Vassily, who beamed a genuine smile.

"Is it an assassination?" said Neil.

"What, other than mine?"

"Who are you trying to kill?" the blond man said.

"No one currently."

"Well, David," the blond man said, "we have as long as you like. You can stay here until you decide to talk to us. Until then, sit and wait."

And with that, they filed out. And I sat. And waited.

It was tough to tell how long I sat there. I wasn't still. I wiggled my arms to see if I could get the tape to give. I couldn't. I strained my legs to get them on the ground. I couldn't. There was a knot in my left thigh and I kind of had to piss. This was not a good beginning.

The door opened. It was a tentative kind of opening. Maybe the person on the other side thought I was dressing and had forgotten they'd taped me to a goddamn chair. Then the door opened all the way and Vassily squeezed in. It was not unlike watching toothpaste come out of a tube, only more homicidal. He shut the door behind him and leaned on it. This was it. Maybe if I was really lucky, he wouldn't eat me. He broke into a broad grin. That made it worse. The light shone off his bald head and his semi-reflective suit.

He said, “How are you feeling, Nicky? Hungry?”

“I’ve been better.” It was the honest answer.

“Oh, sorry about that. Had to bring you in, and there were men in suits with guns.”

“Right. So what happens now?”

He waved one finger at me. I was pretty sure it was bigger than my entire hand. “You weren’t going to tell me, were you? Thought you’d go above my head. Maybe you think you get stripes.”

There is only one thing worse than being taped to a chair alone in a room with a Russian hitman, and that’s being taped to a chair alone in a room with a *crazy* Russian hitman. There’s only one option: play along.

I laughed. “Yeah, you caught me. You know how much I’ve been wanting my stripes. I understand they’re slimming.”

He nodded. “If you told me, I wouldn’t have had to hit you.”

“I should have told you, then.”

“Yes!” He glanced at the door, suddenly worried. Then, quieter: “The others don’t know I’m in here with you. They know you snitch for us, but that’s all. They think you know things.”

“I don’t know much.”

“You know about Chain. You’re looking for it, looking for buyers, looking to make a killing. And you never told old pal Vassily about it.”

“Which, as we established, was my bad.”

“Trying to cut me out of deal.”

“Vassily, how the hell did you find those people?”

“They found me, mostly. Well, Brady found me. Brady—little blond man.” He demonstrated with his hands. “Brady has interests. Wants to keep our interests in line with his.” So Vassily and I were officially *our*. That was a good sign for my continued existence outside of his belly.

"Brady contacted you about the hit on the model."

Vassily nodded. "Some little thing."

"Little?"

He shrugged. "Relativity. What is little to me is big to you. What is big to me is little to God."

"Right. Did he say why he wanted the model dead?"

"No. But Brady is some kind of... patriot." In a Russian accent, that word sounded like a curse, specifically one that describes a deviant sex act with a close blood relation. "Wants to keep government safe. Eh. Whatever is good for business is good for me."

Mina was involved some kind of political assassination plot? Bullshit. I'd known Mina for... not long enough to make that kind of judgment. Still, it didn't wash. Political assassins would either be more ranty, or much more vacant. Really, they'd be more like Raul Diaz. Brady should track his ass down.

"I can see wheels turning," Vassily said.

"Buyers, Vassily. I can make us both very rich."

"Good boy, Nicky. Can you find this Chain?"

"I think I can, Vassily." After all, it was in the trunk of my car.

"You and me, Nicky. We kick enough up the ladder, you get stripes, I get... more."

"Sounds like a win-win." Sounded like Vassily was planning to get the Chain and kill me anyway. But that was a damn sight better than him killing me right then.

"Yesterday, you asked me about contract on Colin Reznick. *You* are Colin Reznick. Who is trying to kill you?"

"That's what I'd like to know."

"Not me."

"What a relief."

Vassily reached into his coat and produced a knife. "Catch is here." He pressed on the black rubber handle and a triangular blade popped out, serrated and ugly. He put the blade away and pressed it into my hand. "Maybe you had it on you all along. Maybe you cut your way out. Maybe you escaped."

"Sounds plausible."

"Good job, Nicky."

Vassily left. I wiggled the knife into position, balanced against the arm of the chair and my palm. I wasn't sure how I was going to cut myself out without slashing my wrists. I hit the catch. The blade popped out.

The door opened. I dropped the knife. It landed right between my legs. I opened them quickly and closed them. Getting that knife back was going to be a bitch.

I looked up. Oana Constantinescu was there, shutting the door with the same move the Whale had just done. She was looking at me with the same stern expression, too. "Oana. Is this because of all those times I made fun of your name?"

She flushed a bit. "Stop screwing about."

"Look, I know that Daphne wants you to kill me. Before you get started, I'd like to give you some reasons why not. Number one, I'm a big fan of the Olympics and bronze is really good."

She cut me off. "I'm not going to kill you."

"That's reassuring. Not to tempt fate or anything, but is there a reason why? I'd be surprised if it was because of that Olympics thing."

"I've been watching you." It even sounded creepy when a tiny woman said it. "You've protected Mina Duplessis several times."

"I didn't want to toot my own horn."

"Daphne believes you killed Mina and are only pretending to hold her as a hostage." That last part was true. I *was* pretending to do that.

"And that would interfere with Daphne's plan," I supplied. "After all, how could she arrange to have Mina killed in a public place if I were to off her quietly?"

Oana's face hardened. "You have proof?"

"I have suspicions."

"I have those, too."

I asked, "Why are you here? With them? I mean, two of them are actively involved in trying to kill Mina."

"Keep your enemies close. They're convinced you're some kind of traitor, which you are, but not to me."

"How can you be sure?"

"It doesn't matter. I have to protect Mina, and you have done this, so even if you're betraying the organization, our goals are the same. Where is Mina now?"

"Were you not... uh... were you at the parking garage?"

"I was. We came out onto the roof—there was some kind of light overhead that vanished. Vassily hit you over the head and we came back here."

"Mina is... missing."

Now I'd made her mad. "What?"

"We were both in that parking garage, but after the bullets started flying, we got separated. I don't know what happened to her." It's always important to be honest when lying.

"Can you find her?"

"Was planning to do that once I got out of here. You know, assuming you aren't all going to have me killed."

"Vassily the Whale wants you dead."

"To be fair, he wants most things dead."

"I can help you," she said. "Can you get out of this room?"

I looked at the door. "Yeah, I think so, as long as there isn't a padlock on the other side."

"There's not. When you get out, go straight ahead and at

the first intersection, go right. You'll find a high window. That will be unlocked. Understand?"

I nodded.

She said, "Find Mina. Try to find proof that Daphne is setting her up. If we can prove this, we can bring new leadership to V.E.N.U.S. Maybe someone with a stronger conception of loyalty."

"That all sounds great." I wondered which hippo would take over, and if there would be a ritual combat. I pictured them all in Starfleet uniforms, equipped with unlikely polearms. That didn't help.

"If you need to contact me, use this number." She handed me a slip of paper that looked like a fortune, with ten numbers grouped in twos. Common trick: it didn't look like a phone number at first glance.

Oana didn't make any sound when she moved, and somehow even managed to open that massive metal door silently. So we were the core of a new V.E.N.U.S., an organization dedicated to the continued breathing of one Miss Mina Duplessis. It was a refreshingly concrete goal that didn't lend itself to schisms.

I opened my legs. The knife was lying between them, blade up. All I could think about was the story in *Clerks* that ended with the kid breaking his own neck. What a way to go, and all I could look forward to was a knife in the mouth.

I was leaning forward with my mouth open when the door opened. I sat bolt upright and hid the knife. Oana or Vassily? Neither.

Neil. He shut the door and scampered over. "Colin, are you okay? It's all I can do to keep these maniacs from doing something horrible."

"Yeah, I'm fine." There was a pattern emerging. "So I take it Stan doesn't want me dead."

"No. I looked into it as much as I could, and I didn't find anything. Then Oana calls and tells me you're nosing around V.E.N.U.S."

"You know Oana?"

"We... uh... we dated."

"On whose orders?"

Neil squirmed. "Stan's."

"Stan was at a V.E.N.U.S.-sponsored fashion show... wait. How long was I out?"

"Six hours, I think? You got knocked out, and I think it became sleep. You were snoring when we taped you to the chair."

"Stan was at a fashion show last night, then. Do you know why?"

Neil shook his head. "Why?"

"No, I was asking you."

"Then I don't know."

"Neil, what the fuck are you doing with those people? I mean, this little cabal that looks like a grab bag of shadow organizations. What are you supposedly after?"

"You."

"I was afraid of that."

"We all want the Chain of the Heretic Martyr, and when we have it, the plan is to kill you. Stan knows I'm involved in this, and now he knows about your whole information-gathering web."

My stomach started to breakdance. "He knows?"

"He was really impressed that you infiltrated all of them, even if you didn't infiltrate that far. Looked like great foresight to him."

"Glad he was impressed. What do Stan and the Masons want with the Chain?"

He shrugged. "Dunno. But if we get it, we can call the

shots, at least with regards to the Templars... That's Knights Templar, if you don't know. Not to mention V.E.N.U.S. and the Anas." The weird part was that Neil was lying to me. He was trying to talk like a fanatic, but he was coming off like someone selling way too hard. He was offering me sixty bucks for a jellybean.

I had to draw him out. "Leverage is good," I said. "Depends on who has it. The Chain is important to everyone, but I don't know that anyone should have that kind of power."

"What were you planning to do with it?"

"Get it off the streets, for one thing."

"What if there were a place it could be taken? Off the streets? In the right hands?" he said slowly.

"I'd be willing to listen."

"We'll talk. When this is over, we'll talk."

"I don't know if you'd noticed, but I'm locked in a bunker in San Pedro."

"San... how did you know?"

I gave him my best annoyed/cocky smile. I probably looked like a giant asshole.

"Right. Can you get out of this room?" I didn't bother to look at the door. I just nodded. He reached into the pocket of his hoodie and handed me some car keys. "Gray Taurus, parked a block north." He stuck the keys in my pocket, which was more than a little uncomfortable for both of us. "I've got to go. I only had a small window to say hi." He scampered back out.

They say that good communication is the key to any successful relationship. This little conspiracy of theirs really should sit down and compare notes. The problem was that somehow they had all found out about my conflicting loyalties and they were openly planning to kill me, even if they seemed to have private reservations.

It was a long time before that door opened again, and I still hadn't managed to fellate the knife out of my crotch, but it was beginning to look like I wouldn't need it. I shifted a little to keep the knife out of obvious sight and I waited to see who the next one through would be.

It was the gray-skinned guy, grinning ear to ear.

"Wow," he said. "The famous... you!" I didn't want to be famous.

"Let my right arm go and I'll give you an autograph."

"I'm afraid that doing so would result in my immediate dissolution and all that entails."

I wasn't sure what it all entailed, but I didn't think that now was a good time to bring that up. I tried to ape his speech patterns and at the same time make it sound like this was how I wanted to talk all along. That was a challenge.

"I'm a little afraid that my dissolution is imminent."

"Negative, negative. LAM would prefer your continued existence."

LAM, from a sketch by Aleister Crowley of his spirit guide. Show that sketch to any alien abductee and they get immediate post-traumatic stress disorder, if you take my meaning. It meant that gray-skin was working for the Little Green Men, which I had guessed as soon as he'd opened his mouth.

"What do you have in mind?"

"Hubba hubba," he said. "Your cells are missing three electrons. You have the signs."

"Uh-huh." These types were all alike. Mind-wiped one too many times, brains replaced with a gestalt. The problem with the gestalt was that it had the mental capacity of a six-year-old with a large and outdated vocabulary. "Do you have a designation?"

"Victor Charlie."

"Well, VC... want to... uh... explain the actions of LAM in

the relocation of my... uh, lady friend?"

VC frowned, which only made his eyes pop out further. "Lady... friend? The dame! Bore the designates, relocated, examined, unfit except as container."

"The dame is not to be... whatever LAM was going to do, don't."

"LAM is amenable to an exchange. The dame hits the skids, you enter the celestial temple."

"Listen, Viet Cong..."

"Victor Charlie."

"That's what I said. What does LAM want with the Chain?"

VC let out a truly horrifying giggle. "LAM wants what LAM wants. Neil Greene called me, LAM sent me, I am here."

"That's wonderful."

VC leaned in close. His breath smelled like a hospital. "The others want to give you the dirt nap. LAM would prefer your continued existence."

"We went over that. Are you going to help me out?"

VC reached into his coat. This close, I could see the back of his head. There were sections where the skin had come loose and was hanging in small flaps. He removed a syringe from his pocket. I flinched.

"You're not sticking me with that."

He giggled. "Negative. Sticking you would give you the dirt nap. Molecular acid." He carefully put the syringe along my right arm and squeezed. Smoke, a hiss, and the tape melted. "Be still, or your appendage suffers dissolution, dig?"

I could hear the acid eat through the tape and start to work on the chair.

"Victor, I'm curious. Does LAM have any agents in... uh..." I gave him Raul's address.

VC blinked. "The question doesn't conform to the required parameters."

"Tell me about it."

VC blinked again. He had completely lost the thread of the conversation. I was worried that he would start drooling from those rubbery lips.

"Never mind."

He giggled again, and this close I could see through the shades. His eyes were completely empty. In that moment, he reminded me a little bit of Diaz. "LAM awaits the exchange."

"Where?"

"The desert. Go east. LAM will see you from a thousand eyes, and you will see LAM."

"I can't wait."

VC backed off and flashed a peace sign. "Twenty-three skidoo."

With that, he was out the door. Four down...

I waited for two reasons. One, I wanted to give that acid as long as I could to settle down before I put my bare skin any closer to it than it already was, and two, I was expecting Brady. He didn't disappoint.

He came in more smoothly than the others had. Still worried about being seen, but nowhere near the nervousness of Vassily, let alone Neil.

"Hi, Brady. I was just wondering, is that your first name or your last?"

"Is David Antonucci even your real name?" That was my Hermetic Secret Service name, so I could say for certain where Brady was from.

"I'm sorry about my handler," I said.

He nodded. "Thank you. Hazards of the job, I'm afraid. I am glad she didn't live to find out about your duplicity."

"I think it's closer to quintuplicity. Is that even a word?"

Brady didn't smile. I don't think he knew how. "Let's talk, Dave. You know, the others want you dead. I'm the only thing standing between you and them."

Oh, Brady. If only you knew. "Then talk. What do you want from me?" I tried to keep the accent off *you*.

"They want the Chain of the Heretic Martyr. They think it will settle the troubles here, assuming, of course, it goes to their group."

"So I gathered. You think I have it?"

"I think you were looking for it before most people knew it was in play. That tells me that you have the best chance of finding it."

"Tell me something. How did you find that out?"

"Apparently your... quintuplicity hasn't gone unnoticed. You were careful enough that it took a long time to uncover it, though."

"By you, I take it."

Brady didn't smile, but the corners of his watery eyes crinkled. "No."

So there was someone. Someone else, that is. Someone who decided to link these five freaks? Someone who wanted the Chain?

I said, "The assassin at Union was for me."

"That much I do know."

Someone who wanted me dead. Me *specifically*. Why? It hit me like Diaz's rock. I blinked, gasping for air as it all rushed out and over me. There was another me out there. Someone flitting through the conspiracies. Someone who knew what I was because *they* were that, too. Someone who had maybe put this group together. Someone who knew what they knew and more. I thought about Diaz: the girl, the girl, the girl.

Brady steepled his fingers. He had small hands, but long, graceful fingers. "What? You know something."

I tried to cover. "It's not every day you find out that you're targeted for death."

Brady didn't look like he bought it, at least not entirely. "No. Not *every* day. So, tell me, Dave. Do you know where the Chain is?"

"Call me Jonah," I said.

Through his teeth: "*Jonah*. Do you know where the Chain is?"

"I think I was closing in. Can you tell me something? Who stole it from the Templars originally?"

"Unknown. Several factions have motive, of course. I can tell you this: it wasn't the Guardian Servitors of the Anorectic Praxis and it wasn't V.E.N.U.S."

Which practically confirmed that Eric had been the one to steal it, an inside job to lift it from the Templars. There was something else nagging at me, but I couldn't put my finger on it. "You still haven't told me what you want, Brady. I'm going to guess that you and the people out there don't see eye to eye on everything."

"No, not everything. Tell me something. Why are you protecting Mina Duplessis?"

"Just thinking about what the man said that jumped naked into a cactus."

"What?"

"Seemed like a good idea at the time."

"She wasn't at the parking garage. Where did you stash her?"

"Stash her? She's not porn." Brady glared. "Why do you want her?"

"I want her out of play. She's confusing the issue, bringing in the gender war where it isn't needed."

"I can do that—but I'm the only one she trusts."

Brady reached into his coat and dropped a leather wallet in my lap. My picks. "You might need these to get out. I imagine you can get out of some duct tape without too much help."

Yeah, I only needed one person to help with that.

"Count slowly to one hundred and make your break. I'll have cleared out the others by then," Brady said.

"No problem."

Brady nodded and was gone. My doppelganger was going to have to keep a closer eye on his foot soldiers to keep them from working at cross purposes even as they thought they were on the same side. It was enough to give me an aneurysm. I tried my right hand. It came loose. I grabbed the knife from between my legs and cut myself out of the silver web. Had it been a hundred yet? I'd forgotten to count. I counted to fifty, figuring that was enough. The door was locked, but I made short work of that with my picks.

I peeked out into a large, circular concrete room covered in rusted piss stains. There was more trash, more graffiti. It was abandoned. There were double doors, but I remembered what Oana had told me. I looked to the right and found a short hall. This was the remains of a bathroom. She was right; there were windows, the kind you see in basements, about seven feet off the ground. I saw grass poking up into the white light streaming in. I thought of the parking garage.

I jumped, tapped the window. It was open. I jumped again, caught the edge, and hauled myself into the sun.

FACES ARE IMPORTANT. SO IMPORTANT, IN FACT, that the human mind naturally creates faces where none exist. It's a phenomenon called pareidolia, and it's why people keep seeing Jesus in toast. Basically, given vague information, the human mind will fill in the blanks until it has a face, then fill in a few more until the face has some significance. Helps us feel like we're not alone in the world.

We grant faces to things we can't see, as well. The terrifying experience of death becomes the Grim Reaper. Holiday cheer becomes Santa. We do this because it makes them feel less like forces and more like people we could know in our lives. People we could have over for dinner. People with families and pets. People we could club over the head and loot if things got dicey.

I was thinking about my phantom enemy, and I gave him a face, or the faceless equivalent: a name. Mr. Blank. It helped a little. Granted, there was a decent chance I was thinking of Mrs. Blank, or Ms. if she didn't want to give away her marital status, but for now I thought of Blank as a guy. I was looking forward to actually slapping a face on him, probably because it would be a face I'd already seen.

As I popped out of the window, I got my bearings. It looked to be a little after noon. I was in San Pedro, on an open hillside overlooking Pacific Coast Highway and the ocean. A breeze whispered in, cool on my freshly duct-tape-waxed wrists. The hillside was dotted with old bunkers, built during World War II when everyone was convinced that the Japanese were ready to launch an invasion. At least, that was the official explanation. The real reason was something I didn't like to think about very much, and which was why I didn't go on cruises. Well, that and my being under fifty years old.

I ran to the street as best I could with a throbbing head and feet that were still half-asleep. One block north meant inland. A quick walk, and I found Neil's Taurus. The keys even worked.

I drove, trying not to think about Mina. That I had to get her back was a foregone conclusion, but going off half-cocked wouldn't do anyone any favors. VC had offered a deal, but whether he was telling the truth or not was anyone's guess. I couldn't even be sure he knew the difference between the truth and a lie.

Lunch was McDonald's, and crappy food never tasted so good. It was more about comfort than anything else. My head hurt and my confidence had just been pantsed in front of its entire eighth-grade gym class. Diaz had been after me all along. Diaz knew where I lived. Chances were good his handlers knew where I lived, which meant going home wasn't an option.

Unless Diaz had followed me home from some point in the previous evening's adventures. My V.E.N.U.S. affiliation seemed to be more or less common knowledge; maybe he had picked me back up there. Maybe he had been too messed up from his conditioning to impart any sort of useful information to anyone who'd ask. I could think of one way to find out, and I needed to talk to the guy anyway.

I drove back to my car, and it was right where I'd left it. I checked the trunk. Phones, all there. Rock and chain, there. The weird flail was sitting on top of some old comics, and the gray dust had taken root. In places, it was beginning to turn into the same crust I'd seen on Diaz's coat. It looked a little like one of those growing rock gardens you could buy in the backs of comic books, only the Day-Glo stalactites were a uniform glowing gray.

I picked up Colin Reznick's phone and texted Neil: "Car where you found me. Thanks." I threw on a clean shirt and my badge.

Considering where the cops picked Raul up, he would be at Hollywood/La Brea. They would still be holding him for another twelve or thirteen hours, and if I knew people, there would be one detective who noticed the mirror image that was the other man in the house. On a normal day, I'd be getting a call from one of my employers to put that detective off the scent, to lose a piece of evidence, or even do some surreal intimidation. This wasn't a normal day.

I drove back into Hollywood. The streets were packed. It occurred to me that it was Saturday. The police station was busy, cops streaming in and out, cars lined up outside. The desk sergeant gave me an annoyed look, so I flashed my badge. "Detective Saroyan," I said.

"What can I do for you, detective?" He needed a couple thousand more cups of coffee.

"You picked up a man yesterday for harassing a family in Hollywood. Talking crazy, trying to get into the house, saying he lived there?"

The sergeant was suddenly suspicious. "What do you

want him for?"

"We've had a couple similar incidents in Van Nuys. I was hoping I could talk to this guy."

"You're about two hours too late."

"Why?"

"We were transferring him to Burbank..."

"Wait. Why were you sending him to Burbank?"

He shrugged. "We get the orders, we send him. Not my problem."

"And...?"

"And, when we took him to the parking garage, a guy came out with a gun and had your guy dead on the ground before we could do anything."

"The shooter—you arrested him, right?"

The sergeant gave me a look that said: *Do I look stupid to you?*

I said, "Can I talk to the shooter, then? Maybe he has some kind of connection to my home invasions."

"Suit yourself."

The sergeant let them know I was coming back, and soon I was sitting in an interrogation room. I rested my arms on the rusted metal table between the two bars that looked they should be helping handicapped people use the bathroom. I kept still. No need to telegraph any nervousness. It wasn't like the guy would be carrying a gun. As far as I knew, Detective Arto Saroyan's name was still off the conspiracy radar. No telling how many of the rest of my names were compromised, how many IDs I'd have to burn, assuming I was going to live through this.

The door opened, with a uniform escorting a familiar face in shackles.

Eric Caldwell, Knight Templar.

The uniform clipped Eric's cuffs to the bars on the table,

nodded to me, and left the room.

"Squire Max?" Eric whispered. I think he was actually a little bit shocked.

"How about we leave names out for the time being? I understand you haven't given yours up."

"Fair enough."

"First things first. I know you stole the Chain of the Heretic Martyr."

Eric was probably a good liar, but he wasn't faking the confusion on his face. "Is that what you told Sir Richard?"

"You didn't steal it?"

He shook his head. "I didn't even know it was missing."

Great. It wasn't an inside job. Or if it was, it wasn't Eric. Instead, I tried the one thing I knew for damn sure he *had* done. "Why'd you kill Diaz?"

"I didn't." He sounded serious and even slightly smug, in a terrified sort of way.

"According to everyone in this building, you shot Diaz to death. You're being held for murder."

"Oh, I shot him. Three times through the heart."

"You're going to have to walk me through this one. Why wouldn't that kill him?"

Eric dropped everything other than the fear. "Because Diaz is a vampire."

"You've got to be fucking kidding me."

"There are vampires out there. Diaz is one of them."

"Okay, I'm going to say this slowly. There. Are. No. Such. Things. As. Vampires."

Nearly religious serenity: "Yes, there are."

I suddenly wished for the Vic Mackey interrogation pack: a phone book, bottle of booze, and a loaded handgun.

He went on. "I have proof. Go to my apartment. Look for a book called *Year of the Condor*. It's a big hardback, in the back of my closet. You can't miss it. There's a sticky note that'll prove it." He gave me an address in Irvine.

I sighed. "If you were so sure he's a vampire, why did you shoot him?"

"I used silver bullets, but I can't be sure they worked."

"Silver bullets are for werewolves."

His eyes went buggy. "Werewolves are real, too?"

"Oh, Jesus. All right, why were you the one sent to kill Diaz? Why not your friend in the gay bar?"

Eric's expression hardened. "You might not want to mention him again."

"Right, right. He's the top dog. The head honcho. The big cheese. *El jefe*. The big kahuna. I could keep going."

"Please don't."

"You were responsible for Diaz. Why did you send him to kill me?"

Eric jumped like he'd been electrocuted. "I didn't."

"You didn't activate him?"

"No... I... Max, you have to get me out of here. Get me out of here and I'll tell you everything you want to know."

"Tell me now."

"No. No way. I need assurances. Get me out of here and I'll take you right to Diaz's handler."

"The girl," I said.

I didn't think it was possible for Eric to look any more scared. "You're gonna get me out?"

"I'll do what I can, but that's not much. Short of a jailbreak, which is about as likely to work as me playing starting center for the Lakers. Statistically, the best bet is to wait for your bail hearing, but you seem antsy."

"And you don't want more brainwashed assassins trying to shoot you."

"Wait, what?"

He frowned and tried to talk me through his cocky threat. "You know, more assassins coming after you for whatever you know."

"No, you said 'shoot.' It was pretty distinct and I have good ears."

"Yeah, shoot. You know, with a gun?" He didn't mime it, but I could tell he sort of wanted to.

"Right, with a gun, because that's what you guys give them. Not homemade flails. Of course."

Eric broke into a nervous smile. "Yeah. You okay?"

"Oh, I've suffered some head trauma recently."

I got a weird look for that one.

Eric sighed. "Doesn't matter. I'm not getting bail. Five cops saw me shoot that bloodsucker."

I thought about yelling at him about vampires and their lack of existence, but it was probably pointless until I had a look at his "evidence." "You'll get arraigned, some hardass judge will refuse you bail, and they'll ship you off to county. You'll never get there, though, because you'll get out at the courthouse. Security's lighter, and you can sneak out of there."

"In this," he retorted, pinching the shoulder of his bright orange jumpsuit and giving it a dubious wiggle.

"Orange is a nice color on you." He didn't find that funny. "Give your guys the slip, make it to the men's room on the third floor, go to the last stall. Move the panel in the ceiling, and you'll find a suit there. I'll plant it as soon as I leave."

"How do I get out of my cuffs?"

"Fucking magic," I said. He didn't get it. A little sleight of hand and I made a lockpick appear. "Please tell me you can work a lock."

He nodded. "A little."

I slipped him the pick and he palmed it. "When are they

taking you over?"

"Two hours."

"I'll be waiting for you outside of the west exit. When this is all over, there's something you need to remember: you spill your guts, then you get the hell out of LA, got it?"

"I understand."

"You're not a fucking Templar. You're in ghetto witness protection."

"What if it goes bad?"

"It's *already* gone bad. That's what being in police custody for murder means. Smile." I had Reznick's phone out, framed him, and snapped a picture. I went to the door and knocked. The uniform let me out, and I resisted the temptation to give a significant nod in Eric's direction. It wasn't a question of *if* the cops in the building were loyal to something beyond the safety of the citizenry of Los Angeles, but *what* they were loyal to. Sometimes I wished everyone would just get their conspiracy tattooed on their foreheads: combination third eye and Hello My Name Is badge.

I sighed and went back to my car.

On the stereo: "Party."

I picked the proper phone and dialed. Familiar voice, complete with a teenaged-Dracula accent. "Hello?"

"It's Jonah Bailey."

"Have you found her?" Oana said.

"I have a location, but I need your help. Meet me in MacArthur Park in an hour."

I had a stop to make first; I picked up a suit downtown for cheap and planted it where I had told Eric it would be.

Then I drove over to MacArthur Park. My ID guy had an office nearby, in the back of a newsstand. I parked at a meter and made my way up a sidewalk that looked like the hide of an elephant with skin cancer. Each little blemish was someone's gum, turned black from dirt and car exhaust. The newsstand was actually a shop, its formerly glass walls plastered with a collage of magazines and beer ads. It managed to look like circus pornography, despite the absence of clowns or bare breasts.

I walked in, passed the sleeping man at the counter, and headed for the back. I opened the door marked "Employees Only," went down a short hallway that looked like it should be part of an abandoned hospital, and through a men's room door marked "Out of Order."

My ID guy was Javier dos Santos. He looked a lot like Edward James Olmos in *Stand and Deliver*, down to the male-pattern baldness and glasses like satellite dishes. Javier blinked at me as I walked in, focusing past his fluorescents.

"Hey, John. Another ID?"

He had everything he needed to mock something up: laminators, a nice lit table, lights, X-Acto knives, an old computer. I felt like I'd wandered onto the set of *The Andromeda Strain*.

"Yeah, but not for me." I handed the phone to him. "Picture's in there."

He plugged it into the computer and retrieved the picture of Eric. "I take it you want me to change the color on his jumpsuit."

"Yeah, make it navy or something."

"What name you want?"

I thought about it. You could take the boy out of fifth grade… "Holden Balzac." I spelled it for him.

"Got it. How complicated?"

"Just enough to pass casual inspection. I need this yesterday."

"Double normal."

I handed him the cash.

He said, "Come back in an hour."

MacArthur Park was a small expanse of rolling green hills, palm trees, and a lake with a fountain in the middle. It was also a magnet for every crackhead, junkie, and wino within five miles, and that lake was only good for stashing bodies. I picked a bench and tried to avoid eye contact.

Oana was on time. She came walking in from the east side, strolling casually down the path. She wanted me to know she was alone. I waved her over to my bench. I had a nice view of the fountain, even if the bench was probably going to put a splinter in my ass.

She didn't waste any time. "Where is she?"

I squinted at her through the sunlight and fatigue. "Government installation out in the desert." A blatant lie, but I wasn't sure how well she was going to take the truth. She knew VC, so it was possible that she was more initiated than I thought.

"And what do you need me for?"

"Look, I'm basically a bagman. I have some skills, but I've never been asked to do any of them in the Olympics."

She nearly smiled at that. It was probably a laugh-out-loud moment for her. "So you need the services of a gymnast."

"I need the services of a dirty-tricks specialist. In point of fact, I'm going to ask two other people. People that we're not going to be able to trust."

She frowned. "Who?"

"The Whale, for one."

"No! When the others found that you'd escaped, things got... tense. There were threats. Vassily nearly twisted Neil's head off."

"Lovely. Look, the Whale can be a handful, but we need a brick shithouse."

"My English is good, but I don't know what that means."

"It means someone like Vassily. Big, dumb, and violent

enough to attract some attention."

"He's not that dumb. Who's the other?"

"You don't know him, but if anything, he's worse than Vassily."

"I don't think this is the best idea."

"You and I need to be solid. We go in, we get Mina, we get out. That's what matters, right?"

She threw me a curt nod like she was signaling the time-keepers before a vault.

"Good." I gave her the address of a burger place in Venice, somewhere nice and public. "Meet me there at six."

With that, I got up.

"Where are you going?" she said.

"Errand." I paused. "You're going to follow me, aren't you?"

"Yes."

"Then come along. If you're going to watch, I want you close enough to watch back." She hopped up and followed me from the park. I said, "Listen, could you try to walk like a grown woman? I already feel a little creepy here." She gave me a blank look and kept walking like a twelve-year-old in a military parade. Beaten, I sighed, "Better."

Back into the newsstand, back into the back. Javier looked from me to Oana. "She need a fake ID to go drinking?"

I rubbed the bridge of my nose.

"I'm twenty-six," Oana said.

Javier wasn't buying, but he handed me Eric's new papers. "None of my business. Mr. Balzac won't be fooling experts, but he might be able to get a credit card."

"Who can't?"

Oana had to move the passenger seat of my car forward about a foot. I was commuting with a hobbit.

We drove to the courthouse and I parked on the west side, across the street. We had some shade. I hunkered down and got to watching. There were a few people out front: a fat man at the bus station, a blonde on the steps drinking from a large bottle of water, and a few suits moving in and out of the building.

"What are we doing here?" Oana asked.

"Parking. Waiting. Look, if you want to go hide in some bushes to watch me, that's fine, too."

"I feel fine here."

Eric should be in there by now. I tried not to let the paranoia creep up on me. He'd been caught trying to escape; he'd been shot. Someone had already gotten to him, either the girl or the old man. There were a lot of ways it could have already gone wrong.

I heard a zipper. It was Oana, going through her purse, a tiny handbag with an angry penguin on the side. She removed a plastic box with a checkerboard pattern, opened it, and emptied the pieces into her hand.

"Travel chess," she said.

"I know what it is."

She set up the board. She moved: e4.

I said, "It's been years."

"Don't be chicken." Her voice went up several octaves and she flapped her arms. "Cheep cheep cheep." That was weird enough to get me to move: b6.

"So what happened in Sydney?" I was still smarting from the Bluthian chicken noise she threw my way. She moved: d4.

"I missed the landing on my vault." That wound seemed fresh.

I decided we needed some bigger guns: Bb7. "Was it worth it? Becoming a hobbit, I mean."

She looked at me as though I was a really interesting insect. Bd3. She didn't answer.

I went ahead. "I mean, you sacrifice a lot. Mornings,

weekends, a normal-sized neck, menstruation." My move: f5.

"Do you think you're being funny?"

"A little, I mean..." I glanced at the door of the courthouse. Eric was coming down the stairs in the gray suit I had gotten for him, trying to look as casual as he could. "Showtime."

Her gaze followed mine and I was out of the car. Eric spotted me, and for a moment looked relieved. The blonde woman tossed aside her water bottle. She was very thin. Skinny, even. Fucking anorexic. Shit.

Eric turned and was about to yell when she kicked him in the face. Perfect Muay Thai form, too. Textbook.

I tried to get a decent look at her. Blonde hair past her shoulders, and thicker than I would have expected. Smallish eyes, thin lips. Good bones, which was fortunate since that's all there was of her.

"Son of a bitch!"

I ran through traffic. Eric was still rattled by the kick; the fact that he wasn't lights out said he was tough as hell. The woman punched Eric in the temple, landing it perfectly. Nobody was *that* tough; he was out.

I hopped on the curb. I wasn't sure what I was going to do. I thought maybe I could grab her. As I lunged, she spun and kicked me in the belly, digging her heel into a jumble of my organs. I crumpled. Pain replaced breath. I couldn't move beyond holding my gut and trying to inhale.

A van roared up. The stick woman easily picked Eric up over her shoulder and threw him into the van. She glanced my way, but didn't have the good graces to shoot me a cocky grin before hopping in after Eric. The van was gone before I could get up.

I devoted my first breath to a stream of curses.

"She was Ana." Oana helped me to my feet.

"You're fucking-ay right."

"Who was the man?"

"That's the last we're going to see of him."

Eric's apartment was not crawling with cops. That made me a little nervous. The man was dead. The very least they could do was systematically violate his privacy like a freshman arriving at an English boarding school. I picked the lock on the front door and went inside.

Old clove smoke had turned the oxygen in the house into an oppressed minority, consigned only to the ghettoes inside. Eric kept his house dark, and not just because the lights were off. He had black drapes on every window, drawn tight. Shadows turned out to be black furniture and bookcases. The walls were lined with fantasy art, the scary Boris Vallejo/Frank Frazetta knock-offs where everyone, man and woman, was six feet of corded muscle, wearing only G-strings and using disturbingly phallic swords to fight disturbingly phallic dragons. The medieval weaponry on the wall was intended either for decoration or theft deterrent. He did keep everything neat and clean, and for that I was grateful.

Eric's bedroom was in the back. It somehow managed to be darker than the rest of the place. I wondered how the men and/or women he brought home reacted. They probably weren't sure if he was going to have sex with them or sacrifice them to his dark gods. Really, that might have been a plus to them. I decided I didn't want to think about Eric's sex life anymore.

I opened up the closet and saw that that wasn't going to be possible.

"What's that?" Oana said, pointing at something I wanted to unsee.

"I don't know."

"And that?"

"Please stop talking."

I found the book Eric was talking about under some squeaking vinyl. It was a big book and could be a part of his medieval weaponry collection in a pinch. I opened the page marked by the protruding sticky note. I must have made a noise, because Oana said, "What?"

"What" was a picture of Raul Diaz, dead. Not alone, either. The picture showed a pile of bodies stuffed into what looked like a classroom. The bodies had been executed with single bullet wounds to the head. The caption said: "The disappeared, victims of Operation Condor."

Condor was the CIA code for the assassination and overthrow of Salvador Allende. Bunch of left-wing Chileans vanished, and later some of them turned up in mass executions like the one in the picture. Others were never heard from again. They were called "the disappeared." Apparently, Raul Diaz had died in 1975. That was fine. Didn't make him a fucking vampire.

I tried to cover my shock. "Horrible picture."

"Yeah."

I searched the rest of the apartment, but I didn't find anything else that I hadn't expected, other than six cans of Aquanet in the bathroom cabinet and two more in the trashcan. I wondered why Eric was doing his hair in 1985. The shaggy medieval look he went for didn't call for that kind of hold.

I drove from there to Venice and parked out by the beach. The door was open, and I was sitting in the driver's seat, feet on the ground. Oana was perched on the hood. It was a little hard to get upset with her for sitting there. After all, it's not like she weighed anything.

I made two phone calls. The first was to the Whale. He answered immediately. "*Shto*?"

"It's Nicky."

"Nicky! I was impressed. Picked that door with nothing but a knife."

"Uh... yeah."

"I put on show for the others. Nearly twisted Neil's head off. Made them believe."

"Vassily, a point."

"You have Chain."

"No, but I know where it is. Look, before you say, 'Good, go get it,' keep listening. It's not where I can get at it. I know *you* can, however."

"You need, what, cat burglar?"

I wondered what kind of cat he thought he was. "The opposite. This place is a research station. Government grants. Links to things like SETI and JPL. I need you to go in hard and loud."

Vassily started laughing. "Just like sex!"

"Security shifts change at midnight," I said. This was a blind guess. "Head in then. And Vassily, bring your guys."

"I will. I get Chain, we split cash. Good doing business with you, Nicky."

"My pleasure." I hung up. To Oana, I announced, "We have our diversion."

She turned around to give me a dubious look. "And the other?"

The second phone call was to Hasim Khoury. "Hasim, it's Len."

"How're you doin'?" I could smell the booze over the phone.

"Can you get ahold of Tariq Suliman?"

That sobered him up. "What do you need him for?"

"Can you get him?"

"Yes. It's not really a good time."

"What do you mean by that?"

"Oh, a bit of a situation. Nothing to be concerned about."

"Then find Tariq for me." I gave Hasim the same meeting place I gave Oana earlier, the burger place in Venice. It was a short walk from where we were.

"He doesn't like being summoned."

"Then phrase it as a request. Talk to you later, Hasim."

Oana was suddenly right in front of me. I jumped, then noticed that she was at eye level when I was sitting down. That put me in a better mood. "Who is Tariq Suliman?"

"You'll like him. He's creepy. I feel like I should warn you, though, he currently wants Mina dead."

"And you thought it would be a good idea to bring him to her?"

"Well, no. The fact of the matter is, Tariq will keep coming until he's dead, and there's only one thing I know of that might be able to take him out."

"Which is?"

"You don't want to know, but we're going to where they live."

I was pretty sure Oana thought I was completely insane at this point, and was probably regretting having helped me escape. A million guys in the information underground, and she had to wind up with the one who talked in the riddles you find on Popsicle sticks.

We waited at a table outside the burger place. I wasn't hungry and I was pretty sure she was a vegetarian, judging by the way she looked at the burgers. Instead, she took her travel chess set out again and made me play a game. She didn't actually *make* me—I mean, she didn't pull a gun, put a knife to my throat, or physically move my hand—but I didn't want her to make that chicken noise again. It was disconcerting and weirdly infectious.

People were everywhere. It was afternoon going on evening, so families, tired and red from a day at the beach, were heading inland, turning the beaches over to the night people: high-school kids and the homeless, anyone who wanted to get drunk on a bed of sand.

I saw Tariq when he was still twenty feet away. I was pretty sure that meant that he had gotten within breathing distance, determined it wasn't a setup, and doubled back. Oana saw him as soon as I did. Clearly, she was expecting something else.

"That's him?"

"Yep."

"He looks like Goofy the dog."

He kind of did. Tall, lanky; sub in ears for dreads and make his clothes a little less garish. Bam. Goofy. I said, "You should tell him that."

Tariq took the empty chair. He wasn't grinning at me, but he wasn't glaring, either—a strange halfway expression that suggested either sudden violence or impending bromance. I was more comfortable with the former.

"Who's that?" Tariq demanded, pointing at Oana. "Someone trying to kill her, too?"

"Just some Uruk-hai."

Tariq burst out laughing. "Hell yeah! What up, peck?"

Oana opened her mouth to say something, but I jumped in, and not to point out that Tariq had his fantasy little people mixed up. "Tariq, listen, I'm sorry about earlier."

The laughter stopped, and his expression suddenly *was* a glare. He'd decided. He was going to try to kill me with what was on the table: a Styrofoam cup, a straw, a half-full ashtray, and some travel chess pieces. I really hated how my mind was filling in those blanks.

"What the fuck?" Tariq snapped. "I should kill you, just because."

"I'm saying sorry here."

"Man, I got kids to feed."

"... You do?"

He shrugged. I had no idea if he was being serious. "You're like Cain, and you know what happened to Cain in the story."

"He got a mark that made sure no one would ever hurt him?"

Tariq said, "You don't know shit. So, come on, I'm here, what do you want to say to me?"

"Your target is still alive?"

"Busty St. Clair?" he said.

"Mina Duplessis," Oana snapped.

"Why didn't you kill her?" he asked.

"The Russian mob has the contract on her, too. They, uh, knocked me out and taped me to a chair."

He shouted to the sky, "D'OOOOH!"

"So I'm saying as a peace offering, I'll give you a location."

"And I give you?"

"Another thirty years on the planet, for starters."

"I like this deal!"

I gave him the location. He held his hand up. I did the

same and he slapped me five, hard. Then he walked away and was gone before he was ten feet distant.

"Let's go. He'll need a couple hours to prepare," I said.

"And us?"

I didn't answer her. We got in my car and drove east. The sun set on us, and soon we were in a David Lynch movie. The desert at night, the sky gets bigger and the ground falls away. There's the patch of ground in the headlights, the shining lines of the center divider and stars. It becomes an asphalt tightrope over infinity.

On the stereo: "Let Me Take You Home Tonight."

To my horror, Oana started singing along. It wasn't that she was a bad singer; it's just that I was having trouble reconciling what she was doing with the act of singing. It was the perfect counterpoint to the desert around us. I shrugged and started singing, too. We weren't going to win any karaoke contests.

I turned off the road at the right mile marker, then off again onto a dirt road. There was a base not far from here. When we hit the rise, I pulled the car off to the side and killed the lights. From ten feet away, it would look like part of the hill.

I got out of the car, popped the trunk, and grabbed a few things.

"Get your gun," Oana said.

"I don't have a gun."

"You don't have a—how are you planning to get Mina back?"

"Thought I'd ask nicely. You catch a lot more flies with honey than with vinegar, you know."

"You catch even more flies with a flamethrower."

"You don't know what 'brick shithouse' means, but you know the English for flamethrower. That's Romanian education for you." I started up the hill.

The desert is not exactly quiet at night. Compared to the city or to anywhere with trees, it is. But there are insects, birds, all the usual noisemakers. They're not as boisterous. Really, the desert comes off like an upscale movie theatre in a rich neighborhood: there's stage whispers, but not enough to screw up the film.

At the top of the hill, we were able to look down on the complex. It wasn't much to look at, really. The small valley gave it about three hundred feet on all sides to the hills. The fences and razorwire enclosed a larger area with distinct sections. On the south side, there was a makeshift town. It was supposed to look like a '50s road stop town, a barracks that didn't feel like one. Over the fifty years since it had been built, it had been partly reclaimed by the desert, becoming one of those *Road Warrior* settlements that dot the southwest. A herd of cows wandered between the buildings. The north side sported a perfectly square patch of pavement: the airstrip. Of course, it was much too small for an actual plane to use. Next to that were the warehouse-sized hangars, lit with floods. In the center was a central building, creepily designed to look like a large '50s-era mansion, with smaller "cottages" that were actually labs.

What there wasn't was men with guns.

To the naked eye, there was no security beyond a high fence and some floodlights. To be fair, they didn't really need to keep people out.

Oana and I walked down the path. It was coming up on midnight, but we should be in before Vassily showed up.

Floodlights are usually described as making small sections of daylight. That's not accurate. Floodlights give a light whiter than anything that's not under Sirius. Shadows become the parabolic electron orbits of atomic symbols. Beneath a flood, we become nuclear. That was the scene Oana and I approached through the desert.

The dirt road led to a gate in the fence. It was partly open, but not all the way. Somehow, that made it worse.

"You know these people?" Oana asked. She knew the answer. Presumably, VC had informed her of that connection.

"There's one word in that sentence that's wrong."

Her head snapped toward me. "So UFOs are aliens?"

"Some of them. Look, this is the kind of thing that ends up driving people crazy."

"Are you saying you're crazy?"

"No, but I'm in an amazing level of denial."

I squeezed through the gate. Oana didn't have to. I was getting a case of nerves. The compound was silent, apparently empty. Oana kept scanning the terrain.

The front door of the central building opened. No one touched the door.

"Oana, what time is it?"

"Eleven forty-five."

"I hope that fat fucker is punctual."

The man that stepped out of the building before us almost looked like Steve Buscemi in *Reservoir Dogs.* Same suit, same pasty skin, same sunglasses, but he'd traded the facial hair for a fedora. His suit looked about a size too small, and he walked like he was having trouble doing it. He didn't look drunk, exactly—he looked like he was new to the whole bipedality party and was still getting the hang of it. He was completely focused on me; I'm not sure he even saw Oana. Granted, she was very short.

He said, "Oftentimes, the visitors appear in skies devoid of meaning."

This was not a code. I really had no idea what to say to that. "Victor Charlie told me that the Zetas were willing to make an exchange."

He said, "When the stars fall, they bring with them promises of a new age."

"Is that a yes?"

"Containers are abundant. They need only the guidance of the visitors to be put to proper use."

Oana whispered, "Containers?"

His head turned slowly, as though it were on greased ball bearings. "Visitations have been known in times of great peril." He did an about-face and walked back toward the building. When we didn't follow, he stopped. He didn't turn his head. He didn't beckon. He didn't make some joke about us dragging ass. He just stopped. When we started, he did, too.

Inside, it looked like an office building. Clean, linoleum, lots of shatterproof glass and white walls. The man led us down a hall. We passed an open door, and as I glanced in, I saw a pair of scientists talking to a short, bald man with a huge bulbous head. The little man's back was to the door. His skin was gray-green. He was not human. I didn't break stride. They wanted to get me with that gag? I invented that one.

Oana said, "Did you see—"

"Sure didn't."

Our guide turned and entered a room. When we followed, we nearly ran into him. He was standing just inside the doorway.

He said, "There are specific patterns in the stars that could be read, if only they would stop moving."

He sidestepped us and left.

"I think he wants us to wait," I said.

The room looked like a waiting room in a doctor's office, but all the magazines were from the '60s. At least I could read about the breaking news of Kennedy's assassination. Almost the instant I sat down, one of the scientists I had seen from the other room, a balding moleish man, bustled in. He said,

"Mr. MacGruder?"

"Yeah," I answered. I didn't bother to get up. He shook my hand. His felt like inflatable suede.

"I'm Dr. Beaman. My, ahem, employers, believe you have something that belongs to them. Something that they want back." He pulled a small machine, almost like a price scanner, from his lab coat. "May I?"

"Depends on what that is. If it strips my skin off, then hell no. If it gives me superpowers, then yes."

He chuckled. "Neither, I'm afraid. There's an, ahem, energy signature if you've had contact with the item."

"The same signature you found on my friend."

He blushed. "Yes, the woman was, ahem, uncooperative."

Damn right she was. I hoped Mina punted the first Zeta that came at her.

He held the machine up to me. It made the appropriate noises. I wondered if they programmed it on purpose, just so the layman could think that he was getting his science-fiction's worth when he ran into something like this. I'll be the first to admit that it enhanced the experience.

I watched Beaman's face. It changed as he read the machine. I said, "I take it I'm positive for the relevant tachyon field."

"It's actually not, ahem—well, yes, you are. Quite so. Mr. MacGruder, I've been informed that you have been a loyal, ahem, employee for three years, seven months, sixteen days, and, well, a few more hours than it said in the file. In that time, you have performed forty-two tasks. This new task would seem easy in comparison."

"Bringing you the item you're sniffing all over me. Can we cut the shit and call it what it is? You want the Chain just like every other person."

"Chain? What chain? We want the stone."

Well, fuck me. "What's the stone, Beaman?"

"That's not, that's not really..."

"Beaman!"

"The Genesis Stone."

When people get really paranoid about the Masons, the Genesis Stone is one of the things they mention. It was the fruition of a Masonic plot to end the world. The plot started with the atom bomb, moved to the assassination of Kennedy (as a stand-in for King Arthur, for those wondering why his administration was called Camelot), and culminated when the astronauts brought moon rocks to earth. The largest one was named the Genesis Stone, and it remained one of the most treasured artifacts in Masonic possession.

And someone had bolted it to a sacred chain and tried to cave my skull in with it.

"Who stole the Stone from the Masons?"

Beaman said, "I have no idea. They have it shielded at all times. Suddenly it was out. We thought your, ahem, friend might know where it was."

"And she didn't tell you."

"Like I said, uncooperative."

A keening wail echoed through the complex; the howling of a hypothetical robot dog. Beaman said, "I have to..."

That's all he got out, because Oana kicked his left knee out from under him, grabbed his arm, and twisted it at a truly horrible angle. She did this so quickly I couldn't say anything until Beaman was on the ground with a look like he was trying to pass a kidney stone the size of a corgi.

"Holy shit," I said. It was the smartest thing that popped into my head at the time.

"Where is she?" Oana demanded.

Beaman couldn't talk. Oana loosened her hold slightly, and I swear I could hear his ligaments creaking. His eyes fluttered and he lost consciousness.

"Damn," she said.

"I was thinking the same thing."

The keening continued. That was Vassily or Tariq. Specifically, that was the alarms in response to one or both of them. I was looking forward to introducing those guys. Either they'd kill each other or take over the world together. Either way meant plenty of work for me.

I flipped Beaman over and went through his pockets: keycard, ID, the scanner, another device I didn't recognize. All of that was mine now.

My Assassin phone rang. Barely heard it over the keening. I answered it. "Not a good time, Hasim."

"I am not Hasim." The voice on the other end was not human. It was a monotone, undercut with buzzing that sounded like television snow. It brought the hairs on the back of my neck to attention.

"Who is this?"

"We have met once before, in the Diaz household."

It sank in. "I remember."

"Exit the room. Turn left."

I skipped the distrust. After all, there were easier ways to kill me. The way the voice was guiding me, it was starting to seem familiar. I'd heard this one before somewhere, but I wasn't sure where, and now was hardly the time to go looking for a memory. Oana followed, but worry was starting to crack her game face. I exited the room and turned left.

The voice didn't wait for me to tell it I was done. "Follow the hallway. There will be a staircase on your left." It hadn't misled me yet. I opened the door into the stairwell with Beaman's keycard. "Go up the stairs, turn left."

"That's a lot of lefts."

"Left is better."

I followed instructions. Up on the second floor, the world had turned white, and not eggshell, or Navajo, or off, or any one of a dozen shades of white. This was the white that turned all other colors to memory, a white that nearly rendered me blind.

"She is behind the second door. Dr. Beaman's card will provide access."

I was about to hang up.

"Do not hang up."

It could see me? Better not think about that just now. No, ESP, right? Another piece of that particular puzzle. I swiped the card. The door clicked, opened. A short hall led into a hemispherical room with human-shaped depressions in the walls. They looked soft, but one touch revealed they felt like ivory. Mina was in one of these depressions, perfectly sized for her. That was great foresight. She was wearing some kind of bodysuit, a silver layer over her, covering everything but her head and hands. It was not flattering. I went to her side. She was completely still. I couldn't tell if she was breathing or not. I looked for some kind of control panel that would release her. There was nothing.

I put the phone to my ear and was about to issue a demand, but instead I heard the voice say, "Hold the telephone to the wall next to her."

I did. There was an ear-splitting wail. I felt the phone heat up in my hand and had the sensation that I was on a boat in some choppy seas. I fought down my gorge. Mina popped from the wall into my arms. The wall shifted in front of me, and suddenly the indentation was generic, no longer conforming to Mina's very specific figure.

Mina's eyes fluttered, opened. I wasn't in the best of shape, and I was having a hell of a time trying to keep her upright, but I'd be damned if I would drop her. It would have ruined the whole moment.

"I didn't think you would come for me."

I said, "Are you okay?"

She nodded. "They scanned me. I think they wanted to keep me... intact."

"You kicked someone, didn't you?"

She nodded again, this time adding a smile. There was a pause. I was trying to think of something to say, and Mina seemed like she was waiting for me to say it. I went through about half a dozen things before settling on, "Oh, Mina, this is Oana. You two know each other. Right. Sorry."

I set Mina on her feet. She was a little wobbly. Mina and Oana shared a look, one I hoped was just recognition rather than, "Hey, you knock him out and I'll take his keys." I was, in that moment, committing a serious crime against a group whose technology was light years past mine, in the presence of members of a single conspiracy. And to top it off, I was on the phone with a monster.

Monster. Oh, shit. That's who this was.

There were times when I loved being me. Then again, there were times when I should probably just save everyone the time and feed myself to some hungry dingoes.

I said into the phone, "Still there?"

"Exit the room now, and return to the stairwell."

"Follow me," I said to the ladies.

"Who is he talking to?" Mina asked Oana.

I supplied the shrug in my head. If Oana really wanted to find out, she could put that armbar on me. She was probably thinking about it. I opened the door and went back to the stairs.

The voice on the phone said, "Down the stairs. Do not hesitate."

I didn't. We were in the central hall. Outside, I heard the

sounds of gunfire: light pistol pops punctuated with machine gun crackling. I burst out of the front door. Past the gate, I saw a convoy of cars, all expensive and foreign. Amongst them: lights like flashbulbs. On my side of the gate, there were three of the bulbous-headed midgets. There were flashes around them, too, the bullets exploding in midair before hitting anything visible. Five men who could have been Victor Charlie's brothers stood in the open, near the midgets, firing pistols back. Every now and then a bullet would hit one of them, and he would fall, apparently dead. I couldn't tell if it was a gunshot from the attackers or a ricochet from one of the Little Green Men. I really didn't want to know.

"Is that...?" Mina said.

"Yep."

"Can we...?"

"Nope."

I pulled her toward the fake town. Oana jogged along with us, her eyes welded to the firefight at the gate. One of the little ones put a hand up like he was about to answer Mrs. Smith's question about state capitals. There was a flash, and the first car melted into mirrored slag.

We took cover behind one of the houses in a tiny shadow, about big enough for half of me. The streets formed what was sort of a residential neighborhood, houses that were half Dick van Dyke and half shack. Between the houses was a single-lane dirt road, and past them I could see a gas station. Past that, the fence, and from there, darkness. The herd of cows had gathered behind one of the houses, as far from the gunfire as they could get, lowing with panic.

The voice on the phone: "Beware, there are guardians in the buildings. When you see them, show no fear. Think only of blood." There was a click. He—it?—had hung up. At least he hadn't told me about any collapsing bridges. I pocketed the phone.

Mina asked, “Who was that?”

“A mutual friend.”

She didn’t get it, but she didn’t have to. She really looked ridiculous in that silver thing. Someone would have to have the body of a sexy fetus to look good in it, and I wasn’t sure that was even possible. Not that people would stop searching for that brand of creepy perfection.

I didn’t see it coming. I was walking, then suddenly I was on the ground. There might have been a flash of light. There might have been an impact. I was dazed as the pain hatched across my left eye.

Tariq was standing over me. “Bam! Tyson to the face!”

Oana attacked him. She was faster; he was stronger. Mina hauled me to my feet. “What the hell is *he* doing here?”

“I invited him.”

“Okay, if we get out of this, I’m going to tell you all the reasons that’s stupid. Come on.” She let me hang onto her while my legs remembered how to work. We were next to one of the houses, so she hauled me to the door. Unlocked. After all, who was going to be breaking in?

It was dark inside, and smelled like Vegemite. I wondered if Tariq had hit me so hard I was having the most Australian stroke on record.

It was a kitchen, a sort of dusty trailer-park kitchen. The room was dark, the shades were drawn, but the white light from the floods burned in through the gaps. I could hear Tariq and Oana fighting outside. I was hoping Oana would win, but it wasn’t a big hope.

A hiss bloomed from deeper inside. Mina swooned, suddenly sleepy. I caught her. “Sorry,” she said. “Do you hear that?” She yawned.

I knew what that sound meant. It was the whole reason

I'd invited Tariq along.

"We need to get out of here. Now."

"As opposed to before, when we were thinking of moving in?" she griped.

I had an appropriate response locked and loaded, but I never got a chance to finish it. I saw the silhouette approaching through the darkness, about the size and shape of a chimpanzee. I grabbed Mina's hand and we were out the door.

We nearly tripped over Oana. She was breathing through her mouth. The bridge of her nose was swollen and would have been purple if the shadows let color in. I picked her up easily.

In the distance: the keening alarm, the crack of gunfire, then a sound halfway between a cat's yowling and a goat's braying. It was answered from inside the house behind us. I ran.

I crossed into the open ground between the two streets, Mina just behind me. I saw motion to my right: Tariq, moving to intercept. He looked like he was carrying a kitchen knife, running with a herd of terrified Holsteins.

He shouted, "Choppy choppy hold the *sake*!"

The gunfire stopped. Vassily had just lost. I wondered if he would be probed for his trouble. I wondered if they had a machine big enough.

The cat-goat yowl-bray started up again, now answered from three separate places, all closing in.

"Which..." Mina was out of breath. "Which one... should I... be worried about?"

I didn't have the heart to tell her all of them, especially with our hardest hitter out. Mina turned her head and, somehow, she managed to scream.

There were four of them, heading toward us in a pack. About the size of chimps, they either ran along on their knuckles or glided on the webbing that ran under their armpits like

Romita's Spider-Man. They had the big almond eyes of the Zetas, but theirs were blood red. They looked like the product of a wild evening in which an alien had gone down to Tijuana and had a threesome with a monkey and a vampire bat.

I really hate chupacabras.

Tariq looked shocked, even letting out a "what the fuck?" as the little guys loped past. They smelled blood: blood coming out of a cut above my eye and coming out of Oana's broken nose. The thing from Diaz's living room had given me some advice. It hadn't steered me wrong yet. It wasn't like I had other ideas.

I stopped. I set Oana down and stepped in front of her.

The chupacabras were getting closer. Tariq had slowed. I straightened up. I had heard rumors about these things, but I'd only seen them the one time. It had been hard getting it into the van. I did feel bad for the kids that went to that petting zoo the next day. I'm not a monster.

"What are you doing?" Mina whisper-screamed.

"I don't know," I said. That wasn't exactly true. I had an idea. My friend on the phone was trying to tell me to find the intersection of belief and perception with these things. Prey runs. Prey fights. Prey hides. Prey does not do what I was about to do. After all, there was one thing I was pretty sure could take Tariq, and here was a pack of them.

I picked the closest one and locked eyes with it. It hissed again, and I felt my stomach churning like it had when the alarm went off. I pushed that down. I thought about blood. I thought about head-butting Tariq at Mina's fashion show. I thought about the blood that was trying to drip into my eye. I thought of Oana's blood-mustache. The chupacabras stopped. They formed a semi-circle around me, like kids listening to a story. I suddenly regretted having left my copy of *Goodnight Moon* in the car.

Tariq was walking now. "Now you're Dr. Moreau." He raised the knife.

This was the hardest part. I forced myself not to flinch. Instead, I visualized the knife going into Tariq, pictured the blood.

The closest chupacabra leapt at him. He was barely surprised. He swung, striking the thing on the arm. It made a sound like hitting a drum. The others surged forward at him. I picked Oana up and started walking, briskly, but not running. Mina was looking at me like I had sprouted a third arm.

"What the hell was that?"

"Death by chupacabra."

Oana didn't come around until we got back to the car. I found a hole in the fence big enough for all three of us. Mina was silent, maybe listening to Tariq's distant cursing or the drum sounds he made whenever he hit one of the little monsters with his knife.

Finally, when we were just climbing the hill, she said in a queasy voice, "At least he won't be trying to kill us anymore." She didn't like that she was relieved, and I didn't like it either. I liked it even less that it had been my plan.

I didn't say anything. It was still possible that she was playing me. Also possible that she was fishing for a sign of conscience, or maybe she was trying to lighten the mood.

She nearly tripped over my car before I hit the key to unlock it. I stuck Oana in the backseat, then opened up the trunk. I handed Mina my sportcoat to complete the most unflattering ensemble possible. She looked like Captain Picard's lawyer.

"Thanks," she said.

"It was just lying in the back. No big deal."

"Not what I meant." In the moonlight, skin turned to silver, she was beyond beautiful. There was still fear in her eyes, her breath still quick. She was close to me, almost too close. Her lips parted, and I saw dark movement past teeth that shone like stars.

Of course, I'm emotionally stunted. "Yeah, don't mention it." I got into the car. Mina did, too, but she slammed her door.

Oana stirred in the backseat. Mina turned around as I started the car. Oana was a little disoriented, and the broken nose wasn't doing her any favors. "I can't move my hand." She sounded like she had a cold.

I heard rustling. "It might be broken," Mina said.

"Painkillers in the glovebox," I said.

Mina found them. "Here," she said. I heard Oana swallow them, and I felt bad for not having any children's Tylenol, and then I felt bad for smiling a little at that thought.

"What happened to Tariq?" Oana asked.

"He's out of the picture," I said.

"We're going to get you to a hospital," Mina added.

"I'm fine."

I said, "Bela really did a number on you, didn't he? Look, it's okay not to play hurt, and it's okay to have bacon every now and then. While we're at it, glitter just looks silly on athletes. I don't care how feminine it's supposed to make you." Mina and Oana were staring at me. "Right. We're taking you to a hospital."

They were quiet after that. I caught Oana wincing at every slight bump, cradling her wrist.

On the stereo: "I Need Your Love."

Mina said, "I really didn't think I'd miss Boston."

I turned away a little so she didn't catch the smile.

We drove back into the city. Mina didn't want to leave Oana alone at the hospital, but the little gymnast insisted. She gave me a look that graphically detailed all she would do to me if harm befell Mina, then gingerly shuffled into the ER, minuscule against the iodine shade of the walls. I'll give her this: she was tough for a tiny person. Hell, she was tough for a linebacker.

When Oana was out of sight, Mina turned to me. "I need you to answer a question for me."

"Sure, shoot."

"No. When I ask it, no in-jokes, no cryptic comments. You have to actually answer the question."

"Okay, got it."

"What were those things back there?"

"Chupacabras."

"Wait. I've heard of those."

"Yeah. They're little blood-drinking monsters. Cryptids. Whatever. They're mostly known for attacking livestock, but they'll go after humans in a pinch. They're great security."

"Wait. You told me there are no such things as vampires."

"There aren't. Those were chupacabras."

"Which is Spanish for 'vampire.'"

"No, it's Spanish for 'goatsucker.' Spanish for 'vampire' is... I don't know, probably *vampiro* or something."

"They drink blood. They had wings like a bat and fangs. Those were vampires."

I was getting a little heated. It's just because every single person, once they learn about one of the cryptids that are out there, insists that vampires are next. "Look, those weren't vampires. If you showed one to a fourteen-year-old girl and she started swooning, I'd concede the point. Until then, there are no such things as vampires."

She let that sink in. Then, "I think those were vampires."

I almost lost it. I took a deep breath. I looked at her. My eyes narrowed. "The button again."

Her innocent look was less than convincing. Apropos of nothing, she blurted, "I need shoes."

"I thought those things were like footie pajamas."

"They are, and I think I've already made a couple holes in them."

"Soon as the stores open, then."

"And I need something else to wear."

It wasn't quite dawn yet. The newspaper, that flimsy dinosaur, was practically wet when I bought it. We stopped at the first Denny's we found that was open. The hostess didn't give us a second glance, despite Mina's outfit and the cut over my eye. I cleaned up a little in the bathroom and joined Mina in a booth. She already had coffee for both of us. She probably wouldn't have had any poison on her, and I didn't think the silver bodysuit had any pockets.

"You drink coffee, right?"

"It's practically a job requirement," I said.

The waitress returned, and Mina ordered breakfast, and lots of it. I wasn't sure how long it had been since she'd eaten, but the way she was ordering, it was probably measured in the eons. I ordered a burger and regretted it as soon as the waitress walked away.

Mina started packing her coffee with enough sugar and cream to turn it into an off-white paste. She fixed her eyes on me. "Okay. Tell me. All of it."

I thought about lying to her, but I had an unspoken rule that I made up on the spot: never lie to a person after their first alien abduction. I started with the revelation I'd had when the gang of five interrogated me in the bunker in San Pedro. I told her about Mr. Blank.

"Someone like you?" she said. "So he wants you dead. Over something you saw? Something you know? Something you have the potential to put together?"

"Any one of those things. Possibly all three. I don't know."

"He has plans, then. What, to end the world?"

"The apocalypse is hardly important enough to kill anyone over."

"What?"

"The world ends every couple years or so. It's no big deal, just a minor re-ordering of priorities."

"You say these things, and it's like you're trying to make me make silly faces at you."

"Those faces do cheer me up."

"Then whatever *is* a big deal, then. That's what Mr. Black wants."

"Mr. Black is some other guy on some other job. This is Mr. Blank."

She blinked.

I said, "Sorry. *Reservoir Dogs.*"

"Mr. *Blank,*" she said, accenting the word. "Okay. Can you explain my... I guess the term is abduction?"

I did. I told her about the Genesis Stone, and the role it played in the apocalypse back in '69. I told her about who wanted that. I told her about what happened to Eric Caldwell.

"What about the old guy in the gay bar?"

"I'm thinking that the old guy might be our Mr. Blank. Oh yeah, and I learned from Eric that his Candidates use guns."

"I'm lost," she said.

"If the Stone is missing, I need to know why the Masons never thought to mention it. I'm the kind of guy that could have helped them get it back. They might not have told me exactly what it was, but they never said they were down one rock. It would also be nice to find out how Raul got his hands on the weapon."

Our food arrived and Mina tore into it. I nibbled, using the side of my jaw Mina hadn't kicked yet, and scanned the paper. No mention of anything related to what we were doing. Not that I was surprised. What, there was going to be a headline about me? I'd be in a hell of a state if I was looking for clues in the paper.

On impulse, I took my Assassin phone from my pocket and checked the call records. I didn't recognize the number the thing had called from. I dialed it.

A normal voice answered. "Jack In the Box?"

"Where are you?"

"Glendale Boulevard in Echo Park."

"Were you there a couple hours ago?"

The voice was nervous, but in fairness, I was asking stalker questions. "Uh... yeah?"

"This is going to sound strange, but a couple hours ago, was there a seven-foot weirdo with big red eyes using this line? Hello? Hello?"

Mina had a triangle of pancake on her fork as she watched me. "You know, not everyone lives in this world you made."

"I'm beginning to realize that." I shut the phone and put it away.

"How *did* you make it, anyway?"

I picked up a French fry and drew a Voorish Sign in my ketchup. "Are you asking my secret origin?" She gave me a "keep going" gesture with her fork. "If you're looking for my radioactive spider or rocket from my home planet, there's not really a flashpoint event. I have a hunch that this life is sort of like prostitution. One day, you're an aspiring actress, you go a little too far, and suddenly you look up and you're blowing a hobo for his methadone."

"Seeing that rock coming at your head, that was your methadone-addled hobo."

That wasn't a question I had to answer for either of us. "Student loans," I said instead.

"Student loans."

"You know that year after college when you have no idea what you're going to do with yourself? You've been in school for so long that's all you know. After I graduated, I kept having this nightmare where I started school all over again. So in my dream, I'm this twenty-two-year-old guy in the first grade. It was like *Billy Madison*. You know, the Adam Sandler movie."

"I don't like Adam Sandler movies."

"Yeah, but did you see that one? Doesn't matter. My point is that when I graduated, I realized I was lacking a few things. Goals, for one. An idea of what to do. And, most importantly, any sort of marketable skill. Not one." I watched the syrup get tacky on her fork. "What I did have, were student loans. I had to pay those, so I started looking for jobs. Craigslist, Monster, pretty much every place that listed any kind of job. I looked for the ones that had no experience required. I had some office jobs, but it turned out that I'm no good in an office. I was legitimately worried that I'd snap and kill everyone. So, one time I answered a job for security work. It was for a club that was a front where the CIA met with the local Kosher Nostra. I went in with a feeling about this place, so I used my old fake ID from high school. I was on the right side of a coup, but I didn't do anything other than carry some messages. I did more odd jobs, and I started being able to recognize the codes in the job ads and websites. I just showed up where I was needed and did what had to be done. And now I'm as you see me."

"What's your real name?"

"Does it matter?"

She thought about it. "Yeah, it kinda does."

"Sorry."

"What, you're going to tell me you forgot it?"

"More like the other way around."

We ate the rest of the meal in silence. I paid the check and we walked back into the parking lot. The sky was turning red. I used my Mason phone to call Neil Greene.

His voice was thick. "Hello?"

"Neil, it's Colin. We need to meet."

"What, now? It's like..."

"Five-thirty in the morning."

"Where?"

"The Temple. And call Stan. I want him there, too."

Neil was wide awake now. "I said he was impressed, but you don't have that kind of authority."

"Tell him I want to know why he's not looking for the Genesis Stone." I hung up on Neil and drove us to the Masonic Temple.

On the stereo: "Didn't Mean to Fall in Love."

Sunrise in Burbank is not romantic. Even, hypothetically, had Mina and I been making out, as opposed to standing silently about five feet apart, even if the Russian mob hadn't marked her for death and a would-be mastermind wasn't hunting me, it wouldn't have been romantic. Really, best-case scenario, the sun peeks over the Verdugo hills and turns the industrial wasteland pink, and for a minute, you can pretend you're in a John Waters movie. Doesn't exactly scream romance.

The look on Stan's face when he saw Mina was pretty priceless. It was around six, and Stan hadn't shaved, so he had a silvery layer of fuzz on his craggy cheeks. He was blinking sleep out of his eyes and moving a half-step slow.

Mina was still in the bizarre costume the Little Green Men and I had assembled, and it affected the way she stood, sort of one leg forward, hands clasped below her waist, alert against the constant threat of cameltoe. Mina was still impressive, though now constantly tempting the mental use of unfeminine adjectives like “sturdy,” yet also inspiring immediate regret if any actually passed the frontal lobes.

Neil drove up right as Stan made it to us.

“Neil didn’t tell me you would be bringing a friend, Brother Reznick.” He managed to make “friend” sound both leering and distasteful, like a Thai hooker who reveals his penis after the money’s been spent.

I resisted the obvious reply, since that put Stan in the driver’s seat. “Did Neil tell you everything?”

“He told me you were... we need to speak in private.”

“You can talk in front of her,” I said.

“No.” He was using a special-ed-teacher voice on me. “No, I can’t. This is business, between members.”

Mina said, “No pun intended.”

Stan glared. “You should...”

I snapped, “Oh, shut the fuck up. Do you know who she is?”

Stan looked at Mina. He had been at the show the previous night, but had he seen pictures of her before that? He was struggling to recognize her, but this was Mina, sans makeup, sans push-up, sans dress. This was some brassy redhead that was giving him crap on his front doorstep. He finally said, “No.”

“Exactly, big guy. It’s called ‘caution.’ Look it up.”

Neil approached, seeing Stan turning red, watching the metaphorical smoke rising from his head. “Hey... everyone.”

I dove in. “Now, why did neither one of you tell me the Genesis Stone was missing? You didn’t even have feelers out for it, by name or otherwise.”

Stan broke into a huge smile, one of those smug asshole smiles that were etched in cocaine back in the ’80s. “That’s because it’s not missing.”

“Bullshit.”

“It’s perfectly safe. I don’t know where you’re getting

your information, but it's in our vault, under guard, completely safe. I saw it yesterday."

I mumbled, "So did I." Then, louder, "I want to see it."

"Absolutely not. You don't have the rank. You wouldn't understand the mysteries."

Neil said, "Stan, maybe we should let him. You said yourself that Brother Reznick's initiative meant he was going to advance. Maybe this will help him? Besides, show him it's where it should be and he'll calm down, and we can find out why he thinks it's gone."

Stan thought it over for about a millisecond, then threw a curt nod at Neil. He led the way into the Temple. The guard in the foyer patted me down and did the same to Mina. She didn't kick him, but that might have had more to do with the 9mm in the man's shoulder holster than an improvement in her mood. Stan gestured, and the guard produced a black blindfold that he handed to Mina.

"What's this?" she said, looking at it with bewildered distaste.

"Put it on," Stan said. "If we're letting you in, we're doing so blind. There are things in there that a non-initiate couldn't possibly understand, let alone a woman."

"Yeah, ESPN and circle jerks are pretty big enigmas." She put the blindfold on. I went to her and put her hand on my shoulder. She held on. I tried not to read anything into that.

We went past the meeting hall, behind where the pulpit should have been. At that moment, we were officially deeper into the Temple than I had ever been. There were a few halls, some doors, and stairs descending into darkness. Stan led us there, and for a moment, the paranoia kicked back in. Being led into basements is never fun, and that doesn't change no matter how many times my job has required it.

The basement was clean and modern, and here and there

were uniformed guards, suddenly sitting bolt upright as we walked past. They gave Mina a strange look. Considering how she was dressed, she might as well have been an alien. She was probably the first woman who'd ever been down there, and I started thinking of the guards as subterranean mole-men. I could practically hear them thinking: *What's that strange creature with the extra heads coming out of her chest? Does she wish us harm?*

Neil gave me a weird look when I giggled a little. I shook my head at him; it would take me too long to explain and probably wouldn't be funny when I was done.

Halls, guards, guns: this place was secure. No matter where I looked, there wasn't a giant hole leading from the sewers. There was no false ceiling for cat burglars to creep around in. The guards looked like they belonged, and both Stan and Neil seemed to recognize them. Maybe they were right. Maybe the rock that had come at me was just a rock. Maybe the Little Green Men had turned Mina and tricked me to get her into the Mason vault. Maybe Mina had hidden lasers in her eyes.

Maybe I needed to get some sleep.

There was a vault, which Stan opened. The plan was gaining steam. The vault was huge, with a door thicker than Vassily. No way we could have broken it, and yet Stan opened it for us. Inside, the vault was bare, except for a single thing: a rock. It was exactly the size and shape of the one in my trunk, only this one was sitting on a pedestal like a Mesoamerican relic in an adventure movie.

"See?" Stan said.

Mina took off her blindfold. I felt her eyes on me. I knew what she was thinking.

I couldn't hesitate. I took three steps forward. Stan and Neil both shouted at me to stop. I heard guns cocking. I picked the rock off the pedestal. It was heavier than the real one in my trunk. The room turned fire-engine red and an alarm went off. I lifted the rock as high as I could and threw it at the ground.

It didn't shatter. Well, there went my theory.

Everyone was staring right at me, mouths open, completely disbelieving. "Uh... that was supposed to shatter. Because it's a fake."

Stan was livid. "Well, you can see it's not."

Neil looked like he was trying to talk to a crazy person. "Now, who told you it was missing?"

I looked down at the rock. Betrayed me. First its double tries to kill me—twice, even—and now this. It was the most one man had suffered at the hands of a rock since Abel. I picked the rock off the ground and pushed it back onto the pedestal. The alarm fell silent.

"Come on, Colin. Tell us," Neil said.

I looked at my hands. Gray rock dust covered my fingers. Just like the real one. I rubbed them together.

No, not rock dust.

Paint.

Fucking gray paint.

I pushed it off the pedestal.

The alarm sounded again. Stan was swearing now. Neil shouted, "Colin, what the hell are you doing?"

I shouted back over the siren, showing my hand as evidence. "It's a fake!"

I walked to the other side of the pedestal. Neil, Stan, and Mina clustered around me. They saw it, too. The paint had scratched away, leaving the luster of solid gold.

I knelt by the rock and started scratching. Paint came away in sooty dandruff flakes. I uncovered all I wanted to see, then stepped away to let the others see it.

There. In the middle, carved into a depression of the rock, was the next best thing to a signature. Inch-high letters that read: KALLISTI.

I shot a triumphant look at Neil and Stan, both of whom were gaping.

Mina just looked blank. "What the hell does that mean?"

AND NOW, A LESSON IN MYTHOLOGY. *KALLISTI* is Greek for "to the prettiest one." Pretty harmless, but it was a phrase that started a whole religion.

Eris is a central figure in conspiracy lore, which is pretty good for a Greek deity that was fairly obscure in her heyday. She was the goddess of discord, confusion, and mood swings. The story goes that all the gods and goddesses were invited to the wedding of Peleus and Thetis, except for Eris—this lack of an invite known in some circles as the Original Snub. An outside observer might see the wisdom in not inviting the goddess of discord to a wedding, but Eris didn't feel that way. She found herself a golden apple, carved the word "Kallisti" into the side, and rolled it into that wedding like a grenade.

Being goddesses, Hera, Athena, and Aphrodite all decided that the apple must be for them. The wedding descended into a catfight that only got broken up when someone had the bright idea to have a young Trojan named Paris judge between the goddesses. Each one tried to tempt him into awarding her the prize. Hera and Athena had apparently never met a man before this, because they tempted him with power and military victory. Aphrodite was smarter; she promised the love of the most beautiful woman in the world. Paris chose Aphrodite without thinking twice.

The problem was that this wasn't a hypothetical woman that Aphrodite promised. She was talking about Helen (yes, *that* Helen), who was, at the time, married to a powerful Achaean king (AKA, Greek). Helen left old Menelaus for Paris, and that was how Troy got wiped off of every map.

The lesson is this: when a group of women asks who the prettiest one is, run. Don't look back. Just run.

I explained this to Mina in response to her question: "Who replaces a worthless moon rock with solid gold?" After I told this story, she asked the question again.

"Eris still has a cult. There was sort of a revival in the '60s started up by a buddy of Oswald's. As in Lee Harvey. They sort of softened her a little and combined her with the psychedelic culture that was going on then. Basically an excuse to do weird stuff to point out absurdities. A Discordian is the kind of person that would chant 'Death to fanatics.'"

Mina was still unconvinced. "They sound fun."

"They can be a little tiring."

"Yeah, if they're always on."

"They're always on something."

On the stereo: "What's Your Name."

Discordians, of course, meant a drive back out to Azusa, where the Brotherhood of Sisterhood hid at the mechanic shop. I'd just been there on Thursday, picking up a box and planting it in Silver Lake, so we should be in good standing. Hell, they might not even know about the whole "quintuple agent" thing, like half the rest of the information underground seemed to.

When Mina and I arrived, GOOD FISH had her flock of

seagulls stuck under the hood of a Volvo. Her friend was in the front seat, door open, foot on the ground, ready to turn the key. They wore coveralls that didn't cover much, and the grease on their faces seemed carefully applied, like warpaint. As I got out of the car with Mina, the other one saw me. She perked up when she saw Mina, and whispered something to GOOD FISH, who turned. The sunny expression wasn't just gone; it had disappeared and didn't leave a forwarding address.

GOOD FISH stayed put, but the other one came to meet me. Her eyes still had the same homicidal look as before, but they softened whenever she glanced at Mina. That put me in a good place hormonally and a bad place socially. Funny how those things were roommates.

"Nobody called you, Zeke."

"Yeah, I know. I need to see Gehenna."

GOOD FISH said, "She's not seeing anyone." Her charm bracelet jingled.

"He's not seeing *you*," the other one said.

"She/he can make an exception, I think."

Mina leaned over, and in a helpful whisper, told me, "It's polite to use the pronoun of the gender they are inside."

I had never seen the other one smile, let alone laugh, until right then. Hooking a thumb at Mina, I said, "She's new."

"I can tell. Where'd you find her?"

"Star Trek convention. We got in an argument over what sucked worse: *Voyager* or *Enterprise*. That led to a round of latinum dances and Dabo, and before you knew it, she was assimilated. Are you letting me in or not?"

"Gehenna's busy, and besides, you fuck off until she calls."

GOOD FISH had abandoned the Volvo, and had her arms folded, holding a wrench like her elbow's erection.

"You make a good point. I have no reason to be here. Hang on." I went back to my trunk. Mina was getting worried. I removed the rock and chain, and hefted the flail over my shoulder as I walked back. To say they were shocked was an understatement; they had been impaled by invisible lightning bolts while wearing suits made entirely of pennies and standing in full kiddie pools. "I wanted to discuss this with Gehenna." I gave them a minute to gape. "Yeah, I thought so."

I didn't brandish it, just let the rock dangle as I walked past: my swinging moon-testicle. Mina jogged to keep up. "What does 'she's new' mean?"

"Well, you are." She kept glaring at me. "Oh. You're thinking of a transsexual—some poor bastard that got born in the wrong body, which is exactly right. The problem with Gehenna is that he/she shouldn't have been born one gender, but both."

"Sounds exhausting."

"Did you just quote *Big Lebowski*?"

She gave me a Cheshire cat grin. "Those were, what, bodyguards?"

"Sort of, yeah."

"The one by the car, the one that barely talked? She seemed sad."

"She probably found out that Flock of Seagulls broke up like twenty years ago."

Mina looked back over her shoulder. "You two could commiserate about all the effort that goes into truly tragic hair."

We walked past where the pumps would have been had this still been a gas station, heading toward what was probably an office once upon a time. It looked like a shack with the white paint peeling from it. The window was bordered with red lights and wallpapered with pictures torn from magazines: ads, jeans, perfume, vacations, promises of better lives for a low low price, now repurposed into a sweaty self-esteem-crushing nightmare. It looked like the collage that would sit above the bed of a sixteen-year-old girl about twenty pounds over her fighting weight who walked with a slouch and was sensitive about the bits of acne at her temples. It was a collection of unattainable, airbrushed beauty, all shapes and sizes, both genders, and blended in ways that not only suggested androgyny, but shouted it while grabbing your lapels and shaking you like a hysterical scout leader. I stopped.

I said, “Want to tell me why you’re on this window?”

She was. I didn’t recognize the picture, but it was definitely Mina. They had Photoshopped her, turning already smooth skin into something like ivory, and her expression was probably aiming for sexy but settled for sleepy. Her hair, normally a soft copper, looked here more like Ronald McDonald’s, and they had thinned her neck a bit. It was Mina, but a plastic version of her, the robot that someone had projected onto; perfect, but in that perfection, fatally flawed.

“Oh god,” she said. She sounded genuinely horrified. Possibly she didn’t know why she was on the window. Possibly she didn’t like having her head pasted onto a muscular man’s body while he was straddling a volleyball. I would have believed either.

“This isn’t a bad intro to Gehenna, come to think of it.”

I went into what would have been the office. It started where the desk should have been: red cloth artfully rumpled into a velvet waterfall. Not that the cloth was visible nearly anywhere but at the borders; there were frames and shelves, boxes and books, all of which held ritual objects from every religion I could think of. There were sacrificial daggers and kachina dolls, an alligator head and a six-inch-tall human skeleton, a clay Venus and a plastic Jesus, wads of computer wires and vomit-stained finger bones, a pistol with runes carved into the handle and idols of every pagan god demonized in the Bible. It was an altar that could have provoked the most casual Easter Catholic into a killing rage. Over it all, the sun shone through the wall of people, casting their reflected gaze on it like that of perpetually horny angels.

Mina didn't say anything. I walked past the altar and to the door beyond. It was the kind of door that really should lead to a dingy basement. The kind of place with a single bare bulb and a nice big hole that you could fill with unfortunate coeds.

It wasn't.

The space beyond was padded. It looked sort of like a Nerf version of the back of an '80s dance club. The pads were vinyl, black with red and white arabesques that somehow looked Greek, and neon tubes running along the hall. The stairs were carpeted, but frayed by Eris-knew-how-many lustful feet. The music that throbbed down the hall didn't sound like a heartbeat, but something more like a drummer on a slave ship who was jacked up on Red Bull and methamphetamines.

I knew what I was going to see when I opened the door at the end of the hall, the one painted like a woman's mouth. I couldn't decide if she looked angry, horny, or hungry—or all three. I looked over at Mina to ask her opinion, but she was blinking at it, and I could tell she had the exact same question.

I said to her, "Yeah, I don't know either."

"Have you ever been down here?"

"No."

She opened her mouth. "I was going to ask a question, then I realized it was answered for me already."

"Yeah."

I opened the door. Mina gasped. I think I might have if I hadn't already steeled myself and started picturing things that would have made the Marquis de Sade vote Republican. The carpet was flesh, and not good flesh, either. Not all of it was loose and hairy, but so much of it was stretched over silicone, tanned into leather, and tattooed with patterns that the only thing that could have screamed "do not touch" more effectively was the yellow on a poison arrow frog. The squirming and pumping actually was sex, right there in front of me, but it didn't suggest sex. It suggested a replicant trying to swallow a bearskin rug.

At the center of it all: Gehenna Tattoo. I think that once Mina set eyes on Gehenna, all the confusion upstairs resolved itself. The porn channel suddenly became unscrambled, and she saw something that was going to be painted on the inside of her eyelids for a long time. Gehenna wasn't involved in the actual fucking. There was part of me that was convinced that Gehenna was a virgin, the same part that was convinced that McDonald's burgers were made of worms and pigeons were created by the dirt lodged in traffic lights. Gehenna was naked, showing off the surgeon's work between two overly veined legs. Gehenna had a pair of breasts that would only be seen in a very specific brand of Japanese porn. Nearly everything was pierced. If Gehenna could put metal through it, under it, or in it, that metal had been inserted: airport security nightmare. Gehenna topped it all off with a very complicated beard that made me think of Spartans.

There's very little as awkward as being one of only three people in the room not having sex. Gehenna pulled it off. I was having trouble.

Gehenna's voice was in between male and female, modulated to make actually determining gender impossible, deep but smooth. Gehenna had to shout over the music and slapping. "You finally decided to join us. And you've brought a guest!"

I let the chain play out so the rock dropped in front of me in a sort of lunar puberty.

Gehenna's face tried to fall, but the surgery kept it in a Botox-lifted mask.

Mina nudged me, but I ignored it. I had to stay focused on Gehenna. "Want to tell me why you made this?"

Gehenna smiled. "Why not? Get the Genesis Stone *and* the Chain of the Heretic Martyr? You try to avoid mating them."

The smell of fluids, both natural and factory-made, was getting overpowering. I wondered if anyone had ever succumbed to fumes like that.

Mina nudged me again. I kept ignoring her.

"You didn't just *get* them. You stole them."

Gehenna held up a finger. The nails were surprisingly reasonable, even if the fingers were tattooed to look like screws. "Our people stole the Stone, but the Chain was a gift."

"I didn't think we were so cozy with the Templars."

"*We're* not. The Chain was a gift from the First Reformed Church of the Antichrist, something about Eris as a consort of the Devil. Superstitious nonsense, but I'm not going to look a gift horse in the mouth."

Mina was muttering under her breath, then, out loud, as she remembered, "Zeke!"

I turned to her. She was pointing at the mass of bodies. "Doesn't that look familiar?"

"Have I not been totally clear about my orientation?"

"No! The man doing it?"

"Looks a lot like Che Guevara. That *is* weird."

"You're an idiot. The other one!"

My assassin was engaged and completely oblivious. I took a step into a clear patch of ground as the flesh carpet shifted like the floor of Indiana Jones's nightmare. I reached down to grab him, but thought better of it.

"Who the fuck is that?"

Gehenna shrugged. "How should I know?"

"Because someone that looked exactly like that man swung *this* at me."

I nudged the man with my foot, and immediately wanted to boil it. He freed up his mouth and gave me a confused look, then reached for me.

"No, no," I said. "Who are you?"

"The walrus." He went back to what he was doing. An insult sprang to mind, but it struck me as too obvious a pun to actually sling.

Gehenna said, "So I might as well ask. How did you get that? Did you open the box?"

For a moment, I just frowned at Gehenna. My brain was fumbling after the statement, trying to grab hold and wring some meaning out of it. But there it was. "The box?"

"The one you were supposed to plant the other day."

Then it clicked. The box GOOD FISH had given me on Thursday. The one that I planted by the Silver Lake reservoir. Somehow, Mr. Blank had gotten to Gehenna—or *was* Gehenna—and had arranged for me to plant my own murder weapon as a final irony that would make him smile late at night.

Gehenna continued, barreling right through my realization. "I thought it would be fun to make a weapon like that and put it in the hands of a nobody. Suddenly, someone with no connection to anything at all is in possession of an artifact that half the information underground would kill for. Of course, that person would then have the power to fight back. Could lead to some fun! I'm a little disappointed in you, though."

"I *did* plant it," I said, a touch insulted about the jab at my professionalism. "How did you choose who to tip off about the drop site?"

"Only one way to do that. I picked a name out of the phone book."

And this was critical: "Which phone book?"

"I don't know. I asked Stacy to fetch one and she did."

"Which one is Stacy?"

"She has GOOD tattooed on one hand, and..."

Before Gehenna finished the sentence, I was running back for the surface, hoping that GOOD FISH would still be there, but I knew she was long gone. When I burst out into the morning, the other one spun around to glare at me.

"Where is she? Where's Stacy?"

"She left. Got in her car and drove the hell away."

I let out a stream of profanity. Some of it was fairly creative; I might have even coined some phrases in there. Finally, I spluttered and spat, "Phone book."

"That wasn't even a swear," she said.

"No. Phone book. Stacy had a phone book. Where is it?"

She pointed to the garage. I saw yellow pages, striped with grease. I ran to it, picked it up. Mina had joined me and was giving me her concerned look, the one that made me feel like an old man with dementia. I picked up the book and let it fall open. I picked a name at random.

Raul Diaz.

I tried it again. Same result. Son of a bitch.

I closed the book and handed it to Mina. "Pick a name at random."

"Okay," she said. She opened the book and pointed. "That's weird." She held up the book and showed me. Her fingernail rested on Raul Diaz.

"Try again."

She did. "That's *really* weird."

"Stacy had a gimmicked phone book. Open it, point, and nine times out of ten, you're getting Diaz. Crease the spine just right, shade the name a little darker, you always get the same guy. A random test that just so happens to point to a Templar-controlled Manchurian Candidate."

"Mr. Blank."

The other one had the good graces not to act annoyed when I took her phone book. At that point, we were probably beyond quibbling over things like that.

"I'M GOING TO COME UP WITH A NICKNAME for you," Mina said. She was sitting low in her seat, half asleep. We were parked a block away from the Brotherhood of Sisterhood, waiting for the orgy to get out. I had no illusions that my presence would have caused much interruption. I had heard that these people had fucked through the Northridge quake.

"Uh-oh."

"No, nothing bad. Just so I have something to call you."

"You have something to call me. You can pretty much call me any guy's name there is, and chances are I've got an ID that matches."

"Yeah, but none of those names are yours."

"Okay, what have you got?"

She shifted, somehow getting even lower in the seat, shading her eyes with one hand. I tried to sit up a little straighter, suck in the gut, cut a nobler profile. It didn't happen.

"Hmm..." she murmured. I knew what she was thinking: not tall enough for a height nickname, too fat to be Slim and too thin to be Chubby. "What about Tweener?"

"Please no," I said. "I'm not eleven. I've never seen the Jonas Brothers in concert. I've never read a single *Twilight* book."

"Yeah, it does make you sound kind of bad."

"How about Microwave? You know, because I heat up quickly?"

"That makes you sound like a slutty girl." She shook her head. "Besides, what am I supposed to call you, Mike?"

"I have a couple IDs with that name."

"See? Square one." She thought about it. "Okay, a doctor's called Bones..."

I burst out laughing.

"What?" she said.

"Just wondering what they'd call you, then."

"Very funny. Seriously, though, it's your job, right? What do they call people like you?"

"I call people like me suckers. Agents. PAs. Brothers. Initiates. Acolytes."

"Why do you call people like you suckers?"

I explained the octopus. She laughed. "I'm not calling you Tentacle."

"That would be awkward."

"Rabbit," she said, nodding.

"Rabbit? Not even a cool animal? Like a wolf? Or a snake with like a gun?" I tried a gunlike gesture.

"You know the old stories about Br'er Rabbit, right? That's you. Whether or not you like it, that's what we're going with."

"I can live with that," I said to her.

The people started coming out of the mechanic's in ones and twos, looking relaxed. Made sense. They were like deflated water balloons. My assassin's double was in the middle of the pack, heading to his car.

"You know, there's a surefire way for him not to know you're following," Mina said.

"Yeah, I know, get there first. Problem is, I don't know where he's going."

"It's that house, remember? Where, you know..." I did know.

I said, "That's assuming this guy is a double. He might be a triple."

"Or a grand slam." I looked at Mina. She looked guilty. "I'm getting punchy."

I started my car and stifled a laugh. I was getting pretty bad, too. I hadn't slept for a couple days, unless one counted getting a Russian upside the head the other night. I couldn't imagine Mina's UFO abduction had been all that restful, either. When this was over, we'd get our sleep, assuming Mina didn't remember her mission and try to kill me. She probably thought I'd forgotten about that.

I followed the grand slam though the streets. I kept expecting him to head to a freeway, but he didn't. He crept down to Colorado and followed that. He wasn't heading for Hollywood.

On the stereo: "We're Ready."

As he rolled into Pasadena, I realized exactly where he was going. I didn't bother with the tail; I just turned down some streets and found the closest edge of Caltech. It's easy to lose Caltech if you've never been. It's hidden just south of Pasadena's main drag and on the outskirts of a pretty sleepy suburban neighborhood. I always expected it to be heralded by chemical lasers lancing from the sky and buildings exploding with popcorn. When I finally saw the horrible late '60s architecture, it was a bit of a letdown. The best part is underneath.

The famous steam tunnels can be reached through nearly

any of the buildings. The trick is to get in, which is easy if you have a keycard and know where to look, which I did. I found the basement with the ladder down. That led to a small room lit with a bare bulb that helpfully illuminated where some *Hitchhiker's Guide* fan had spray-painted "Beware of the Leopard." From there, the corridor led off into the tunnels themselves. Pipes ran along one wall, alternately hissing and clicking.

"Where the hell is this?"

I pointed to some relevant graffiti.

Mina said, "Oh. Hell, apparently."

The graffiti didn't stop there. There's a great old tradition at Caltech of writing on any available surface. Many walls are covered with little messages, and down in the steam tunnels, where things aren't painted over nearly as often, it was possible to see the age of the college, assuming there weren't people in the '90s desperately in favor of impeaching Nixon. Not that they meticulously covered one wall and then moved on. It was like looking at a substrate that had been stuck in a bag of Shake 'n Bake. As other vandals moved in and wrote around the previous generation's graffiti, it formed a tangled web, connecting the generations with ligaments of swear words and Monty Python bits.

After a few minutes of reading the walls, Mina asked, "Who are we going to see?"

"Remember when I told you about cloning technology?"

"Right. You said it had spread all over the place."

"It has, but it started with a single source."

"Let me guess: Nazis."

"Sort of. The correct answer is actually Thulians."

"That sounds like a *Star Trek* alien."

"You're thinking of Tholians."

"No, I'm really not."

I took a deep breath. "Thule is a lost-continent legend, sort of like Atlantis or Mu, but it has a distinctly Teutonic spin. Anyway, the legend of Thule was an inspiration to Heinrich Himmler, who was the architect of the SS and a committed occultist. According to the legends, each generation only has seventy-two 'true men' who are the descendants of the sons of Thule, the Nordic-looking guys who escaped the cataclysm that sank the island. Anyway, the idea was that these seventy-two could be increased a thousandfold if they could be faithfully reproduced on a genetic level, which led to the first cloning experiments. Himmler's people never got it right during the war, but the technology left Germany with the Odessa ratlines, and was perfected in South America."

"Right, Nazis."

"Yeah, okay, Nazis."

"So who are these guys?"

"As it turns out, Nazis are a fractious bunch. Without a charismatic leader, their natural bloodlust takes over and they start getting misty over *der Nacht der langen Messer*. There were also some in the younger generation who believed in genetic purity but thought that actually rounding people up and exterminating them was cruel."

Her deadpan had improved, "Gee, how progressive."

"These are Nazis, remember. Baby steps. Anyway, the group started splintering. Meanwhile, the CIA had started getting very interested in South American affairs. They shot pretty much every president down there and installed what they called friendly dictators. Basically any sadist with anti-Commie bona fides got his own banana republic. The point is, they were down there and they already had access to incomplete technology from their dealings with the Little Green Men."

"How do you keep all this straight in your head?"

"I saw a flowchart once. One of these Nazi splinter groups got infiltrated by the CIA and they sort of... merged. They became the Clone Wolves. We're going to see their LA office."

"So they're not Nazis?"

"They don't give a crap if you're Jewish, if that's what you're wondering."

"I'm not Jewish."

"I know, I was just saying. The Clone Wolves are about unity. Ever see *Invasion of the Body Snatchers*? Imagine that, minus the seedpods and psychotic behavior. If the body snatchers were rapists, the Clone Wolves are more like that guy who drives a van with wall-to-wall carpeting and way too many Dire Straits CDs. Basically, they want everyone to get along, and the best way to do that is eventually make everyone identical at a genetic level."

"That's really creepy."

I paused. "So, what, you're Catholic?"

She was quiet while her brain found the track mine had taken and boarded the appropriate train of thought. "Uh... sort of. I was, I mean. Before V.E.N.U.S."

"The first time you meet an angel, that kind of thing goes right out the window. Talk about assholes. Oh, here we are."

I didn't have to look to know she had that annoyed-Mina look on her face, those big blues narrowed at me, forehead scrunched up like a pug. I loved making her make that face.

"Here" was a doorway. It looked like any of the others we'd passed: a service door. There wasn't even a spray-painted symbol to denote that this was the headquarters of one of the more bizarre conspiracies in LA. The door had a lock, and I had the key.

The door opened up into an amphitheater-styled room. Instead of rows of seats, tiers of portable labs ringed the central pit. A metal staircase led down, strewn with landings that led to each tier. Light came from two sources: one, desk lamps that were clipped to every available surface. The other source was in the center of the room, a structure that looked like a bunch of grapes, only each grape was man-sized and glowing brightly. Within the grapes, there were silhouettes. Human.

Distinct groups roamed the room, both the tiers and the bottom floor: white-coated men and women, all of whom were stunted and moleish. Each group had exactly five members, and looking closer, each group was made up of exact duplicates that moved, even unconsciously, in unison.

They ignored us until we were halfway down the stairs.

Mina whispered, “Why did you leave the rock in the car?”

I turned. A pack of them lurked on the stairs above us now. They were Brian, my Clone Wolf contact, the socially awkward wall. I turned back. Two groups were at the bottom. All had the same unblinking stare. One group licked its lips. The other flexed its right hand.

“I thought we were clear, Mr. Hoyt. When we want you, we will let you know,” said the group on the bottom. Their name was Bess, a woman that looked like a clean-shaven Wolverine.

“Sorry about that. I had some potentially damning information that I wanted to share with you.”

The other group spoke up. Their name was Steve. They were larger, looking closer to a modern basketball player. “You could have called.”

“But then I couldn’t see your lovely faces.”

Bess said in stereo, “Why do you bring us this one?”

“She’s interested in what you had to say.”

“You don’t have the authority to...”

The group behind me spoke up. “No. Mr. Hoyt is spreading the word. It was a good thing.”

I turned around. That group, Brian, had its attention on

Bess, but they looked to be focusing on the top of her head instead of her eyes. Brian, who I had seen a few days ago on my delivery, always looked awkward, but this was awkward even for him.

Steve, all of Steves, said, “What’s the information?”

“You have a clone family that’s been compromised.”

Bess and Steve exchanged looks. Between the ten of them, that took a little bit of time. “Come down here.”

I nodded to Mina. Brian was above us, all five of him swaying a bit, not knowing what to do. She followed me down, and Bess and Steve parted in perfect choreography. I felt like I was in the middle of a dance number, only I had forgotten all the stage direction and each of my legs weighed sixty pounds.

“You sold one of your people to the Brotherhood of Sisterhood, didn’t you? I’m fairly certain that individual has been compromised. Not to mention the rest of that family.”

Bess and Steve had pretty good poker faces. “What are you getting at, Mr. Hoyt?”

We were amongst the human-grapes now. I tried not to look too closely at them. “Security, mostly. If your agents are turning, you’d think you’d want to know. I guess I was wrong.”

I turned to leave. Brian was still on the landing. All five of him.

Steve said, “Mr. Hoyt, we’re sorry. It’s just... we’ve been on eggshells lately. We’ve had to sell a few of the families. But your concerns, well, they aren’t concerns.”

“Let’s be clear. The family that I’m talking about has a member named Raul Diaz that was killed the other day. For the second time.”

All ten of them nodded. My skin tried to crawl off my body and make a break for it.

“The man that killed Diaz wasn’t the buyer, was he?”

"No. The buyer was, we believe, an agent of the Anas. You are familiar with them? The fashion ascetics?"

Mina snorted.

"Yeah, we've heard of them here and there." Didn't take too much to know who that was. Again, I remembered Diaz: *the girl, the girl, the girl*. The skinny blonde outside the courthouse. The woman who murdered Eric. "Don't suppose you'll give me a name on the buyer, will you?"

"Mr. Hoyt, that information isn't pertinent..."

"I have reason to believe that they're turning your clones into assassins, and not the fun, pot-smoking, capital-A kind. They're turning them into the real deal, Sirhan Sirhan, dead-eyed killers. Whoever this Ana is, she has connections, I think to more than a couple other groups, through a specific individual—someone that just hinting about has gotten *me* shot at and *her* taken by a goddamn UFO."

Before Bess could stop him, Steve said, "Her name is Ingrid Brady."

Brady, skinny, blond. The Ana, same. I thought back to it: the mustache could have been fake. The girl's hair had to be a wig since the Anas started going bald pretty quickly. There wouldn't be much of a woman's figure to hide, and that g-man suit could have done it. Brady had pulled a d'Eon on me and I hadn't seen it. She had practically screamed it back in the bunker. She had called the Anas the "Anorectic Praxis." Everyone else used the pejorative. I should have caught it, but I was too busy being shocked there was a Mr. Blank at all.

Mr. Blank had a name, and he was a she.

"What is it, Mr. Hoyt?"

"I've met Ms. Brady. She's lovely when she's not kidnapping Templars and kicking me in the guts."

All ten gave me confused looks. "Mr. Hoyt, while we have you here, have you reconsidered donating your genetic material?"

"No."

"All we're offering you is the chance to live forever."

"As a mind-controlled assassin. No, I'm good."

"And your friend?"

"She's not interested either."

"She can answer for herself."

Mina said, "No, he's right. Not interested."

I blinked as a thought caught up with me. "He really did look like Che Guevara." I focused on Bess. They might as well have started rubbing their hands together. "He was one of yours, too? Guevara was killed by CIA-trained Bolivians. Let me guess, one of them sent the head back here as a paper-weight?" I asked them.

"Correct in the generalities. Not in the details."

I looked up at the faces in the shining grapes. I turned back to them. I remembered the picture in Eric's book. "That's where you got them, isn't it? *Los desaparecidos*. Good source for bodies. Who's looking for someone that vanished thirty years ago?"

Bess took two steps toward me. I was suddenly very aware that I was underground in a room with five sets of five clones. Even if they were lab rats, they outnumbered Mina and me twelve and a half to one. "Mr. Hoyt, that kind of information is pure speculation."

Steve said, "Really, we wouldn't have to do that sort of thing if some of our agents didn't have such phobias about cloning."

"It's not a phobia. It's just, I can barely stand myself. I couldn't imagine standing four more."

Bess said, "You know a great deal about this. More than one of our agents should."

I felt Mina getting closer to me, watching our backs. I

hoped she had that kick ready. We might need it.

"True. Blame the person that sent one of your clones to kill me armed with a Templar and alien relic." That stunned them. I took Mina's hand and started purposefully up the stairs. "I'm going to get to the bottom of this." I glanced around at the underground lab. "The figurative bottom, I mean. It wasn't you, but you should know what your little utopian seeds are being used for."

Bess exclaimed, "Brian! Stop them."

Brian, all five, stepped out onto the landing in front of us. Brian was a fairly big guy, and even if leaning over a microscope had given him a mighty hunch, he still had a full head on me. One Brian could probably throw me down the stairs without much effort, but all five could have a boot party. His eyes were focused on my chest. I braced myself. Maybe I'd get in a kick to the groin. Maybe I could get past the glasses and gouge an eye or something.

The backmost Brian passed something to another Brian, who passed it to another Brian, who passed it to the one in front of me. He looked sheepishly at the Brian next to him and held it out.

It was a box, wrapped in Santa Claus paper, tied with a clumsy pink ribbon.

I took it. Light. Too light for a bomb.

Brian, all of them, stepped aside.

"Brian! Stop them!"

Mina and I walked up and out into the steam tunnel.

We were above ground when Mina said, "So what is it?"

"There's a part of me that's convinced it will be the head of a Girl Scout."

"The box is the wrong shape."

"It disturbs me how quickly you said that."

"I've been hanging out with you since Friday night."

I put the box on the car. It was light for a big bomb, but it's possible that Brian the beefy Clone Wolf had put something small in there. A little plastique could mean I was about to say goodbye to my thumbs, and I rather liked those. They really tied the hand together.

Mina said, "This box looks like it was wrapped by a twelve-year-old."

I looked at the wrapping paper. Crinkled, sure. Bunched up in places. Lots of tape straining to keep it shut. Certainly not a professional job. "Doesn't look so bad to me."

She rolled her eyes. "Open it."

I did. I tried to probe the paper first, make sure there

were no needles filled with horrible plagues. I ripped carefully, worried about a contact toxin. I opened the box away from me, because you never know. When I finally looked inside, it's fair to say I was morbidly disappointed.

Mina asked again, "What is it?"

"A dress."

A cute one, too, in a drooling juvenile fantasy sort of way. I mentally took back every bad thing I'd ever thought about Brian. I wanted to get him a Christmas card.

Mina snatched it. "What size?"

"Yours, I think."

"Are there shoes? Tell me there are shoes."

"No shoes."

"Do we have time? I'm getting shoes."

What the hell had just happened?

As we were driving, she looked it over. "This *does* look like my size."

"That's what I said."

"No, that's weird. I'm sort of strange in terms of, you know, relative sizes of things."

"I hadn't noticed."

"Every other sentence you've said has been addressed to my breasts."

"I didn't want them to feel left out."

I wasn't sure how familiar Mina was with the area, but she had suddenly developed radar. She directed me to the nearest mall, and I found myself sitting next to a similarly forlorn guy as Mina ran off to the dressing room.

The guy gave me the once-over. "Which one's your wife?"

I pointed to an Asian lady who looked just north of a hundred. "It's a May-December thing."

I think he knew I was fucking with him, but he nodded over to his wife. She was pretty, in a sort of Orange County way. "There's my wife. Remember when Sundays were fun?"

"Not really."

He chuckled. "What do you do?"

"I kowtow to a bunch of psychotics who would just as soon see me turned inside out as talk to me."

"Yeah, I work in an office, too." He stuck out his hand. "Davis."

I picked a name out of a hat. "Zeke."

"Got kids?" I shook my head. "Me neither, but that'll change soon."

"It's supposed to be a lot of fun."

"So's sleeping for eight hours a night."

"You make a good point."

Mina came out of the dressing room. She had on the dress that Brian had picked out for her. Suddenly, I didn't want to get him a Christmas card. I wanted to bolster his Christmas tree with every single geek fantasy I could think of. I would drown him in Jack Kirby *Silver Surfer*s and *Babylon 5* DVDs. I would somehow obtain every episode of *Droids*. I'd use necromancy to get him signed copies of *The Hobbit* and the first *Monster Manual*. I'd find him a Sarah Conner, a Princess Leia, a Zotoh Zhaan... and I was getting off track.

Put simply, the dress fit. Perfectly. If Mina's figure previously had been an hourglass from a Boggle set, she had been turned into one of those two-handed antiques capable of keeping time while beating a serf to death. She twirled, letting the skirt flare out just a bit.

"What do you think?" she said.

I crossed my legs. "You look nice."

Her face fell a little. Not sure why. I'd said she looked nice. "I'm going to get a pair of shoes."

"Yeah, I'll just wait here for a little while."

Mina walked away. I watched her and tried very hard to

think about my dead grandmother playing baseball on the toilet.

Davis spoke up, sounding like I'd just given him the secret of fire. "That's your girlfriend?"

"It's... uh... complicated."

"Friend zone, huh? Yeah, that sucks."

"I should..."

"Yeah. Nice talking to you. Take it easy."

That was pretty good advice. I stood up, and fortunately, I wasn't having a junior high moment. I found Mina trying on shoes. She hadn't seen me. The posture of someone who doesn't know they are being observed has a vulnerability to it. Their subconscious takes over. They sing under their breath along with the tune in their head. They flex their hands and wiggle their fingers, maybe conducting the same music, maybe making a speech, maybe in the throes of *esprit d'escalier*. Their pretense melts away, and their face takes the expression underneath—in her case, a secret smile. Their bodies relax, letting the natural weight pull their spines into comfortable curves.

Mina looked up. Her back straightened. She swallowed the smile. "Can I pay you back for the shoes?"

I wanted to say something along the lines of "My treat," but all that came out was, "Yeah, no problem."

When I got back to the car, my briefcase was buzzing. I opened it. Voicemail on one of my phones. I sifted through the clacking plastic and found it: Assassins. That would be a fun conversation. "Say, Len, have you seen Tariq?" "Gee guys, no. Last I heard, he was going to cover himself in squid juice and jump in the shark tank at Sea World. You haven't seen him since?"

I called the voicemail and heard Hasim's voice, sober for once and sounding more than a little like Hudson, even if he never actually used the phrase "game over." I listened to it, but before I was done, one of my other phones started ringing. I answered it and tried not to sound annoyed.

"Squire Max, it's Sir Richard." He sounded a little like Hasim. I wondered if they were having similar problems.

"Yes, Sire?"

"We need you to come to the Castle, as soon as possible."

"Give me an hour."

He hung up without saying goodbye. I wondered where they had found Eric's body, and in what state.

I started the car. Mina said, "You're popular."

"A bit too popular. We're going to see the Assassins, then we're going back to the Templars."

"They were the ones at Medieval Castle?"

"Yep."

"I wanted to kick that one guy."

"Again, reserve the kicking for me."

"Whatever. So tell me about the Assassins. All you said before is that they're the originals, whatever that means."

I laid the rest out. It all started in the 9th century, when a guy named Hassan-i-Sabbah created a sect of trained killers who didn't mind dying. He took the standard-issue religious fanatic and decided to crazy them up a little more. He created this bizarre pleasure palace, stocked it with fruit trees, sexy women, and streams that literally flowed with milk and honey. He then got these fanatics, usually impressionable kids, really high on the best hash he could find and let them into the palace, telling them it was heaven. So yeah, he convinced them that if they killed for him, they would get right into heaven where all their puerile teenaged desires would be exceeded. The sect was known as the Hashishin—users of hashish—which was corrupted into the modern word assassin. Supposedly the sect was wiped out in the Crusades, and the Templars tried their damnedest to do it—there's still some bad blood there—but actually, they just went underground.

Which brings me to William Randolph Hearst. Hearst was a lot of things—newspaper magnate, flamboyant philanderer, sledding enthusiast—but his biggest accomplishment was something that most people are entirely unaware of. Hearst was a tireless enemy of the demon weed. Most people who know this fact will tell you this is because Hearst owned timberlands, and the more efficient hemp would undercut his prices and slice into that famous fortune of his. That's not true, at least not entirely, but I'll get back to that. The point is that hemp made Hearst send his yellow journalism machine into overdrive. He linked pot with violent behavior and promptly scared lawmakers into criminalizing it.

Which makes no sense. Pot only makes you violent from the perspective of a box of graham crackers.

For his actions to make any sense, Hearst had to have known about the Assassins, and, in fact, he did. He first learned of them when they killed a friend of his, while the guy was celebrating his birthday aboard Hearst's yacht. This friend was the director Thomas Ince, who, according to public record, died from either a heart attack or cramps. Witnesses blamed his demise on the bullet hole through his head. In any case, after Ince's death, Hearst turned his attention to the man that killed him. When he learned about the demon weed, that's when he went on the offensive. Hearst had pot outlawed to fight the Assassins.

Mina said, "They didn't mention any of that on the Hearst Castle tour. Why did the Assassins want Ince dead?"

"That's a whole other story. Look, when we go in there, don't mention chupacabras, okay?"

"I wasn't planning on it. The Assassins still have the contract out on me, right?"

"No. Tariq specifically has the contract on you. As long as they think he's still alive, you're safe. As soon as they know he's dead, someone else gets the contract and you're back in danger. In a lot of ways, the Assassins are nicer than the Russian mob."

By all accounts, the Assassins back in the Holy Land were more of what you'd expect: dour fellows whose hobbies included bomb making, knife sharpening, and scripture interpreting. The local Assassins had gone native. They were much more pleasant to be around. That's not to say they wouldn't stick six inches of steel through your eye if someone paid them to, but they wouldn't be dicks about it. They didn't even mind using an infidel like myself to pick up their dry cleaning and plant their getaway cars. The simple fact that they had getaway cars to begin with showed just how native they'd gone.

I wasn't too worried about meeting with the Assassins. If there was one group I was pretty sure Ingrid Brady hadn't infiltrated, it was them. I had to find out what the hell had Hasim's panties in a bunch and see if they could help me track my Ms. Blank.

I pulled up at their beach house. A high fence ringed it, but as soon as you left the gate, turn right and there was the Pacific Ocean. I went ahead and let myself in.

That turned out to be a mistake. Assassins who weren't waiting to kill me were still waiting, and they were still armed. Before either of us knew what was happening, we were grabbed from behind, had guns pressed to our temples, and were being forced to inhale breath that smelled like old milk.

Hasim came charging out of the house, hands up. "Wait! Don't shoot him!"

I said, "Them! Don't shoot *them*!"

"Right, that too."

The guys let go, backing off and glancing around at the

surrounding rooftops. That's when one of them sprayed blood out of his chest. I didn't even hear the gunshot.

Hasim screamed, "Get inside!"

Mina and I ran. The man that had been holding her was just behind us. I heard bullets kicking up along the walk, then heard the man fall. We burst through the door, falling onto hard wood. Hasim slammed the door shut behind us.

I looked around at the living room. Couches and chairs tipped over for cover, some pocked with bullet holes. They had six opened boxes of cereal, several half-empty bowls, and a bong that had the top broken off. Assassins were scattered around the room, already behind cover, armed and terrified.

I yelled at him, "What the fuck did you get me into, Hasim?"

"We need your help! Get behind something!"

"I'm behind the fucking *door*!"

Mina had more sense; she hauled me into the adjoining kitchen and pulled me behind the fridge. I heard the door get kicked in. Then, silenced gunshots that sounded like how I imagined laser weapons would. There was a scream, a shot, a thud, then silence.

Hasim poked his head around the door. "You can come out. It's safe for the moment."

"The hell it is! What's going on?"

"Assassins. We're knee-deep in them."

"Do you want me to point out the irony, or are you already there?"

I crept out of my hiding place. There were more bullet holes around the room, one of the cereal bowls had been shattered, and Che Guevara was lying in the living room, dead. Hasim pointed at him.

"We've had guys like that tracking us all over the city. We lost three of our people before we holed up here. We thought we were good until one of them showed up on our doorstep at five in the morning and killed Khalid. We're under siege, Lenny!"

"And you thought you'd call *me*?"

"You're just a rafiq. You can find out what's tracking us, right? They're not tracking you."

"Well, in point of fact, yeah, they are."

"Shit. Shit! *Shit*! Sorry. Look, you shouldn't have brought your lady friend."

"Well, you could have mentioned on the phone that I was walking into a gunfight."

"But then you might not have come."

I really wanted to hit Hasim. I swallowed that impulse, and instead, said, "These assassins attacking, we're talking Manchurian Candidates, right?"

"No, none of them are Chinese. They look Mexican or something."

"Not a movie buff. Okay, they all have blank expressions, incredible strength, that kind of thing? Maybe they keep muttering the same thing over and over? They really like *Catcher in the Rye*?"

"I don't know about that last part, but yeah. They're all old-school assassins, only they don't have any connection to us. There's that rumor about other groups making something like we used to, but it was just a rumor, and they sure as hell weren't coming after us."

"You said you lost three guys?"

"Three guys definitely. No one's heard from Tariq since yesterday. We're hoping he's holed up somewhere."

"Yeah. It would take more than these guys to take him out." Like a pack of genetically engineered killing machines, for one.

"Okay. Look, we can just stay in here, and whoever is

sending these zombies at us, maybe Tariq will track him down and solve the problem."

I almost put my hand on his shoulder. Couldn't give away the store, though. "I need to get out of here."

"No, man! We're safe in here." We both looked around at the bullet-riddled room. "Safer, I mean."

"I think I'm going to take my chances out there. How often do they attack?"

Hasim shrugged. "It varies, but the frequency is going up."

"Hasim, you have to get the hell out of here. This is a death trap. Whoever is sending these guys is just going to keep sending them until one of them gets lucky, and then you'll be dead. Get out. Leave town."

Hasim gave me a weak smile. "Nah, man. Safer in here."

Well, I tried. "Good luck." I turned to Mina. "Ready?"

"Oh yeah."

Mina couldn't look at the corpse we had to step over to get to the kicked-in door. How many of these guys had the Clone Wolves made? And how many had they sold? I was getting to the point where I was going to start pointing guns at every set of twins I passed, on the off chance they were Candidates. I peeked out the door. It looked safe, other than the two Assassins lying dead on the front lawn.

"Just run."

Mina nodded.

We bolted for the gate. No shots. Opened it. Closed it. Ran more. No shots. Scrambled into the car, started it, peeled out. No shots.

Mina said, "That was a lot of bodies." I glanced at her. She was staring at her lap. I hadn't seen her look quite that shaken before, but she was right. That *was* a lot of bodies.

"Yeah. Sorry you had to see that."

She shrugged. There was part of me that was convinced

this was an act. My guard was so low as to be completely nonexistent, which is just where she wanted it, regardless of whoever she was actually working for. But there was a bigger part of me, not to be egotistical, that wanted to believe her.

Normally, a trip to Medieval Castle is something that's done maybe once a decade. When the nieces and nephews are in town—not that I had any, but it was the kind of place I imagined taking them when I imagined having them, an occurrence which usually involved alcohol of some kind. I always wondered if that was normal: if women fantasized about having kids, and if men just fantasized about hanging out with them for the excuse of seeing guys in armor wale on each other with swords.

The show wouldn't be on until eight, but the cast would be there, gearing up, doing the last-minute rehearsals. It was important to be faux-authentic. For every "yo, Brad" that replaced a "forsooth, Sir Bradley," there was disciplinary action. I parked where I had on Friday night, just for symmetry's sake.

Eric's car wasn't there. I don't know why I expected that it would be. Poor guy. He was a complete asshole, but he probably didn't deserve whatever had happened to him.

I walked in the stage door with Mina, and no one bothered to stop me. Max Gross had a reason for being there. I passed guys in black t-shirts carrying equipment and clipboards. I heard the ring of steel on steel coming from the show area and ignored it. Richard had a dressing room to himself, while the other knights had to make do with a communal one that was more locker room than anything else. I knocked on Richard's door. I got a shouted "What?" in response.

"It's Max."

The door opened. Richard was on the other side, looking pale. At least he didn't look as bad as Hasim, which made me feel a little safer. "What happened to you?" He was wearing a robe. I couldn't tell if he was wearing pants, but I was tempted to pray to everything I could think of that he was.

"Bad day."

"You brought your friend? Can she..." He trailed off, gesturing.

"Mina, could you wait over there?"

She nodded. She was still subdued from the carnage at the Assassin beach house. I went into Richard's dressing room and shut the door behind me. Richard sat down and gestured toward a sofa that was pretty much just a loveseat. I really hoped he hadn't auditioned many serving wenches on it.

Richard's dressing room was half swinger's pad and half monastic cell. There was a nice big cross on one side, a small altar, and it didn't take much to imagine panties hung over one side of it. I wondered if he angled them so Jesus was always looking at them or always looking away from them. He had a stereo with an iPod dock, but I didn't want to know what kind of music he liked. I imagined a lot of Enigma.

"Eric Caldwell was found dead outside his apartment."

I tried to express some surprise, but Richard wasn't looking at me. He was looking at his hands, like he wondered if maybe he had strangled Eric with them and forgotten about it. I settled on a neutral response that I tried to inject with that same little bit of dismay that I'd felt when Brady took Eric. "How?"

"He was shot twice in the chest with a 12-gauge, thrown through a plate-glass window, run over, and set on fire. The police are calling it suicide."

The really sad part was that wasn't the most ridiculous "suicide" I'd heard of. I said, "They always do."

"I suppose so." He'd forgotten to call me "squire." He seemed really broken up about the whole thing. I was going to have to change my opinion of Richard a little bit. "I have contacts within the police," he said. Yeah, me, only he didn't know that. "The investigation is already closed."

I decided to cut the shit. I'd been shot at, and I knew who did it. No reason to let Richard stew like this, especially if he really was hurting. God, Mina was turning me into such a schmuck. "Eric was kidnapped from the jail by a woman named Ingrid Brady. She normally goes around dressed in a man's suit with a little blond mustache. Ringing any bells?"

Richard's mouth worked like a fish.

I said, "Yeah, I know. Brady's an agent of the Anas, and possibly part of a conspiracy to break the peace with V.E.N.U.S. She also might be trying to wipe out the Assassins, but that could just be a coincidence."

"How do you know all this?"

"And that reminds me. The Chain of the Heretic Martyr was stolen by the Satanists, who then gave it to the Discordians, I think for religious reasons. It's been... altered since you've seen it."

"Squire Max?"

"I know, disconcerting, right?"

"It's a lot to process. This agent, Ingrid..."

"Brady. I'm trying to track her down."

"Good. You do that."

I got up. Richard was collecting himself. When I got to the door, he said, "Squire Max, wait."

I turned around. He was holding a dagger. Goddamn it. Not him, too. I braced myself for an attack. He flipped it around, offering me the handle. "Take this. You might need it."

"I'm not a big fan of weapons."

He sheathed the dagger. "Not really something one expects to hear from a squire in the Knights Templar. If it makes you feel better, think of it as a cross. Go with God, Squire Max."

I looked at the thing. It seemed like an antique. The blade was dark, the grip worn smooth. I slid the blade out a little from the worn leather sheath and touched it. Sharp. And probably a vector for tetanus. “Thanks.”

There aren't a lot of Buddhist conspiracies. Sure, there are some. The Tibetans that fought for the Germans against the Chinese in World War II were one. The Undying Samurai that kept bothering people in the Pacific during the '60s and '70s were sort of Buddhist. It's not that Buddhists are better than the rest of us—they're really not—it's just that most of them actually believe in the tenets of their religion. It's sort of jarring.

Despite the name, the Anas aren't a sect of Buddhists. They'd like you to believe that they are. The name of their goddess, Anamadim, is supposed to sound vaguely Indian with maybe a bit of Hebrew, in order to cash in on the whole Kabbalah fad. They're a fairly new cult that blew up with the rise of the internet. If there's one thing the internet loves almost as much as porn, it's new religions. It makes it hard to keep up with, but it also keeps providing me with new jobs, so I can't really complain.

The Anas are ascetics in their way, but they're also very concerned with the here and now, especially the part of this present world which relates to love handles. They've been steadily kicking V.E.N.U.S.'s ass for the past couple decades, too, and considering that V.E.N.U.S. claims a prehistory, where most conspiracies merely have a history, that's pretty impressive.

We were driving toward their temple in the Hollywood Hills.

Mina said, "You realize these people want me dead."

She was right. Brady, in her disguise as a Fed, had hired the Russian mob to take Mina out. "Hey, look on the bright side. It could have been your own people."

"Even if it's not, that doesn't change anything."

"Perfect cover. You go in as you. You tell them that V.E.N.U.S. set you up. I recruited you, and you're there to hear the sales pitch. We get the run of the place. I need to get more information on Ingrid Brady."

"And I get some truly insane dieting advice."

"You have to like laxatives."

She made a face. "Okay, Rabbit. What do I call you in there?"

"Ivan. Or Angelbutt."

"That would *so* not be your pet name."

"What's wrong with my butt?"

"I don't have enough evidence to make an informed judgment."

Now, when a woman says something like that, God, Eris, the Devil, maybe the Cosmic Trickster or the Universal Unconscious conspires against you. You fart. You spill a drink into her lap. Or, in my case, you arrive at your destination, and don't have a good excuse to continue the conversation. More than anything, I wanted to get out of the car and curse at the sky, even thought it was wholly innocent in the matter.

The temple of the Guardian Servitors of the Anorectic Praxis looked like it was bought with drug money. Specifically, coke money earned in 1984. It looked like a stack of white blocks that some kid arranged haphazardly on the way to failing an IQ test. In the LA sun, it shone so brightly I wanted to turn away. The wrought-iron gate was wide open. The lawn was trimmed. There was no breeze, no one around. I had the feeling that I was going to open the door onto a slaughter.

Mina lagged behind me, probably hearing the same alarm bells I was. We reached the door. I knocked. The door drifted open. I nearly shrieked.

I was immediately glad I hadn't. I would have looked like an idiot and I still kind of wanted to impress Mina. A woman, though telling gender is tough with the Anas, wandered in front of the door, looking like she was on her way somewhere and just happened past at that moment. She wore a flowing white gown that looked designed, and nicely showed off her skeleton, clearly visible even though she had skin stretched over it like Saran Wrap. There was a little bleached blonde hair coming from her scalp like she had just come from ground zero at a nuclear test. She saw me and grinned, her eyes unfocused and sleepy.

"Oh, hey. I know you, right?" The Anas could be a little spacey. Something about not eating. Still, it was a good idea not to let your guard down. They were capable of some pretty impressive feats in short bursts, as Ingrid Brady had so ably demonstrated.

"Ivan Cohen. I work for you."

She nodded gingerly. "Oh, good. What can I do for you?"

"I'm here to see the Reverend Mother."

"She's leading meditation and... by Anamadim!" Her sleepy smile was gone, replaced by stark horror. She was looking over my shoulder at Mina.

"Hi," Mina said.

"Wha... wha..." The skeleton was having trouble.

"I'm here to talk to the Reverend Mother about a possible new recruit."

The skeleton swallowed. Probably more nourishment than she'd had all week. "Of course. Right this way."

She shuffled along the hall like she was worried about breaking a hip. The halls were wide and plain, the walls white and smooth. There was minimal art hanging, and that was modern, usually something I didn't understand. I could hear ghost sounds within the mansion, a soft shuffling that sounded like the wings of pigeons. As we got closer, more sounds joined them, a whisper-hum that grew in volume. The hall opened up into a vaulted room that I knew was in the center of the structure. There would be no windows in there, but the room was lit in bright gold: 147 candles. I didn't have to count.

We got to the doorway. In three rows, one of three and two more of seven, were more of these wraiths in various stages of emaciation. They sat in lotus positions, wearing designer clothes, everything pure white. Candles and incense burned around them. At the head sat the Reverend Mother, a shriveled thing who, through concentration and sheer willpower, had turned herself into a thousand-year-old goblin. She hunched over, eyes closed, humming. She had a small crucible in front of her, and stacked by it were cookies, a candy bar, and what looked like a Taco Bell burrito.

Our escort raised a claw, but made no sound. Still, the Reverend Mother opened her eyes. I saw horror register when she saw Mina, but it was a fleeting thing. She controlled everything else about her—why not that, too? She rose from her lotus position and, in a voice that sounded much too young for her appearance, she said, "Excuse me, students. Keep concentrating on the sculptor of flesh. I will return to you shortly."

She shuffled over to us. "What brings you here, Ivan?" One look at Mina and she knew what I'd say, but she wanted me to say it.

"Reverend Mother, this is Mina Duplessis."

The Reverend Mother turned to Mina, but didn't offer her hand. "I know who she is. Why is she here?"

Mina spoke up. She stuttered, but that was probably from the counter-horror of seeing these people. "I'm... uh... I'm here to join." The Reverend Mother was silent, so Mina just bulled on ahead. She spilled the cover story I'd sold her, and she didn't sound completely unconvincing. I kept waiting for the Reverend Mother to stick Mina's hand in a box filled with pain.

When she was finished, the Reverend Mother turned to me. "And you brought her to us, Mr. Cohen?"

"Thought it would help. A defector like this, well, it can't hurt."

"No, I don't suppose it could. Miss Duplessis, will you consent to stay awhile? Mr. Cohen, you may go."

Mina shot me a look, subdued but pleading. I tried to tell her that I'd be around, but my telepathy wasn't up to snuff. I had some quality lurking to do. The Reverend Mother guided Mina into the meditation room. I turned to my guide, the friendly skeleton. She was shuffling down the hall.

"Excuse me?" I said, going after her.

She turned and smiled. "Hey. I know you, right?"

Wow. I wanted to force-feed her a steak or something. "Yes. Ivan Cohen? I work for you?"

"Right. How are you?"

"Can I ask you about someone? We have a member named Ingrid Brady, right? She's blonde? Might be prone to cross-dressing?"

I got a blank look.

"Can you check? There are rolls, right? Member lists, that kind of thing?"

"You're not a devotee of the carver of fat."

"Well, no. But she did buy me a big TV last year."

"Oh, that's nice." The skeleton started to shuffle off. It was pretty clear that questioning her was like playing ping-pong with a wall. One way or the other, it'd end up with me exhausted and flat on my ass. It was time to wander around, and if someone found me in a place I shouldn't be, resort to the "I got lost" card and hope that protein deficiency filled in the gaps in any of my lies.

There were cells in the building, that much I did know. The cells weren't for day-to-day living, but any Ana of sufficient standing would have a dedicated one. The cells would be used in a time of total war, or if an Ana was having trouble with temptation and needed to be kept cloistered. I took a gamble and started wandering down hallways, trying to find a stairway. This sort of thing struck me as something that would be on a second floor.

I found the staircase, and I was immediately terrified when I got up it. The walls were no longer white. They were mirrored. It was like a dance studio up there, with reflections that went on to infinity. At least they weren't funhouse mirrors, the ones that make you look fatter. I imagined that whoever designed the place trusted the warped subconscious of the faithful to do that.

Doors opened in the reflections, but those, too, were mirrored. I felt alone and surrounded all at once. I would see movement out of the corner of my eye, but it was just one of my infinite reflections. Pretty soon, I had to block that out. I really wished that I'd had the foresight of a Hansel or a Gretel and left some breadcrumbs. Of course, leaving carbs around this place would probably get me killed.

I opened the first door I found. Unlocked and empty. It was a cell, and in this place, all the walls were mirrored again. There was a tiny cot, a chair, and a desk. Other than that, the room was bare. I started wondering if they had an RA or a Den Mother.

I was deep in thought when one of my phones rang. I checked it. The Templar phone. I picked it up. "Sir Richard, I'm in the middle..."

It wasn't Richard. The buzzing voice said, "Duck."

I did. I felt the wind over the back of my neck. I spun into the hall to face my attacker, dropping the phone. Ingrid Brady stood there barefoot, in one of those white gowns, recovering from her attempted kick to the back of my head. I could see her ribcage over the scooped neck. She wasn't wearing a wig, her scalp showing through her wispy hair.

"Hi, Ingrid. Or do you prefer Brady? And I'm curious, is that g-man power suit and the fake mustache in the building, or do you keep those offsite?"

She threw another kick, faster than I expected. I jumped backward. That one barely missed. It was only a matter of time before she took me down. She said, "You're not getting out of here."

"Your assassins keep failing, so you think maybe you'll to the job yourself?"

Kick, punch. "Stop talking." She was getting closer. Much closer. I knew from before that a single one of her kicks would be enough to drop me. Abruptly, I was filled with rage at the entire ascetic tradition. Assholes deny themselves comfort and become total bad-asses. It was unfair to those of us who liked our trans fats and ten hours of sleep a night.

Spin, kick. I said, "Why didn't you just take me out in that bunker? Why let me go?"

"You played me!" She lunged forward. That was my chance. She might be a kung-fu asskicking machine, but I had a couple inches and probably a hundred pounds on her. All the kung fu in the world is useless if you've got someone sitting on you.

I went for a tackle. She recovered, grabbed my waist, and twisted. My momentum was her power, and she introduced me to the wall, face-first. The mirror didn't shatter, but it did crack. In another situation, seeing my face like that might have been hilarious. In any case, the sliding sound I made was a little funny.

"Ow."

She kicked. I rolled. She kicked me in the ribs. I kept rolling. Another kick to the ribs. Okay, this was getting ridiculous. I came up on my back with my hands up. "Wait! Wait!"

She stopped. "What?"

"Can I get up?"

"No! I'm going to kill you."

"Okay, fine. But I don't want to die ignorant. Fill in some blanks for me, then you can snap my neck or whatever, deal?"

She sighed. "Fine. Be quick."

"You sent the Candidate after me at Union Station when you found out..." The look on her face said I already made a wrong turn. "You *did* send the assassin, right? After you had the weapon planted because..."

She got ready to kick me. "I'm not going to listen to your lies anymore!"

"Wait!" She held the pose. "You didn't send him? The one you and Eric Caldwell were conditioning."

"He was ours, but we lost contact with him sometime Friday morning."

"You did activate him, didn't you?"

"We did. Not for you, though."

"Who then? Mina?"

She laughed. "Why would we want her dead? No, her contract went through the regular channels."

I was trying to keep up. "You're not Mr. Blank?"

"What the hell are you talking about?"

Oh, crap. Statler. Her boss. "Who's Statler? The guy Eric was meeting in the gay bar? Your boss!"

"That's not something I'm going to tell you. Let me save you some time: he doesn't exist to someone like you. Anything about him is well out of your reach." She wasn't lying, but there was one thing even Statler couldn't escape, and it was waiting in a downtown basement doing whatever it is gods do.

"Who did you send the Candidate after?"

She sighed. "A man named Tariq Suliman. An Assassin. Diaz never made contact, though."

"Then how the hell did he end up at Union Station trying to kill me with the Genesis Stone?"

"I don't know. This has been fun, but you're a threat. It's time to finish this."

"Wait. One more question. Why put the contract on Mina?"

"Nothing personal. Orders from the Reverend Mother." I nearly lost all control of my bowels.

"That was an Ana plot?"

She shrugged. "I thought it was stupid, myself. Kill her young and she becomes a timeless sex symbol that never ages. Still, the Reverend Mother wanted her dead, so she dies."

Suddenly there was a horrible screech. My eyes went to my phone. It was smoking, and the sound that came from it had no relation to anything the machine could have made on its own. Brady and I covered our ears. The mirrors shuddered, cracked, shattered. Glass rained down onto the floor.

I tucked my head in. Shards sliced along the backs of my hands, but my arteries stayed intact.

There was a pop, and the screech stopped. My phone had exploded in a puff of white smoke. Brady and I looked at each other, shocked. The fact that my spooky red-eyed friend wanted me alive that badly said I was at least a little important. Silver Bridge in miniature. He had warned others of that collapse, and they hadn't listened. Now he was warning me, but of what, I had no idea. Probably not worth thinking about while a trained killer like Brady was still within flying-knee range.

I scrambled to my feet. My steps chewed glass. "It was great talking to you, but I have to run. You might want to stick around, though." I pointed to her bare feet and the shattered glass. With a slightly nasty smile, I said, "I understand you people have bleeding problems."

I ran. Brady fumed, but she stayed put. I was not looking forward to our next confrontation when she'd take that out on my hide, but that was later. I only needed my hide for a little while longer. I retraced my steps at warp speed. I really wished I'd thought ahead and brought some chocolate or bacon or something I could throw like a grenade and make the Anas cower in corners, helplessly hissing.

I skidded to a stop in the meditation hall. There were the three rows of three, seven, and seven, but no Reverend Mother and no Mina. To their credit, the Anas didn't stir when I came in. They were deep in some kind of trance, probably all picturing cheeseburgers.

I ran for the back and tore open the door. Mina and the Reverend Mother both started, looking up at me. The Reverend Mother was sitting in the lotus position, and Mina had her legs tucked under her. They didn't look like they had been fighting. They might have been arguing.

Mina's face changed when she saw me. Surprise went to concern. The Reverend Mother's face stayed in her Gollum-mask.

I started babbling, definitely too excited, but I was on a severe adrenaline high. "Hey! How's it going?! Listen, Mina, we should probably be leaving!"

Silently, she mouthed, "What the hell happened to you?"

I smiled bigger.

The Reverend Mother raised an eyebrow. "You should not be here, Mr. Cohen. I was in the middle of informing Miss Duplessis about her cleansing regimen."

"Lots of water and B-12." Mina didn't sound pleased. She couldn't keep her eyes off the right side of my head where Ingrid had slammed me into the mirror. I touched it. Blood. That explained it.

"Oh yeah. I tripped upstairs. Broke a mirror, Reverend Mother. Really sorry about that."

She waved a hand. "It's nothing. You brought us such a promising new recruit."

"Oh, happy to do it. Just thrilled to help out. The thing is, Mina, you're late for that thing. The, uh, shoot with the folks from Pizza Hut."

Mina cocked an eyebrow. "Pizza Hut?"

The Reverend Mother, employing some kind of conversational jiu-jitsu, lectured us. "She should not be performing her job until we can make her presentable, and certainly not for that death-peddler."

Death-peddler was a little harsh. Tummy-ache-peddler didn't really have the same ring, though. "Right! Exactly, but if we want to keep her in good with the modeling community for when she's, uh, presentable, we at least have to tell them why she has to bow out, right?"

"I suppose..."

I grabbed Mina's arm. "I'll bring her right back. You know, after that, and after she takes me to a hospital."

"Yes. You seem to be dripping on my floor."

"Sorry about that. Mina, let's go!"

I hustled her out of the room and that's when I crashed. I stumbled out the front door, but she supported me easily. Bless those hips and their center of gravity. She said, "Whoa. Are you okay? What happened?"

"It's not Ingrid Brady. She's not Mr. Blank." I explained the Candidate's real target.

"Was Tariq at Union Station?"

"He must have been. Probably hunting you."

Mina looked at my head and winced. "You have glass in your scalp."

And that was about it. I made her drive down the hill before I let her check it out. I tried not to bleed on the upholstery and thought about Statler. I'd have to find him, and there was an avenue open for that. It wasn't an avenue I liked, but like it or not, it was what was there. I'd probably end up losing more blood. I hoped I'd have some left when this was over.

MINA SAID, "IT DOESN'T FEEL RIGHT, THAT'S ALL. You'd think the chemicals would, you know, do something."

"What? You think I'm going to mutate into some kind of atomic killing machine?"

Her face was inches from mine. I could see her blue eyes narrow, and I filled in the rest of the exasperated expression. "Or, you know, something actually reasonable."

"That's what Superglue is for. Originally anyway. It sticks to your fingers because that's what it's designed to do."

She said, "Right. Let me fill in the rest. In 1947, Nazi agent Cyrus T. Superglue developed the formula for the CIA, who immediately used it to glue our pouches shut. Oh yeah, and by the way, we're actually marsupials."

It was hard not to laugh, but her fingers and the glue applicator were by the cut on my brow and every time I almost broke up, it shot a new bee sting into my face. "I didn't mention that? Seriously, no. Superglue was originally Vietnam-era medical technology."

"I still say you need stitches, Rabbit."

"The glue's fine. Either way, I'll have the sexy scar."

"What story are you going to tell people?"

"What, you mean I can't tell the truth? That I was beaten up by an anorexic?"

"Your knowledge of women is mostly theoretical isn't it?"

"Well, I only just now found out you guys have pouches. Out of curiosity, where is it exactly?"

"You're going to have to save my life at least one more time."

"It's still early."

I had bled onto my shirt. The bruise on my jaw was starting to turn yellow, but my left eye was still nicely purple. Add to that the red over my right eye, and my face was starting to look like a bowl of Lucky Charms. At least there was no way I could get any orange on me.

Mina said, "So we know for a fact it's the Anas that tried to have me killed."

"Yep."

"And now that they think I'm defecting?"

I shrugged. "It's possible they called off the hit. I mean, we know the Assassins aren't collecting anything, and the Russians are probably a little distracted by that whole 'leading them into an ambush' thing, not that they're going to tell anyone that a bunch of spacemen shot them up."

"So I'm not really in any danger." That got me. She had no reason to tag along with me. Her problem had been solved, at least in the short term. By staying with me, she was actually putting herself back in harm's way. I was a liability.

"Yeah."

"Great. I'm going home."

I tried not to look like she'd just shot my dog and thrown it in a mass grave with the rest of the doggie dissidents. "No problem. Where is home exactly?"

Home for Mina was Silver Lake. She lived a few blocks from the reservoir, on a low hill. Our places were only ten minutes away from one another. She had me pull up to a one-story house with a long driveway that ran along one side. The house was white, with large windows that reminded me a little of a church. It looked like old LA to me, a place where a bit player had probably died in the '40s and was a stop on one of the lower-rent tours. She had a small lawn and even some rose bushes planted under her windows. There were none of the concessions to paranoia that I might have expected from a single woman, but to be fair, my perceptions were a bit warped and I was running on something like two hours of forced unconsciousness.

I pulled up and stayed put as she unlocked her door. She was half out before she noticed I hadn't turned off the engine. She said, "Aren't you coming in? You look like you could use some coffee."

Coffee was only ranked third on what I needed: a *Scarface* mound of cocaine would be number one, and a giant syringe of adrenaline into my left ventricle would be number two. Coffee had the advantage of being both legal and less stabby. I didn't say this because my mouth had chosen that moment to dry out. "Yeah, sounds good."

I turned the car off. Mina pointed to the briefcase of phones. "You should take those. You know, just in case."

This was true. I never wanted to miss a call from that creepy seven-foot bastard, especially if Mina were planning to poison me. I grabbed the case and followed her. We went up her tiled steps and she said, "Could you? My spare keys are inside."

As I knelt to pick her lock, I noticed something. "How scratched was your lock yesterday?"

"I don't know. Why?"

"Someone might have broken in."

"Shit," she said. Yeah, that summed it up. "What's the plan?"

I tried the door. It was locked. "We should go."

"No. I'm going in there. We're going to check it out, stay on our toes, and if someone's in there, we're going to knock them out, call the cops, or both."

I said, "That was going to be my next suggestion."

I picked the lock, paused, listened. Opened the door, paused, listened. If Mina really was loyal, I should probably go first; and if she was gearing up to betray me, better now than later. I listened some more. The place was completely silent.

We stepped into a short hallway. Small arches on the left and right opened into other rooms. Farther down the hall, I could see doorways. There was a door right next to us. Mina opened it. Closet, some coats. Mina reached in and pulled out two golf clubs. She handed me one. "See, now we have an actual plan."

I waved the club. "This is a hobby, not a plan."

She brushed past me, locking her eyes with mine, but she didn't say anything. She made it to the two arches and peeked. Nothing. I followed her. Turned out, they led to the living room on the left and a little breakfast nook on the right. No assassins, upper or lower case, waiting in either. The kitchen was empty; so was the bathroom, which was ridiculously clean and stuffed with products that had fruit and flowers on the labels. We opened the door to her bedroom. No one was waiting. Her bed wasn't made, still mussed from when she had last slept in it. She had a framed poster of *Laura* on one wall, *Double Indemnity* on the other. On the wall behind her bed, a patchwork quilt. Her makeup table looked obsessively organized. The drawers of her antique dresser were closed. Her bookcase had names like Hammett, Chandler, Reichs, and Mankell.

She said, "If someone was here, no one's here now."

"They probably came in yesterday or the day before and just got tired of waiting."

She was silent for a minute. "Do you want an ice pack? For your eye, I mean?"

"Which one? No, it's fine. I'll, uh, I'll go sit down."

I turned around and went into her living room. A window looked out onto her street, and the curtains were open. This was the room she presented to the public, and it was spotless. I put the case of phones on her coffee table. She had some personal knickknacks strewn around. Some of which I expected: the Venus figurine, the collection of Isises and Basts, the subscription to *EW*. Some of which I should have expected, but I never imagined: photos of Mina with a beefy blond guy, an older couple that was probably her parents. She had a rack of CDs that showed taste that I found annoying: everything but Boston. One thing that I maybe should have guessed: a picture of Mina holding a mottled lop rabbit, snuggling it for all she was worth. Her couch was covered in so many pillows and afghans I wasn't sure where the couch part actually was. Still, I sat down. I was looking at her mantle and the flatscreen over it, wondering if I should snoop further. I thought I'd rather lie down for a bit.

The last few days were heavy on me. Maybe I should rest my eyes for a bit. No harm in that. I could still hear Mina if she tried to sneak up on me with an icepick or something. Quick rest, then run the last few miles of this marathon.

Suddenly, I was in that room in San Pedro, but it was also the living room of my apartment. My axolotls were the size of border collies. Mina came in, naked. She gave me a come-hither look and walked back into my bedroom, which had turned into the reservoir. I tried to follow her but I ran into a hammer, but the nice part was that the hammer had made me some coffee that smelled like vanilla. Mina was trying to get me to find her, but she kept repeating, over and over again, "I'm Mr. Reznick's associate. I'm Mr. Reznick's associate. I'm Mr. Reznick's associate."

I opened my eyes. There was a cup of coffee on a coaster sitting in front of me. Next to it, my case, open, cell phones in a pile.

Mina's voice filtered through. "Whatever you want to say to Mr. Reznick, you can say to me."

I blinked. My tongue felt thick. I was lost for a minute. I sat up and nothing swayed. I blinked again, and turned around. Mina saw me and grinned. She was on a phone. My Mason phone.

"If that's the case, be at Silver Lake Park in half an hour." She hung up the phone. To me, she said, "You fell asleep. It looked like you needed it."

"I hope I didn't bleed on your couch." She shrugged. I looked out the window. Red-gold light was coming in: sunset. "How long was I asleep?"

"A couple hours." Mina had cleaned up; put on makeup, too. I suddenly felt very skuzzy. I still had desert dirt on the tops of my shoes. She'd had a ton of time. If she wanted me dead, she could have bludgeoned me in my sleep, drowned me in coffee, thrown me in a trunk.

"Who was that, Stan or Neil?"

She said, "Neil. He wants to meet. It's about the Chain. I thought the Masons were after the Stone, not the Chain."

I rubbed one eye, winced, rubbed the other, winced more. "Dammit. The Masons are, but Neil's not working for the Masons. Well, he is, but he's with someone else, too. I smelled it on him in that bunker in San Pedro. Not sure who yet, but whoever they are, they want the Chain. I'm supposed to meet him in Silver Lake Park, then?"

She nodded. I took a sip of the coffee. Cold. I didn't taste bitter almonds, but I did taste French vanilla. I couldn't recall any poisons that fit that description.

I stood up. I had that hot muzzy nap feeling all over, but I had a meeting to get to. "Listen, Mina, I'm sorry about all of this. Thanks for, you know, the coffee, the place to sleep, the last couple days. You know. That stuff." I stuck my hand out. "Stay safe, okay?"

She had the same look on her face that dogs get when you make cat noises. "Um... okay?" She took my hand and tentatively shook it, like she was waiting for a punchline. I noticed she'd put earrings in.

I took my cellphone back and put it in the case, and took that out the door. "You should feed your bunny. He's probably wondering where you've been for the last couple days."

Her eyes flickered to the picture on the mantle. "He died in March."

"Oh, I'm sorry." That would have to go down in the annals of bad goodbyes: let's bring up her adorable dead pet. I could top that off by punching her in the stomach and keying her car.

"Are you going to be okay? At your meeting?"

"Neil's pretty harmless as these things go. He had some interesting associates, but they like me better than they like him. As for his real loyalty, chances are whoever that is knows me, too. I should be fine." I went to the door, stopped, turned. "Listen, if you need anything..." I opened the case and took out a card and a pen. I wrote a number on the back and handed it over. "Call that."

She raised her eyebrows. "Which phone does this go to?"

"Mine."

"No, which phone? Which conspiracy?"

“Mine.”

Her mouth opened slightly. Blood buzzed in my ears. Her eyes were locked on mine. Something tangible passed in the air between us, a presence. It was there, in that hallway, pushing the floors and walls away until nothing remained but Mina and me.

I opened my mouth. “I should be going.”

And it was gone.

A minute later, so I was I, driving for the park. I didn’t turn to look at the house as I did. Was she in the window? Either option would have probably kicked my ass more than I wanted to think about. At least now when I left her, it was comfortably at home rather than in the belly of the mothership.

I drove past the reservoir, past the place where I had climbed the fence and planted the weapon that was once again in my trunk. That was a nasty trick Mr. Blank—Statler—had pulled on me. I still needed a name on him. Maybe Neil had it, but probably not. There was a source for it, but that wasn’t going to be pleasant. Probably a good thing that Mina wouldn’t be around for that, if only because they were such weirdos. Little Green Men and the Clone Wolves were one thing, but the guys I’d have to go visit for his name were truly bizarre.

I pulled up in front of the park. The rec center was ahead of me, the sandbox and jungle gym directly parallel. I didn’t see Neil. Briefly, I thought about snipers, but then I pictured Neil chowing down on that sandwich in the parking lot the other day and got out of the car. I should probably ask after the rest of his conspiracy. It would be good to know if the Whale was planning to do something horrible to me. I thought of Vassily carrying around one of those inflatable donuts you needed for ass-related injuries and I felt better.

I walked through the gate in the chainlink fence, chose a

bench, and sat. Part of me wanted to lie back down and pretend it was Mina's couch, but that struck me as the gateway drug to homelessness.

I saw Neil coming through the gate on the other side of the park. He crossed the faded baseball diamond and even waved, like we were a couple of friends. Maybe in his head, we were. It was hard to tell what he thought. We were definitely friendly, despite his being part of duct-taping me to a chair. He joined me on the bench.

"You look like crap," he said.

"Good to know."

"You've been up to your neck in this whole thing, huh? Did you ever find out who sent that Manchurian Candidate after you?"

I felt like I'd been hit in the face with ice water. Neil knew about my multiple loyalties. Neil was at ground zero for the theft of the Stone, and there was always the chance he had been the one who gimmicked the phone book. He wanted the Chain: that suggested links to the Templars or the Anas, both of whom had ties to Diaz. There was a serious possibility I was sitting next to Mr. Blank, and Statler was just a red herring.

I tried to hide it. I said, "No. Still coming up empty on that one."

I couldn't tell if he was masking relief. "What about the Chain?"

"That I did find."

He couldn't hide the eagerness. "Where is it?"

"Sorry, Neil. You're going to have to tell me where it's going first."

He looked past me and nodded. Fuck. The bag went over my head and cinched tight. It rubbed against my cut. Neil barked, "Stop moving! You're only going to hurt yourself!"

I tried to curse at Neil, but the bag turned it into some kind of animal growling. I hoped it meant something really mean in Bear, Cat, Wolverine, or whatever the hell mammal I was mimicking. A hard cylinder jabbed into my side, and I almost had time to swear again before the current went through my body. I saw white, felt twisting agony, and smelled burned toast. My body went limp.

There were hands on me. I was hoisted over a shoulder and hustled from the park. I heard a car door open, and I was thrown in a backseat and a big body smashed me against another big body. I felt plastic cuffs tighten around my wrists. The car rumbled, started, and moved out. I heard Neil talking, riding shotgun.

"Stay calm, okay? There's nothing to be worried about."

"Neil? Have you noticed that I have a bag on my head? I feel like I'm about to star in an al-Qaeda recruitment video."

He sounded a little worried. "It's just a precaution. You don't have anything to fear from us."

"Then let's take the hood off and talk about this like people who aren't going to shoot each other."

"Are you going to... look, it's best if you keep the hood on. The orders were specific, and if you show up without the hood, we'll be in trouble."

"Jesus, who are you taking me to see, your mom?"

Neil didn't say anything to that. This didn't feel like an execution or, more accurately, how I thought an execution should feel. Neil couldn't hide the fear in his voice, and some of that fear sounded directed at me. The steroid hulks on either side of me were shrinking away, almost like they didn't quite want to touch me. I briefly thought about impersonating Gozer, but that would probably work better if I'd had the foresight to bring a terror dog. That, and my lack of sleep, made me giggle a little. The hulks both flinched.

I decided to keep quiet, but I ended up drifting off again. I woke myself up when I snorted, and I felt the guys beside me tense up. The car was slowing down. It stopped, shut off. I heard the doors open, and I immediately smelled seawater. My first thought was concrete shoes. I wasn't sure if the Kosher Nostra kept that tradition up. It seemed like maybe the worst way to die, if not the most creatively horrifying. One of the hulks hauled me out of the car, and I felt a clean breeze.

One hulk on either side held my bicep. They walked me forward, and part of me was pretty sure that they were going to run me into something for a good laugh. Neil said, "Careful, there's a step in front of you."

On a lark, I believed him. There was a step. He warned me about another, and I humored him. I heard a door open, and then we were going down a hardwood hall. I smelled thick incense, and up ahead I heard a party: a wall of conversation coupled with light clinks and sloshes. The sounds got louder, and then there was a hush. Instinct told me I was standing in front of and above the party, at the top of a short staircase. I felt eyes on me.

A knife cut my cuffs. The bag was whipped off my head. I expected bright light, but no. The room, a ballroom, was lined with black candles and draped in red cloth. In the center of the room, there was what looked like an altar set within a dry fountain. There were guests: the men in black tuxes, the women in red cocktail dresses. I blinked.

A familiar voice called out, "The guest of honor!"

Everyone broke into polite applause. Some of them raised their glasses at me. The crowd parted for nothing. No, not nothing. I looked down and saw Paul Tallutto, the leader of the First Reformed Church of the Antichrist. He was the primordial dwarf who had been present at Mina's show on Friday, the same show at which I had seen Stan Brizendine.

The little guy had his glass raised—a normal-sized glass, so it looked like he was slurping on a Big Gulp filled with booze.

Paul smiled at me and beckoned me to step into the ballroom. I did. I wondered if I was supposed to kneel or crouch when I talked to him. What was polite? I didn't think pissing off a Satanist, especially in his own home, was a good idea. This whole "guest of honor" thing seemed like one of those "fair is foul" rites that was going to end with me naked and riding a goat.

"Looks like a nice party, Mr. Tallutto."

"Please, call me Paul." He was leading me over to the bar. The guy on the other side looked so self-consciously evil I could barely take him seriously. The scar down the left side of his face I could handle, but the dead white eye seemed like a little much. He held out a martini. I took it. Paul said, "What would you like me to call you?"

I glanced around the room. I saw Neil leaning against one wall, watching me. So he was a Satanist. Now *that* I didn't see coming. Was he a Satanist because he really liked the message, or was it a family thing? Did he really believe in Hell, or was he hedging his bets? Did he sin all the time, or did he block off parts of his schedule? Probably more importantly, what the hell did they think I was?

I said, "Uh... Sam is fine."

"Sam it is."

A pack of Paul's bottle-redheads squirmed through the crowd. Two flanked him, and one cozied right up next to me. I offered her a weak smile.

"Mr.... uh, Paul, what's going on?"

"A party in your honor. I have to admit, I was a little surprised you were right under our noses this whole time."

"Had to be under someone's nose, I guess."

Paul laughed like a Japanese schoolgirl. I was getting distinctly nervous. He wasn't scared of me at all. "That's good. Just remember, what's mine..." a gesture at the women, although from his height, he was basically nodding at their crotches, "...is yours." Same gesture at my crotch. That made me uncomfortable. I felt like I was being propositioned for a threesome, and not the good kind. Before I could awkwardly cite erectile dysfunction, Paul strutted away, cradling the backs of shapely knees.

The woman next to me, who was trying to accomplish mitosis in reverse, said, "So, you want to go somewhere? There's back rooms and stuff."

It had been awhile. She was attractive. I was tired, sure, but I could get untired. She looked willing, maybe even into it. I couldn't really tell, but I didn't think it mattered to her. I nearly shrugged, then I tried to picture her kicking an attacker in the head. I couldn't.

"Maybe later."

"I could get a friend."

I spat out a mouthful of martini. "Uh, yeah. Right. Later. I need to talk to some people." I fled like she was a burning building stuffed with asbestos and C4. Neil saw me coming from across the room. He was severely underdressed, holding a glass of red wine and failing to blend in. His eyes got wide, and he tried to find an exit, but I was already on him.

I prompted him: "So, you're a Satanist."

The fear completely dropped as he gave me a "well, duh," look. "So are you."

"Everyone thinks I'm being judgmental when I say that. I was trying to start a conversation."

"Well, yeah. I'm a Satanist."

"I take it Stan doesn't know."

"Lord, no. Have to be a Christian to be a Mason. By the way, what's your real name?"

"Everyone has a different one, huh? Vassily called me Nicky, Oana called me Jonah... incidentally, how are they?"

Neil shrugged. "I haven't spoken to any of them since we left you at the bunker."

"You wanted to turn the Chain over to the Satanists?"

"Brady wanted it back. He stole it from the Templars, don't ask me how, and handed it over to me. I gave it to Paul, and Paul lost it, I guess." He lowered his voice. "There's been coup-talk ever since we found out he didn't have it anymore. That's sort of what this whole party is about."

I scanned the room. "Who's supposed to take over?"

Same look. He was getting good at that.

I said, "What, me?"

"Well, you *are* the Antichrist."

Apparently I was getting good at spitting my martini across the room.

Neil said, "You are, aren't you? The signs point to you. I saw the way you played Vassily, Brady, Oana, and that freak Victor. No one but the Antichrist could do that."

I tried to control the coughing. "Yeah, right. I'm the Antichrist."

I could tell Neil wasn't quite buying it, even if he wanted to. God bless him, or in his case, Satan curse him. I wasn't sure how it worked. I'd slept through the indoctrination, but I remembered there had been a video.

A soft clinking drove our conversation underground. Paul was standing at the head of the room, surrounded by his harem, all of whom looked like giants next to Mini-Ming. He held a glass of red wine and was tapping one of those tiny grapefruit spoons against the side. It was sort of cute, in a Black Lodge kind of way. I thought about using my authority as the Antichrist to make him say "I am the arm."

"Where is he? Where is the guest of honor?" He made a

show of looking for me, but I was the only guy underdressed and with a face that looked like I'd gone three rounds with Georges St-Pierre. Paul found me and nodded me over. "Sam, please join me."

I approached. If he had a knife, he could definitely reach my junk, and I was hoping to use that at some point in the future. I wound up next to him, and two of his floozies draped themselves over me.

Paul said, "Sam Smiley has given us hope for our future. Before Sam, we were content to be led by those who merely followed the example of our lord, but now, we have his actual offspring. Everyone, let's raise our glasses and..."

His voice trailed off. I followed his eyes to the front of the room. Had I been talking, my voice would have trailed off as well.

It was Mina. She was at the top of the stairs, eyes locked on me. The way she prowled into the room, I could swear I heard jungle drums. A grin played on wet lips, a glimmer shot through eyes like stars. She was an expanse of blue in the red and black. I nearly fell for the whole act, but my paranoia leapt in like a heroic Secret Service guy. Had she been here the whole time? She was a redhead, so she sort of matched. Had she been waiting? Was she a Satanist? Was that necessarily a bad thing when her breasts were that...

Focus.

I realized what she was doing. She had listened. At the intersection of perception and belief, she had found magic. This was her Reagan haircut. She had found a way to simultaneously belong and violate the rule of the conclave. She held the room in her cleavage. Paul couldn't stop her even if he could remember his name at that moment. She was on me, pushing the other women away. I didn't mind. I felt her breath on my face. She leaned in and kissed me.

The kiss wasn't exactly what I was hoping for. No tongue, but she did taste like strawberries, so that was a plus. She pulled away, but kept both hands on my lapels. "Excuse us. I'll have him back in a minute."

She dragged me through one of the curtains into a hallway. She leaned in again, and so did I. I opened my mouth, hoping to encourage her, but when I looked, her eyes were on the way we had come, and she was worried. She whispered, "Are you okay?"

I recovered and hoped she hadn't noticed my faux pas. "Yeah, I'm fine. What are you doing here?"

"Rescuing you."

"Why did you think I needed rescuing?"

"I followed you to the meeting. I saw them put that bag on your head and tase you, so I tailed them here. I got a little closer, snuck around a little, and made my move."

"Wait. You followed me?"

In the dim light of the hall, I couldn't tell if she blushed or not. It seemed like she might have. "I, uh, I forgot to give you my number. You know, if you found out the hit on me was still on. So you could warn me."

"Oh. You realize you just wandered into a coven of Satanists to tell me that, right?"

"Yeah."

I tried to think of something appropriate to say to that. I couldn't. "I think everything is going to be fine. I got a crotch-stabby vibe from Paul for a second, but they think I'm the Antichrist, so it's going pretty well."

"Then why the hell did they tase you?"

"They have a whole fair-is-foul thing. You know, they like to invert established social norms. It's why they put a midget in charge."

"I thought he was a primordial dwarf."

"I stand corrected. But with these guys, a hood and a taser is sort of the equivalent of a firm handshake and a how-the-hell-are-you."

"Well, if fair-is-foul, wouldn't that extend to the party? If you're the guest of honor, wouldn't that actually mean something bad?"

"You might be confusing Satan with Bizarro Superman."

"You're the one who laid out the rules here."

In the other room: a splashing sound, the sharp scent of copper, and an "oooo!" Mina and I exchanged a look. We peeked through the curtains. The fountain-altar in the center of the room had been activated. Blood flowed up through the altar and down into the fountain, drenching everything. The guests were applauding with a little more gusto. Paul stood nearby, holding a curved sacrificial blade. A few of the Satanists dipped their cups into the fountain and drank deeply.

Paul said, "Don't fill up on the goat's blood. Pretty soon, there will be real power flowing through that."

Mina and I ducked back into the hall.

She said, "We're getting the hell out of here."

"Yeah." We went toward the back. "Mina?"

"Yeah?"

"Thanks."

She shrugged, trying out a cocky smile. "Aliens, Satanists, what's the difference?"

"They both seem to have it out for the livestock, don't they."

There's a problem with knowing everyone. Ingrid Brady had put the thought into my head, and now I couldn't get rid of it. She'd given it to me without knowing it, and now I had to go through with what the thought had inspired. And that meant I had to see Fabian Strudwick.

Mina's car was a block or two away. Once we had left Paul's kitchen, we ran across the grounds and into the streets. I remembered Mina's car from the other day, right before she'd kicked me in the head. It was a good sign for my continued neurological health that I had memories around that event.

By now, the Satanists must have figured out that we were gone. I wasn't sure if Neil had spotted my car at the reservoir, but chances were they'd be sitting on it until I got back. That would be fun. I was pretty sure I was going to need it before the night was over.

She drove while I slumped in the shotgun seat. Mina's car was fairly neat. There was a wallet of CDs on the floor even though she had an iPod plugged into the stereo. There was

Kleenex and lotion; throw in a laptop and that was a pretty good Saturday night for me. The iPod wasn't playing Boston; it was playing some kind of British Invasion music that I couldn't stand.

I said, "I know who Mr. Blank is. Statler. Eric Caldwell's friend from the gay bar."

"You're sure this time? Because you were dead set on Ingrid Brady before this."

"I'm pretty sure she's working for him. He had her kill Eric in order to protect the organization when Diaz got arrested."

"So why do you have that horrible expression on your face?"

"Because I don't like where we're going."

"And that is...?"

"How are you with new gods?"

It was a legitimate question. Some of the groups were devoted to old gods, and by old, I meant anything before Joseph Smith. Old gods were deities like Yahweh and Satan, Eris, Athena, or Set. That last one was an Egyptian snake god whose cult had died out a couple years before. Turns out praying at cobras is the second-worst antivenin in the world. Anyway, there were also the new gods, whose cults were usually spread digitally. Deities like Anamadim or J.R. "Bob" Dobbs. I explained this to Mina. She seemed to take it all in and trust I wasn't winding her up.

"Another cult?"

"Another cult. Just be aware that their god is very, very real."

"Well, some people believe..."

"No, I'm talking about 'you reach out and touch him' real. And he might touch you back."

"That sounds ominous."

"Good, that's what I was going for."

Some cults were spread by the internet. This cult *worshipped* the internet. A single incarnation that had a form of consciousness. Unfortunately, like the internet, said consciousness was petty, prone to rants, incredibly vast, and utterly inhuman. Fabian Strudwick was its high priest and one of the most unpleasant people I had ever met. I liked to think that statement carried a certain amount of weight.

I explained some of it to Mina. No one really knew when the internet had gained consciousness, or even really if it had consciousness the way we knew it. With all the information in the world at your fingertips—not that it had fingertips, but bear with me—you would become more than a little fragmented, too. Even though by any human standards it was the smartest thing there was, it lacked the human quality of collating the information in any sane way. It also had a serious problem with memes.

I directed Mina to drive back downtown. Track down Statler and then what? If it *was* him behind all this, what exactly did I have to hold over the man? Blackmail, probably. If he really wanted me dead just for being, there probably wasn't much I could do.

Then again, I could just ask him for a job. He knew I was out there. He might *not* know that I didn't really have any loyalties. A person like that could be useful. I'd managed to talk *myself* into it, and it hadn't taken any time. I felt a little better after that.

I picked up the Shub-Internet phone and hit Fabian's number. When he answered, it sounded like the phone was being held under a faucet. "It's Adam. We need to meet." The phone disconnected. That was normal. After a moment, the phone buzzed with a text. "@ temple lolsacrifice."

Mina said, "What's it say?"

"It says we're going downtown."

Downtown Los Angeles is a collection of skyscrapers. Go watch any movie set here and you'll see them, usually silhouetted against a brown sky. Next to the skyscrapers were the warehouses and factories, some of which were being reclaimed as expensive lofts for hipsters, and others that remained the kind of place that was really only good for shooting a snuff film. The one I was looking for was in the center of this industrialized John Carpenter hell. Go through a maze of trash-strewn alleys, past an army of dead-eyed homeless people, and follow the path of increasingly terrifying graffiti, and that was where the Temple of Shub-Internet could be found. From outside, the building looked burned out. Nearly every window was broken. The walls had gibberish scrawled on them, a weird combination of code and hermeticism. Mina pulled the car over.

She said, "This is good. I was looking forward to being raped and killed tonight."

Silhouettes lingered at the mouth of the alley.

"Stay close."

"Wait, you don't have a joke here?"

"Can't think of one."

Now she was getting nervous. I wasn't sure how to calm her down. I said, "I could try a knock-knock joke?"

She gave me a weak smile. "Let's go."

We got out of the car. The silhouettes were still milling around. They either hadn't decided to descend on us and devour our brains, or they were regular homeless people who couldn't tell if we were worth hitting up for change.

The door was open. This wasn't surprising, since there was no lock. Inside, it did not smell like urine, which was never a good thing downtown. It meant that whatever was in there was too scary to piss on, which was a very short list around this area, a list that didn't always include the cops. There was a stairwell that went down.

I led the way. It was three full flights down. Around the second one, I started hearing a whine, sort of like a dot matrix printer. It kept getting louder. I opened another door into a dark hall, and the sound stopped.

Mina whispered, "Okay, I really want to go now."

Fluorescent lights flickered. The hall stretched off past boiler rooms. Nothing there. The door at the end of the hall spat out light of a different kind, tinged slimy green. I could hear the sounds of expensive sheets being evenly torn.

I said, "You're safer with me."

I forced myself to walk down that hall. It's not every day one meets a god, but on the upside, I knew this one at least slightly.

There's a great fallacy about prayer. Prayer is an attempt to get a message to a deity, which sounds fine and dandy. But really, there's no guarantee that the god wants a prayer, and all you've done is successfully attract the attention of an omnipotent being. It's sort of like fishing for Humboldt squid using your face as bait.

I entered the temple. The eye only goes one place upon entering, and that would be to the Avatar. Gods can be in many places at once, but Fabian had decided to build his god a body to inhabit. This was the first reason I disliked Fabian. What kind of idiot does that?

The Avatar of Shub-Internet was a machine, but what was actually inside that machine was a mystery. It eclipsed the far wall of the temple, a mass of steel and rubber tentacles in constant writhing motion. This was the sound of ripping I had heard: metal slithering across metal. Sometimes the tentacles would part, revealing a speaker or a screen, seldom the same ones twice in a row. The tentacles extended across the room, crawling up the walls, snaking across the floors, tipped in plugs and pincers. The mass stank, like it was rotting, but there was no flesh in it.

The mass was speaking, low and uneven. It had different voices, some male, some female. It was hard to track the conversations, but they were filled with non sequiturs:

"First!"

"I smell synergy."

"They deleted my comment."

"Mmm creepy man on fish undertones."

"Aye and you tell the kids of today and they won't believe you."

"Hey! Relax the sphincter."

The temple was the size of a large school auditorium. Its walls were covered in monitors of all shapes and sizes. Some new, some old, some cracked. All were on, and all were displaying some of the strangest porn the 'net had to offer. It was hard to look anywhere and not see something that threatened the future of my bloodline by making sure that I would never be able to achieve an erection again. On every wall, there were ladders between the monitors and tentacles, going up to little balconies with keyboards where robed men tapped away, finding more horrible porn.

By the time I saw Fabian, he was already lurching toward us. Fabian was the kind of guy that made you question the existence of *any* sort of god. That might have been why he decided to build one, just so when the subject inevitably arose, he could point to the horrible writhing mass of metal and say, "There, see?" He had a lisp and some kind of bowel problem that led to near-constant farting, and not funny loud ones, either. I kind of wanted to club him with a shovel.

He said, "To what do I owe the pleasure?"

"I have to ask a question." I indicated the Avatar.

He ignored me. “You bring an angel, but you don’t introduce me.” He turned to Mina and held out his hand. “Allow me to introduce myself. I’m Fabian Strudwick, high priest.”

“Uh... hi. Maxine. Gross.” I made a mental note to tease her.

“Perhaps there are pictures of you, my dear? Ones that we could sacrifice to His hunger?”

“No. There aren’t.”

“A shame. Seeing you nude would be an experience. There’s so much of you.”

Mina looked at me. “Can I hit him?”

I shrugged. “Shub-Internet won’t care. It barely knows he’s here.”

She cocked a fist. He held up his hands. “I can only assume that Adam brought you as a convert to our cause, and that your connection to our Lord had to be because you were naked online somewhere.”

She hit him. Hard. He hit the ground, eyes fluttering.

None of the acolytes reacted. They’d probably punched Fabian out a couple times themselves.

I walked forward. The tentacles started growing thick on the ground. I couldn’t be sure, but I thought they might be massing around me. I hoped that wasn’t the case. The central mass shifted, uncovering a monitor that was showing some black-and-white zombie movie that was quickly covered again.

I saw something out of the corner of my eye. I turned: the tentacles were rising up on all sides, curving toward me like question marks. It had noticed me.

It whispered in three different voices: “Grammar and punctuation aren’t important in thread hijacking. Not drunk enough, her clothes are still on. It’s really closer to a ratatouille.”

I wasn't sure what to say to that. Around me, the screens had all sprouted blue status bars counting up. They were the worst censor bars I'd ever seen. Above each bar, the word "deleting." The sacrifice. Had to keep the internet running somehow, and after all, the damn thing did eat porn. Why else would there be so much of it?

It hissed. I couldn't tell if it was a happy hiss or not. The tentacles around me didn't move. I knelt down and looked at the tentacles on the floor. They were wet.

Suddenly, one was on me, wrapped around my body and dragging me into the air. Mina screamed. I found myself being yanked toward the central mass and closed my eyes for the impact.

I stopped. I opened my eyes and found myself looking into another eye. Actually, a screen with the image of an eye from a contact lens commercial. The eye changed: this one was from a Korean horror movie. Then it was Janet Leigh's dead eye.

It whispered, "Should have gone with the short version: the freakier you are, the more time you get."

The upside was, it had just eaten. The downside was that it was still a god, and gods weren't known for impulse control.

The screen disappeared under a mass of tentacles. Another appeared and cycled through, I thought, every single lolcat that had ever been produced. It stopped on the goddamn walrus. I was its bucket, apparently. I didn't know if that was good or bad, but I erred on the side of bad. My arms were free. I searched through my pockets. There was the Shub-Internet phone, Adam Roth's phone. Useless. Then I found it: Colin Reznick's phone.

It wasn't squeezing, but it started showing a surveillance video of a 7-Eleven in which the clerk was furiously masturbating into the Slurpee machine.

I scrolled through the phone's memory. I found the picture. I reached out, and Shub-Internet grabbed my hand. I could feel the pressure on my wrist. Damnit, I really didn't need any broken bones. I thought about asking nicely, maybe even promising it some freaky German porn in payment, but it tore the phone from my hand, and rammed a tentacle into its ass-end. I winced. Even watching an appliance get anally violated was unpleasant.

The image of Statler popped up on the screen.

It whispered, "Any movie with J.T. Walsh as a sleazy son of a bitch is automatically awesome."

The image flickered so quickly as to almost be subliminal as more pictures of Statler popped up. I saw him, much younger, on an airstrip in the jungle, talking with men in uniforms and mirror shades. Smiling in a professional portrait. In the background of a news broadcast.

Then files went by, too fast to read. I saw names, redacted sections, words like Condor, Zapata, MK-Ultra. Statler was CIA, that much was clear, or he used to be, and linked with every single bad call they had made since the '60s. Condor meant he was tied to the Allende hit, Zapata to the Bay of Pigs, MK-Ultra to the manufacture of Manchurian Candidates. This was a man, that if he wanted you dead, you ended up dead.

The files slowed down. A name started appearing again and again: Irving Quackenbush, Hasim's "retired security consultant," the man Tariq Suliman was supposed to kill. Statler was Quackenbush's man in LA, the guy that got things done when no one else could.

Then, finally another name: Burt Shaw.

The tentacle unraveled into smaller fiber-optic tendrils, dropping the phone and retracting into the wall. The large screen disappeared under a mass of other tentacles. A new one appeared as more tentacles shifted aside, showing a team picture of a New York Knicks lineup from the '70s. It whispered, "Technically that's known as a Havana Jackoff."

I backed away. The tentacles shifted, writhed. I felt a hand on me, yanking me back. I turned—Mina. She pulled me away from the seething mass and I let her lead me up the stairs and out. It wasn't until we were in the night air that she said something: "Was that normal?"

"Normal for me?"

"Good point. Let's go."

I looked down at my shirt. I was covered in a thin layer of grease that looked and smelled like KY. She saw what I was looking at. "It's okay. You can pay for the carwash."

"Fair enough." I got in the car.

She said, "What now?"

"I arrange a meeting with Mr. Blank."

"I NEED TO PICK UP MY CAR."

Mina said, "Okay, let's fast forward. Assume I'm going to say 'But won't the Satanists be waiting for you?' And I'll assume you'll give me that smile you think is smooth and say back, 'That's what I'm counting on.' Then you assume that I hit you or something and make you explain yourself."

"Got that all mapped out in your head, huh? The way I figure it, I'm about to have a meeting with a fairly dangerous guy. Sure, I get to pick the venue, but that's not going to save our asses if things go south. What I need to do is confuse the situation, which means adding more people."

"More people that want you dead?"

"In point of fact, they want to *sacrifice* me, so it's possible, even probable, that they would rather not see me get the Bugsy Special."

She thought about that. "The mob killed him, right?"

"Little Green Men. They've been running Nevada for years."

The street was quiet, my car waiting for me. I spotted the Satanist tail by the cherry from his smoke. I tried to make him call his buddies, but my Antichrist powers were on the fritz. Mina parked and got out of the car.

"You can stay here. Not here, exactly. I mean, you don't have to come to the meeting."

She sighed. "Look, we can have this conversation if you want. We both know how it ends."

"I don't want to be a killjoy, but you *are* aware that I'm about to call a former CIA agent who probably quit because the agency was getting too sissy for him, right?"

"Yeah, and you're going to need backup you can trust."

"You're backup?"

"I beat you up one time."

"I wasn't ready. And you sucker-punched me. And I hadn't slept well the night before."

"Any more excuses? No? Good. Right now, Rabbit, all you have is me, and I'm not going to drive away and leave you twisting. Besides, I want to see how this ends. You're going to sum up the whole thing, right?"

"I hadn't really thought about it."

"You have to. You have to tell him all the stuff he already knows and how you figured out what he's up to. It's how these things are done."

"Good to know."

She wasn't saying anything else. She was just looking at me expectantly. Maybe she thought I was going to stick to my guns. She had a point. Sure, Mr. Blank—Shaw— probably wouldn't respond to what I had, but chances are he was just as vulnerable to face kicks. I nodded to her. "Let's go."

She got into the car looking smug. "Where are we going?"

I thought about it. "Griffith Observatory." Seemed like a good location. Suitably remote, and if things went bad, hiding in Griffith Park was slightly easier than losing a fistfight with the Hulk. Plus, if it was good enough for the Terminator, it was good enough for me, and I had wanted this thing to end somewhere high up.

"I haven't been there in awhile."

"Yeah, me neither. I wonder if they still have that laser show?"

Griffith Observatory reminded me of an egg laid by an alien chicken. Mostly white and mostly spherical, it was nestled in the brown hills overlooking LA. Long, winding roads took us up there, climbing past dark trees until we could see the city. From this distance, there was some beauty to it, but there was always a part of me that concentrated on what I knew was down there. Lipstick on a pig wasn't severe enough. It was more like glitter on the implants of a forty-year-old former starlet sleeping in the thin paste formed from vomiting up desperation and pills.

I parked near the entrance to the parking lot. Farther to run, but easier to get out once I made it there. I wasn't sure it was the right call.

The parking lot ended at a curb, and beyond that, there was a lawn divided into two sections by some walkways. The building itself was beyond that: three domes connected by an Art Deco façade. Golden lights shined upward across it, like the observatory was telling a scary story around the campfire. Up this high, the sky was divided into two parts: the low haze, where the lights of the city reflected purple, and up higher, which was closer to the sky in the desert.

This was a good place to finish it.

I opened the trunk. First, the rock and chain. The Genesis Stone had taken root. A rock garden had bloomed across some comics and the nose of my stuffed gator. I hoped the thing had one more apocalypse in it, but I wasn't that optimistic. I picked up my case of phones. Half had the batteries in them, waiting for calls. I put batteries back in the rest, just in case.

I started toward the observatory and dialed from memory. I wasn't even sure which phone I was using. The girl with the sexy voice answered. Suddenly, she had Mina's face. I shook it off. The girl said, "Yes?"

"It's Levitt. Tell Burt Shaw that I need to meet him."

"There's no such person here."

"Tell him I have Brian—" shit, didn't know his last name, "and Brian is ready to talk all about Raul Diaz and the others."

There was a pause. "I can send the message through the usual channels, if you like. No guarantees."

"Tell him to meet me at Griffith Observatory in half an hour." I hung up on her. I opened the case and went about the second part of my plan.

When I was finished setting up, Mina and I waited around the right corner of the building. They'd have to drive, unless, of course, he took a helicopter. I wasn't sure what I'd do in the event of a helicopter. I tried to think about examples of people who dealt well with helicopters, your McClanes, Yuens, or Chelioses. There was a common thread there, and it involved guns.

"Mina?"

"Yeah?"

"You wouldn't happen to be an undercover cop with a dark past, would you?"

I don't think my questions surprised her at all anymore, because she simply said, "Nope."

"Cyborg killing machine from the future?"

"Nope."

"Adrenaline-addicted indestructible hitwoman?"

"Nope."

"Print model with ties to an underground feminist conspiracy?"

"Nope—wait, yes."

We sat on the small concrete ledge of a planter that bordered this side of the building. Beyond us, there was some greenery and a couple cigarette butts stubbed out in the soil. It was more than a little mundane. Mina leaned into me. I leaned back. We waited.

I heard the cars before I saw the headlights swing into view. Two of them: black, probably bulletproof. They parked illegally in front of the building. Two men got out of each, men in suits, and an easy bet that they were armed. They scanned the area. After a moment, the door on the left car opened and Burt Shaw stepped out. He straightened his tie and walked toward the building. His men fanned out.

"Showtime. Hang back. If they start shooting, run."

I didn't check to see if she'd nodded. There was, of course, the chance that she was working with Shaw and this was their final gambit to kill me. It was also possible that I was an idiot.

Shaw saw me before his men did. He stopped, his attention fixing on me. His men reacted a half-second later, whirling; two moving back to protect the boss and the other two moving outward to cover me from multiple angles. They were the ones ready to shoot, but it was Shaw that was the scary one. The man's attention was palpable. He could invade my personal bubble from twenty yards away.

He spoke loudly. "Mr. Levitt?"

I nodded to him. "Mr. Shaw."

There was no expression on his face, not amusement, not surprise, not apprehension. He was waiting to see how this played out and any response seemed fine to him. He said, "I was surprised when Ms. Ratliff gave me your message. I had been under the impression that you were happy in your employment."

Ms. Ratliff. Right. "Mr. Shaw, look, I realize you're a busy man, and I appreciate you coming here. I know it was kind of a rude way to get your attention, but I figured I had to scream to be heard, if you follow. I do have a question for you before we go on, and you know, this is just curiosity, and you might be the wrong guy to ask, but... Ms. Ratliff. What does she look like?"

He raised his eyebrows. I think that was his version of the Mina-look of utter shock. "She's mid-fifties, gray hair, very short and plump."

"In this business, faith isn't so much tested as it is beaten about the head and neck with a sock full of batteries."

"What are you babbling about?"

"Not important. I called you here because I know everything."

"Omniscience is generally reserved for God."

Mina was right: this was going to be very satisfying. "Let's start with your bio. You're former CIA. You were involved in Operation Condor, collecting DNA from the disappeared, which you then sold to the Clone Wolves in exchange for future considerations. Specifically, you bought the clones, which you then turned over to specific handlers—people like Ingrid Brady and Eric Caldwell—to turn into Manchurian Candidates. You kept track of these with gimmicked phone books, given to each one of the handlers. The plan was to use your Candidates to remove opposition. You want LA, and with it, the heart of the information underground. You control peace summits. You control hand-offs. You control hits. There was only one possible person that could stand in your way: me. You knew about my divided loyalties. I didn't know about your plan, but I had the tools to put it together, so you arranged my hit. You even had me plant my killer's weapon... this..." I hefted the rock and chain for emphasis, "as a final fuck-you."

"And what did you hope to gain by talking to me?"

I shrugged. "Clemency. You want LA? I don't care. Not

my problem. My goal is to not have my head caved in. Modest, I know, but I find the key to happiness is intimately involved with one's head staying roughly spherical. Alternately, you could kill me, and everything I know goes straight to the papers."

He gave me a thin smile. "You're actually threatening me with the press? Mr. Levitt, I control the press. I could have Paul Newman hack you up and feed each screaming piece to Shamu in front of three thousand people and have the press call it suicide."

I wondered if he knew Paul Newman was dead. It was creepier if he did. In any case, he was right. Eric proved that, even if people like Dorothy Kilgallen and Karen Silkwood hadn't.

He continued, "As I said, I was surprised when Ms. Ratliff gave me your message. I was not aware of you until I saw you on Friday night. I looked into it, and I found out that I had you to thank for warning Mr. Quackenbush about the problems he was due to have with the Assassins. Mr. Levitt, I never tried to have you killed. On the contrary, we were quite happy with you. Emphasis on *were*." His men pulled their guns. Mina gasped.

I said, "Diaz couldn't act on his own."

"True. He was supposed to kill Tariq Suliman, thanks to you. Why he went off-mission is, frankly, a mystery." Shaw reached into his coat. I flinched. He removed an envelope. "Fortunately, it's not a mystery that matters to me. This is a letter from our mutual friend, Diaz's 'father.' It claims responsibility for everything Diaz did." He threw it at my feet. "You can keep that one. I have a copy."

I picked the letter up. Opened it. One look at it, and the whole thing fell into place. For real this time. I thought about goat's blood and the bunker in San Pedro. I wanted to vomit, but that's bad form when four pistols are pointed at you. I had thought that the octopus used the darkness, but I'd forgotten that just because something lives in the dark doesn't mean it can see.

I pocketed the letter.

Then all I had to solve was the problem of the four guns pointed at me. It's not like four was the magic number. It's not like you give me three and they'd be on the ground, clutching mangled crotches and thinking I was some kind of nut-punching dervish, but that fourth gun is one too many. *One* gun was one gun too damn many.

"Okay, so the press thing was a misstep. Sorry about that. How about we discuss this a little more before you do something I'll regret?"

"Sorry, Mr. Levitt, or whatever your real name is. Shooting you seems to be the simplest solution."

"Put those guns down!" Neil's voice, shouting from off to the left. He marched across the parking lot, surrounded by other Satanists. They were still in their tuxes and cocktail dresses, but they had chosen to accessorize with the latest in NRA fashions. They outnumbered Shaw's group at least two to one.

I said, "I hope you don't mind. I brought backup, and mine thinks I'm God. Or... something along those lines."

Shaw had the good graces to look annoyed. Maybe that was the bone he threw me, so if there was an afterlife, I could tell everyone else he'd killed, "Yeah, I got an exasperated eye roll out of him! It was awesome." I'd get some jealous high-fives, and then I could get down to the serious business of finding out where Marilyn was hiding.

I didn't see the signal, but Shaw and his men turned and started firing as one. It reminded me of the Clone Wolves. Apparently, Neil and the others weren't prepared for someone to call their bluff.

"Hey! Wait!" Neil hunkered, he danced, all while the bullets whizzed around him. The other Satanists had thrown themselves to the ground, run for cover, or just plain bolted. It seemed like a good idea.

I turned. Mina was already running. I was proud of her. I caught up and we were at the railing before Shaw called in an irritated monotone, "Would someone kill Mr. Levitt, please?" If Mina made it out, I hoped she would put that on my tombstone. I wondered what name she'd put on it, or if I'd have the world's first multiple-choice grave marker.

She rounded the corner, the planter giving her some cover. I heard a gunshot I was pretty sure was intended for me and I flinched, but I made it around the corner with no new holes. Mina had stopped. She looked scared, but it was a controlled fear. After the parking garage, the UFO abduction, and meeting Shub-Internet, she was getting some steel in those veins. She said, "The summation didn't go as well as I'd hoped."

"The upside is I know who actually did it."

"Are you sure, or is this another false positive that's going to get us shot at?"

I decided to ignore that. There were more gunshots, all of which I'm fairly sure were directed at the Satanists. Footfalls pounded toward us. I pointed Mina toward the planter and moved away from it. She took my meaning. I stood in the open and started whipping the rock over my head.

The spook turned the corner and skidded to a stop. For a second, he was terrified. Then he remembered that he had a gun and I had a rock. That seemed to cheer him up. He leveled the pistol at me.

I tried a turkey curse: "A can of Spam is opened every four seconds. The same can."

He frowned, trying to figure out if what I'd said to him had any meaning at all. Fortunately, he was so focused on me, he missed Mina creeping out from behind the planter, only seeing her when she jumped on him. He fell, his gun clattering across the cement. While he threw her off, I grabbed the gun off the ground and pointed it at him. "Freeze? That sounds so outdated. What's the current term?"

Mina snapped, "Focus." She was getting up and brushing herself off.

"Right. Freeze!"

The spook looked a little nervous. I couldn't blame the guy. I was pretty nervous myself. He grinned. "I don't know how you plan to shoot me with the safety on."

"Oh, har har. I've seen that one. I check the safety, you attack, disarm me, and you have your gun back. I'll just check." I fired the gun. It hit him in the leg.

He screamed.

I felt terrible. "Oh my god! I'm sorry! Are you okay?"

He rolled around, holding his leg. "Son of a bitch!"

I couldn't tell if I'd hit anything important.

Mina said to him, "You stay there. We'll get help."

The gunfire out front had died down. I wondered if the Satanists had gotten anyone. Mina and I ran for the far rail at the back of the observatory. I looked over; it looked like a drop into nothing at all. I'm not generally that afraid of heights, but that view completely petrified me.

"Come on," I said, pulling her along until we found a place where I could see the ground. I hopped down. She followed, fell on her ass, and swore at me.

"Sorry."

She got to her feet. "Better than being shot, right?"

We stood on what could barely be called a path. Just staying upright on the slope would be a challenge. I was about to stuff the gun down the front of my pants, then remembered how poorly that had the potential to go, so I shoved it down the back. I could handle getting shot in the ass. Emotionally, if not physically. I reached out and Mina grabbed my hand. Between the two of us, we might be able to keep from falling down the hill. We picked down the slope along the wall of the observatory and worked our way across the bottom. I could hear Shaw talking to the agent I'd shot, but I couldn't make out what they were saying. Probably something about how I had a gun now. What they didn't know was that the gun was making me more than a little nervous. I kept having waking nightmares of falling and shooting my balls off, even though I'd have to violate the laws of physics to do it. If there was one thing I had absolute faith in, it was the lengths the universe would go for a groin trauma gag.

I picked up my phone and dialed Adam Roth's phone, the Shub-Internet line. I could hear it ring in the distance. The talking stopped. They would be looking toward the other side of the parking lot, near where we went down the hill. Far away from the car.

The talking started up again. I hung up the phone and nodded at Mina, who was really just an indistinct shape with a sweaty hand at this point.

We made our way around the observatory. There was the beginning of another path, probably used by the little deer and coyotes found in the park. Go up that, run across first the lawn and then the parking lot, hope the Satanists had been chased off, and we would be at my car.

I helped Mina up the slope. A silhouette stepped into the observatory's light. I couldn't tell if it was Shaw or not. Mina and I ducked behind a tree. I tried to remember which phone was up there. I guessed maybe my Malta phone. I called it.

On the other side of the park, I dimly heard a ring, then

several gunshots. Okay, not there. Maybe the V.E.N.U.S. phone? I called it. That ring was closer. I peeked: the silhouette's head had whipped around. He'd be rooting through the planter until he found it. I thought about making a run for it. No, better to stick to cover.

I led Mina through the trees, every now and then calling one of my phones. It was a game of full-contact Marco Polo. I called, they shot. I knew they were seeing me in every tree by now. Count on pareidolia. It wasn't Jesus in toast, but I could repurpose it well enough to have them see a low-rent Antichrist in some chaparral.

The car was close now. Just a short hike up a hill, and we'd be in it and away.

Of course, that's right when I got outsmarted.

Shaw stepped out in front of us. He had it worked out. Without the car, we'd be walking down the hill in the dark. "Hello, Mr. Levitt."

"Hey, Burt. Want to help us up?"

"Drop the gun."

I did.

He cocked his pistol. I imagined him giving me a thin smile, but then I saw what was dropping from the sky and everything else in my head vanished. Mina screamed. In fairness to her, if part of me hadn't been expecting this, I might have screamed, too. Our friend from Diaz's house tucked its huge wings in and landed silently behind Shaw. The glowing eyes cast enough light to read by.

Shaw brought the gun up. That was when he noticed the red glow on his hand.

"Shaw, meet Mothman. Mothman, Shaw."

He turned, and I think he tried to say something. Then both shapes rocketed into the sky.

Poor Shaw. Of course, had he decided to talk it out like a

normal human being and not a mass-murdering asshole, he wouldn't be the prey of a time-traveling mutant or fortune-telling alien or whatever the hell Mothman actually was. Shit, I owed the guy my life. I could at least get his taxonomy right.

Mina asked, "Was that the thing from Diaz's place?"

"Nice guy. Saved my ass three times."

"Mothman? What is he, some kind of conspiracy superhero?"

I thought about it. "Yes." Good an answer as any.

We ran up the hill and threw ourselves into the car. Within seconds, we were roaring down the hill at a completely unsafe sixty.

My phone rang. I answered. I knew who it was even before I heard the buzzing voice. "Thanks for the save."

"You're welcome."

"Not to sound ungrateful, but why do you keep helping me?"

"Because you need it."

"Eric Caldwell needed help."

"He made his choices."

If that thing had said that before I had worked everything out, I might have pushed the statement away. But he said it when I was feeling unusually introspective. "And I haven't."

"Not yet. Soon."

"Look, next time..."

"There will not be a next time. You get my help one time. Then I move on."

"Right. You stop this Silver Bridge from collapsing this time, but after that, it's on its own."

"I see all times and all places. No one has ever manipulated probability to such a degree."

"So I'm, what... your favorite show?"

There was a long, crackling pause. "Yes." The line went

dead.

Mina watched me hang up the phone and tuck it back in my pocket. "I don't want to know, do I?"

"I think you do, and no, you don't."

"So Shaw wasn't Mr. Blank?" I shook my head. She sighed. "Then who? Who's left? We've scoured every inch of this city, and your stupid information underground; we should know what's going on."

"I do. We're going to get out of here and find someplace quiet. And then I'll tell you everything. The real summation."

That's how I found myself in a diner on Sunset, the Brite Spot. A nice place, with a lunch counter through the middle and a dessert case displaying dangerously top-heavy cupcakes. Mina and I were at a booth, the vinyl shot through with glitter. The waitress, who had to be more than a hundred, slid a slice of pie in front of me, and a milkshake glass in front of Mina, along with the silver cup holding the extra. Mina looked at me over a generous dollop of whipped cream. "Okay. Speak up."

I took a deep breath. A couple booths away, two cops ate a late-night breakfast. Where were they when I was being shot at? "I know exactly who sent the assassin to Union Station. I know who armed him; I know why he was there. It had to be someone with all of my connections, all of my resources and knowledge. There's only one person like that.

"Me."

The look she gave me effortlessly combined fear, anger, and incredulity. I wanted to bottle it and sell it to extras in disaster movies.

I went on: "On Thursday, Hasim Khoury the Assassin told me that Tariq Suliman had accepted a contract on Irving Quackenbush's life. That's Shaw's boss. He runs a security company. Basically, he's the guy who protects nearly every government installation. Anyway, I told him about the contract on his head. Quackenbush put Shaw in charge of solving that problem."

She said, "So he activated his Manchurian Candidates to kill the Assassins. How did Diaz get his hands on the Genesis Stone and the Chain?"

"Remember when you said that the Discordian, Stacy—GOOD FISH—was sad? That was right after Eric Caldwell died. If you looked at her charm bracelet, it included a Templar cross—the thing that looked like a Nazi iron cross, only in red. She was dating Eric Caldwell. When I checked out his place, I found a bunch of cans of hairspray. He didn't use it, but Miss Flock of Seagulls sure did. She must have taken the gimmicked phone book from Eric. The Discordians selected a Candidate without knowing it because they were using a phone book designed to pick only one person. They tell Diaz where to pick up the weapon, and now he's armed."

"That's why his gun was at his place. He kept the weapon he got last."

I nodded.

"That's confusing."

I said, "It all comes down to goat's blood."

She grimaced. "Explain."

"That goat's blood at the Satanist soiree. I delivered that. It's the first thing I thought of when Shaw gave me this." I removed the letter from my coat and slid it across to her.

She opened it, and made the same face I was pretty sure I made. "This is the same handwriting as on Diaz's secret admirer letter."

"Brian's handwriting. The Clone Wolf that grew Diaz in the first place. Remember him? He wasn't Diaz's secret admirer—he was yours. Brian's in love with you—granted, creepy stalker love, but it's probably the closest thing he's ever felt. That's why he had that dress that was perfectly your size on hand already and wrapped up like a present. That letter in Diaz's place was for you, and the letter in Daphne's office in his handwriting? You were the delivery he was talking about. Daphne was trading you to a Clone Wolf. On Thursday, I delivered a piece of information to Brian from V.E.N.U.S., and that information must have been that you would be at Union Station on Friday. Brian didn't have the courage to talk to you, so he sent the closest thing he had to a friend to deliver you that love letter."

"That's kind of sweet."

"Love to a Clone Wolf means he wants to combine your genes with his and make one super-person."

"Ew. Okay."

"So Brian gave the letter to Diaz..."

Mina finished for me: "Only he was already activated to kill on information you provided and given a weapon you planted. Instead of coming to deliver a letter, he was there to kill whoever came to that locker."

"Yeah. *I'm* Mr. Blank. This whole thing was just the fallout of doing what I do and not thinking about what it means. *I'm* the person I've been tracking. Remember when I told you about how conspiracies are like an octopus? When the gang of five—Vassily, Oana, Neil, Victor, and Ingrid Brady—captured me, each one had no idea what the other was doing. That showed me that octopi can't see in the dark. Metaphorical ones, anyway. I think regular ones can see just fine."

"You nearly got both of us killed because you never bothered to open a goddamn envelope."

I nodded. My chances with Mina, out the window. Good to burn the one bridge I had with a person who seemed able to trust me. "Yep."

She looked at the table. I tried to read her face and couldn't. It was stormy there. There was a good chance I was about to get kicked in the face again, and this time in a restaurant in front of a bunch of teenagers that looked like they had just gotten out of the prom.

"You're paying for this."

I nodded. "Yeah, I understand."

"No. You're paying for this." She pointed at the piecrust and her empty milkshake. "And you're going to find a way to make this up to me."

23

EVERY CONSPIRACY NEEDS A GUY LIKE ME.

They've all got scut work that needs doing, hauling crap from place A to place B. I've never flown a black helicopter, I haven't seen a mutilated cow in what seems like months, and I still haven't killed anyone, including myself, but that wasn't for lack of trying. I haven't hidden any weapons, impersonated any government agents, or called anyone that I didn't know in even longer. Without me, I'm not sure how—or even if—the shadow governments are moving, but frankly, it's not my problem anymore.

Yeah, every conspiracy needs a guy like me. That means there are close to a hundred job openings in Los Angeles these days. All that's required is a limber brain and a willingness to avoid asking the really obvious questions.

Long story short: I'm retired.

I'm not a Rosicrucian, a Freemason, a Templar, or a Hospitaler. My links to double-black agencies in the government are still there, but neither side is talking. I don't know if the various organized crime outfits want me dead or don't care.

I don't talk to the Vatican, the Servants of Shub-Internet, the Discordians, or the Assassins. The Knights of the Sacred Chao, the Brothers of the Magic Bullets, and the Illuminated Seers of Bavaria can fuck off. I don't even think about Symbionia, Thule, Shangri-La, and the Hollow Earth, but I did go to Napa Valley on vacation. I still know who killed everybody, but the difference is, I don't think about it unless I get drunk or Mina asks. The Little Green Men leave me alone, the Atlanteans are too busy talking to fish, and Oswald's clones are in retirement homes. There's still no such thing as vampires, but I do see the occasional chupacabra.

Completely retired. My mysterious red-eyed friend asked me to make a choice, and I did. Pretty simple decision after you realize you'd accidentally arranged your own death. For the time being, I thought I should stick to the lighted areas of the world.

The night after the observatory, I slept in a motel. Mina acted weird when I dropped her off at her car, but I couldn't think why. I promised to call her, which I ended up doing two days later.

I went back to my apartment the next day. Turned out my neighbors had called the cops. Everyone thought I was dead. I did what I do best: I lied. I got what I needed out of there. The strange thing was when I went to the kitchen sink. The axolotls were waiting in there for me, and rather hungry. They had lost their gills and their skin had taken on a mottled look. They had metamorphosed. They weren't supposed to do that. I put them in a salad bowl and was only bitten once.

I tied up the few remaining loose ends. There were no bodies at the observatory, but there were reports of a disembodied voice calling for help. That stopped around eight in the morning. As far as I knew, Burt Shaw was never heard from again. I let Richard know that Eric's killer was no longer a problem and he wanted to knight me, but I wasn't confident that I could get through the ceremony without giggling.

I tracked Ingrid Brady down and sent her a large pizza and a pair of shoes. I don't think she found that funny at all.

Hasim Khoury lived, but decided LA was too dangerous. Last I heard, he'd moved to Afghanistan. I think he's a member of the government now.

Oana Constantinescu started a team of full-figured gymnasts. That's probably going about as well as you'd think.

I kept the Chain and the Stone. They were safer with me than anywhere else. They live in a mini-fridge under my desk. The inside glows pretty brightly even though the light bulb is burned out.

I got a new identity and left the city with my salamanders. I didn't go too far, just a little way up the coast where no one knew me.

I was a little worried about what making things up to Mina meant, exactly. We were past the third act, so any betrayal wasn't going to be timely, unless she was setting herself up for a longer con. I owed it to both of us to stick around to find out. She'd be disappointed if her opportunity never materialized, and I couldn't do that to her.

As it turned out, making it up to her meant dinners in expensive restaurants and seeing movies that starred Julia Roberts and Kate Hudson. This happened several times before it dawned on me that we were dating. It came as a bit of a shock to me, but what the hell. She treated me well, even if she kept asking me what my real name was.

I think she meant the name I was born with.

Instead, I showed her the ID I was using.

"Robert Blank?"

"First thing I thought of."

She smiled at me. "It fits."

ACKNOWLEDGEMENTS

Thanks to the masters of noir for creating such a fun world to play in. And thanks to the theorists, the prophets, the wingnuts, and the deep throats for populating it.

Thank you to my editors, Kate and AnnaLinden. Without you two, I'm not even sure this thing would have been written in English. A second thank you to Kate for wanting to publish me, and for generally being the kind of awesome that's reserved for crimefighters and unicorns.

Lastly, a thank you to my readers. After all, you're the ones I write for.

ABOUT THE AUTHOR

Much like film noir, Justin Robinson was born and raised in Los Angeles. He splits his time between editing comic books, writing prose and wondering what that disgusting smell is. Degrees in Anthropology and History prepared him for unemployment, but an obsession with horror fiction and a laundry list of phobias provided a more attractive option.

FOLLOW THE AUTHOR ONLINE

www.captainsupermarket.com
mrblank.candlemarkandgleam.com
Twitter: @JustinSRobinson
Facebook: http://on.fb.me/JustinRobinson

CPSIA information can be obtained at www.ICGtesting.com
Printed in the USA
LVOW081613190413

330033LV00007B/846/P

9 781936 460366